A GENTLEMAN IN POSSESSION OF SECRETS

THE LORD JULIAN MYSTERIES—BOOK TEN

GRACE BURROWES

GRACE BURROWES PUBLISHING

Copyright © 2025 by Grace Burrowes

All rights reserved.

No part of this book may be reproduced in any form or by any electronic or mechanical means, including information storage and retrieval systems, without written permission from the author, except for the use of brief quotations in a book review.

If you uploaded this book to, or downloaded it from, any free file sharing, internet "archive" library, or other piracy site, you did so in violation of the law and against the author's wishes. This book may not be used to train, prompt, or in any way interact with any generative artificial intelligence program whatsoever.

Please don't be a pirate.

Cover image: Cracked Light Studio

Cover Design: Wax Creative, Inc.

DEDICATION

**To Glenn,
a gentleman in possession of honor**

CHAPTER ONE

"If I might speak very bluntly, Lord Julian, Miss Stadler's family tolerates me." Captain James MacNamara limped the length of the library as he spoke, then did a teetering about-face under the previous duchess's portrait. "They are never overtly rude, but I'm too old, too poor, too damaged, too Scottish... They acknowledge my acquaintance, even as they also constantly allude to my deficiencies."

I wanted desperately to invite my guest to sit. When last I'd known him, Captain MacNamara had been hale and whole, one of the best artillery officers in Wellington's army. In the nearly two years since Waterloo, he'd aged considerably.

His once-jaunty swagger had become a halting, bobbing walk. His left hand was missing the smallest finger. His temples showed flax among the russet of his hair, though he could not yet be five-and-thirty years old.

His gaze was a testament to chronic pain, not all of it physical. I refused to add to the indignities he'd suffered by treating him as an invalid.

"I gather Miss Stadler doesn't share her family's opinion of you?" I asked.

"Miss Stadler finds me acceptable." MacNamara addressed the duchess in her gilt frame. "To be honest, she might well find me acceptable simply to twit her family, but I flatter myself the lady enjoys my company. We are by no means formally engaged, but she has given me leave to ask permission to court her. If we were to plight our troth, I'm sure she'd make me work for it, effort I am more than willing to put in."

MacNamara was far from handsome. His features were rugged—craggy, some might say—and his nose was an aquiline blade. He was nearly as tall as I was—six foot, two inches—and his Scottish burr gave his speech a growling quality. His rare smiles were angelic, and his ferocity in battle had been demonic.

He would make a loyal, protective, and doting husband, but he was not a typical suitor for a viscount's daughter. I doubted he was poor, but he was undeniably Scottish, definitely the worse for his military adventures, and no stripling.

"Might we sit, MacNamara? The steward got hold of me yesterday morning and did not grant my parole until nigh midnight." Hours in the saddle, a dozen tenant calls, acres of newly planted land inspected.

I no longer enjoyed the stamina I'd developed in Spain, but then, I was no longer fighting a shooting war.

"I can sit for a time," MacNamara said, "then I must move, then I must sit again. My gouty auld uncles find me hilarious. I'm suffering just deserts for my incorrigible youth, according to them."

MacNamara lowered himself into a wing chair, his knee able to bend only slightly, which necessitated a perch on the edge of his seat.

I shoved a hassock before him. "My eyes cannot tolerate bright sunshine. I wear blue spectacles out of doors."

"That powder wagon outside Madrid, wasn't it? A grand display and a very great noise." He smiled, propped up his foot, and sighed. "I don't miss it, not in the least, but also, I wouldn't want to have missed it. The Scots, Welsh, and Irish proved themselves over and over in battle, and I don't care what the great man himself says, Wellington was not born on English soil."

Wellington was Irish by birth and ancestry, but when questioned regarding his nationality, his response had famously been that being born in a stable did not make one a horse.

"About Miss Stadler? You fear she's in danger?"

MacNamara extracted a pillow from the corner of the chair and stuffed it under his foot. "Yes, damn the notion, I fear she's in danger. Perhaps not bodily danger, despite being taken from her home against her will."

"How do you reach that conclusion?" The library chairs were seductively comfortable, the morning sunny and just edging toward warm. A soft, grass-scented breeze wafted through the open windows, and sleep tugged at my mind.

Typical of me lately, to toss and turn the night away, then long to nap when the sun was finally up and about his rounds.

"I could say lover's intuition inspires my worries, my lord, which you might dismiss as so much foolishness, but hear me out. I am in the habit of exchanging notes with Miss Stadler. Nothing sentimental. She is a bluestocking, reads voraciously, and we have a sort of competition. She'll quote some old Roman, and I'm to tell her who, then it's my turn. Or she finds a quote and can't unearth the source and challenges me to solve the riddle by Friday. All very harmless and silly."

Not silly. Sweet and surprisingly literary. "I did not know you were much of a scholar."

"I'm Scottish, my lord. We read the way you English drink ale. Besides, sitting about waiting for my wounds to heal, I had few consolations besides books."

I rose, went to the sideboard, and poured two servings of brandy. MacNamara had been too intent on his narrative when he'd arrived to tolerate the courtesies, so I saw to them now.

"To your health."

"And yours, my lord." He saluted with his drink but did not rise, so I resumed my seat.

"Miss Stadler stopped corresponding with you?" I asked.

"Can't really call it a correspondence. More of an exchange of dispatches. She left her notes for me in my fishing cottage. I put mine in her belvedere at the bottom of the steps. She'd warned me that she had a particularly challenging quote to share with her next epistle, but that epistle was never left for me."

An oversight, possibly. "What else?"

"When I called at Pleasant View to inquire regarding my next assignment, Miss Stadler wasn't on hand to receive me. I asked after her, and the viscountess told me Hannah was suffering a megrim. Hannah—Miss Stadler—does not believe in allowing a megrim to lay her low. She regards activity and fresh air as the best tonics."

I thought of my sisters and their many megrims. "Might she have been suffering the female complaint?"

"No."

Everlasting Powers. The matter had just become a great deal more complicated...

"Your expression is priceless, Caldicott. As if you've just blundered into Almack's wearing riding attire and are only now realizing your error. Miss Stadler had just got over the female complaint. She is vociferous—to me—about the injustice and indignity of it all, the inconvenience which a fair-minded Deity ought not to visit on only half of His creatures. She is vociferous about a lot of things."

And clearly, the captain esteemed her for being so forthright.

"MacNamara, at the risk of being called out, might the lady have simply tired of your company?"

"Aye. She tires of me from time to time, and it's off to London to pillage the Bloomsbury bookshops, though perhaps she's in truth flirting with the Mayfair gallants. When travel is in the offing, she tells me her plans, brings me back a few tomes, and onward we march. We are honest with each other, my lord, and beyond that..."

He took a sip of his brandy, made a face, and set the drink aside. "Too fine for me."

"Beyond that...?"

"To meet her, you'd think Hannah was an antidote. She can be brusque. Her sense of humor is unique. She's not dainty, and she doesn't suffer fools. But that woman has the kindest, fiercest heart God ever bestowed on a mortal soul. She cannot abide dissembling. Hannah might tell me to my face that I've grown boring or that she prefers a husband who can dance under the stars, but she would not leave me to fret and worry any more than you'd simply disappear from Miss West's life."

Hyperia West, the light of my existence, the beacon illuminating my days, the lady to whom I had pledged my future, dodgy though my prospects were in some regards.

"Could an explanatory note from Miss Stadler have gone astray?"

"She did not entrust our notes to anybody else. Neither did I. Gave me motivation to walk at least as far as the fishing cottage or the belvedere."

MacNamara got to his feet, which involved taking his foot off the hassock, moving to the edge of his seat, angling his body, getting his good foot under him, and pushing himself upright. Only then did he put weight on the bad foot, and in a tentative fashion.

"What's the problem with your paw?" I asked, rising. One soldier could ask that of another.

"Shrapnel, as best the surgeon could tell. I stood too close to where a cannonball landed. Missing some toes, but he saved the foot. Got what he could, but I was bleeding all over creation, and cauterizing this and that became more pressing than extracting little bits of metal. He said some would work their way out, or they might kill me eventually, especially if the little bits are made of lead."

"You should see a Scottish physician."

"I should. I will, but finding Hannah is more important. I have done what I could to locate her, though the mission wants two sound feet, for starters. Hannah's family has gone so far as to suggest she's taking the waters, as if she's some beldame in need of the cure. When I press for her location, I'm told she's off to the spa towns."

Of which there were many. "You're worried."

He kept a hand resting on the back of the chair. "Would I be here, asking for your help, if I wasn't half out of my wits, Caldicott? I would rather face Napoleon's damned cuirassiers than think that Hannah has come to harm and I've failed her. She doesn't have to marry me, God knows, but to think that she's kicking her heels in Paris because her family objects to me, or that she's been bundled off to some convent in Dublin... I slept well the night before battle compared to how I've been sleeping lately."

Cuirassiers were heavily armored cavalrymen. Death on big, fit warhorses. MacNamara had faced them, as had I. One could not forget the experience, even if one wished to.

I did *not* wish to take on this investigation, which surprised me. I wanted to enjoy the bucolic splendor of Caldicott Hall as spring eased into summer. Haying was a fortnight or so away, and the crop was coming along nicely. My boyhood memories of haying were sweet, while in other regards, I associated warmer weather— campaign season—with hell on earth.

I wanted the security and comfort of Caldicott Hall, wanted to compose long, sentimental letters to my intended and to pop up to Town for a day here and there and treat myself to her company for a stroll in the park.

I longed to dote, to court, to drift for a time. Needed to.

"Say you'll look into this, please, Caldicott. The Stadlers can't ignore you the way they try to ignore me."

I knew the family in passing. Viscount Standish was about twenty years my senior. The heir was my junior by several years, and like me, he had a plentitude of older sisters. The viscountess and my mother were cordial, as one must be in the country with any family of note within ten leagues of one's home.

"Lady Standish might not receive me, MacNamara. You've doubtless heard the talk."

"Bother the talk. You survived captivity. Your brother, God rest his soul, did not, and neither did many others. Are you responsible for every life the French took? I think not. The war is over, and the Stadlers won't snub the son of a duke."

I was, in point of fact, not only the son of a duke, but also my older brother Arthur's heir. The present Duke of Waltham was touring the South of France in the company of his great friend Osgood Banter. I wished them the joy of their travels and hoped to never again set foot in France myself.

"Very well, the Stadlers will be at home to me, but if Miss Stadler has played you false or fallen into a fit of melancholia, they aren't likely to share such a confidence with me."

MacNamara limped away from the sideboard to face me. "That's the thing about you, though. You'd go for a little hack through the Spanish countryside, your spyglass hidden away in your boot. A week later, you'd toddle back into camp, in want of some rations and a bath. You'd have the location of every French unit in the vicinity, its strength in men, cannon, and horses, and a good estimate of its rations. And you'd come by this intelligence without asking any questions of anybody. It's no wonder the French wanted you buttoned up in some dank, musty prison. You likely gave Old Boney nightmares."

"You flatter me." A reconnaissance officer had little value if he could not draw accurate conclusions from his observations.

"Some, perhaps. I would dance with the devil if he could assure me that Hannah is well and happy—if I could dance at all."

MacNamara could no longer dance. He could no longer march. He could, though, ask for reinforcements when the battle was turning against him, and I mightily respected him for that.

"I'll call on the Stadlers later this week."

"Tomorrow, man. Hannah has been gone three days, that I know of. If she's been carted off to one of those private asylums, that could be three days in hell."

Another thought worthy of nightmares. "Tomorrow, then, and you will bide here at the Hall until I have something to report."

"Will I truly?"

"You can hardly put weight on that foot, MacNamara, and you

turned down good brandy because you need all your wits about you to stay ahead of the pain. I'm sending Mrs. Gwinnett to you. Our cook knows every remedy in the herbal, and she is no stranger to grumpy men. You cross her at your peril."

Most soldiers were adept at following orders, though I was taking a risk telling Captain James MacNamara what to do. He had a temper to go with his Scottish charm.

"Your cook sounds like my Hannah. Do we dress for dinner?"

His Hannah, though he was not yet engaged to the lady. "We do not. Country hours. To bed by ten of the clock usually. I'll see you at supper. Borrow any book in the library for as long as you please."

I left MacNamara pretending to peruse the biographies, though I knew for a certainty that the instant I was out of sight, he would be back in the chair, his foot once again propped on a pillow, the brandy gone in a trice.

~

"I don't understand." Atticus, my tiger, peered out the coach window at the verdant countryside. "He's sweet on her, and she's sweet on him, but he lost her? Is she playing hide-and-seek, like?"

Atticus occupied that age hovering below the onset of adolescence, when some of childhood's innocence yet lingered, but would soon be gone forever. I'd found him in service at a country manor in Kent and offered him a post as a stable boy, tiger, and general factotum. He was loyal, observant, an asset in an investigation, and too bright to be wasting his days polishing boots.

He was also frequently stubborn, impudent, and too independent for his own good.

The boy had made respectable inroads on literacy, and he was a natural in the saddle, but a reluctant scholar otherwise. He adored Hyperia, who doted on him, and a recent outing to a race meeting had left him in a horse-mad phase that could last the rest of his life.

"Miss Stadler's family might have suggested she'd benefit from a change of air." That observation came from my mother, Dorothea, Her Grace of Waltham, serenely ensconced beside me on the forward-facing seat. "They might have suggested rather forcefully that the young lady pay a call on distant relatives."

Atticus was in awe of Her Grace, as was I at times. She, having worn the Caldicott tiara for decades, regarded his adulation with gracious good cheer.

"They'd haul her away," Atticus asked, "like press-gangs and highwaymen? Or you mean she's sentenced to the chapel for a week?"

Mama's perfectly matched brows drew down. "Sentenced to the chapel?"

"In the parish house, if you was bad, you had to sit in the chapel. Place was colder than a well-digger's—"

I winced. "Language, young man."

"—boots. Dark and spooky, and there was graves under the flagstones. You could hear the souls of the damned moaning when the wind was up, at least that's what headmaster told us."

The little scamp liked using the word *damned*, if his grin was any indication.

"Fortunately," Her Grace said, "you no longer reside in such surrounds. The Caldicott family chapel is a cheerful place, though it can be chilly in winter. Julian, you mustn't frown so."

"Your face will get stuck like that," Atticus added helpfully.

My mother sent me a half-exasperated, half-smirking glance. Were Atticus any older, he would not ride inside in company with Her Grace. But the day would be long—a good thirty miles of travel— and sending the boy up to the box for the whole distance might result in John Coachman giving notice.

Then too, Atticus was my eyes and ears belowstairs, and I had yet to give him his orders.

"The young lady's name is Hannah Stadler," I said. "She's been missing in action for several days, as far as Captain MacNamara knows. She was in roaring good health when last he saw her. She did not mention upcoming travel and has ceased a regular, informal correspondence without notice or explanation. She might well have sent him a note explaining a pressing need to admire ocean vistas, but if so, that one note went astray."

"What's she look like?" Atticus asked.

Well, blast the luck. "I don't know, other than she's robust, tallish, vigorous, and... That's all I know."

"Miss Hannah Stadler is a brunette," my mother said. "Has sky-blue eyes that are often obscured by spectacles. Wears her hair in a plain chignon, has a heavy tread for a lady, and can ride in the first flight all day. She is the fourth daughter, the only one yet unmarried. Her memory is prodigious, and she is an outspoken advocate for reform. She believes more women should have the vote, for example."

Atticus's mouth formed into an O. "I guess the guv gets it from you, ma'am."

Her Grace smoothed her skirts. "I beg your pardon?"

Atticus should not be addressing the duchess at all, and his observation seemed to have rattled her nigh impregnable serenity.

"The guv sees all the details, don't forget nothin'—except when he forgets everything—and makes a picture where the rest of us see only lines and shadows. He'll find the lady, but first he'll get all remote and think-y, and then he'll go grouchy and hare about, mutterin' and annoyin' folk. Miss West will have to sort him out a time or two, or Lady Ophelia will, and then it all comes right just when you think the guv has bit off more'n he can chew. He does that too. Don't have no sense, sometimes, and don't you be glarin' at me, guv, because I'm an honest boy speaking the honest truth."

A loquacious boy. One in need of a reprimand, though I would not injure his puerile dignity with a set-down before the duchess.

"I could not have said it better myself," the duchess murmured. "Julian, do you recall the Stadler heir? He was some years behind you, and he did not serve in uniform for the obvious reason."

Not only was the Honorable Mr. Strother Stadler his papa's heir, he was the sole scion of the house. That he remained unmarried several years into his majority was a testament to gross negligence on the part of the matchmakers, or incorrigible bachelor tendencies in the young man.

"Mr. Stadler and I have met, of course, years ago. Doubtless at some hunt meet or neighborhood gathering. He's tall, brown-haired, and I seem to recall him being of a self-important nature, but perhaps that's a phase most young men go through."

Atticus snorted.

"Have you something to say," I asked, "or have you taken to indulging in gratuitous rude noises?"

"I believe," said the duchess, "that Atticus remarks on present company's propensity for self-importance. You do become very focused on your investigations, my lord."

Atticus silently mouthed the new word: *pro-pen-si-ty*.

The boy had a *propensity* for collecting big words as crows collected shiny objects. "A capacity to remain focused on a goal increased the odds of my survival in Spain. My apologies if either of you find my company objectionable as a result."

The duchess's expression smoothed into her characteristic calm dignity. Atticus resumed gawking out the window.

Bad of me. The search for Miss Stadler wasn't even properly under way, and I was already out of sorts.

"Apologies all around. I have no excuse for ill humor. We don't even know yet that the young lady is truly missing."

The duchess and the boy both sent me glances that suggested more might be said at a later time. I hadn't noticed any resemblance between them previously. She was a statuesque redhead of mature years and aristocratic provenance. He was a skinny, dark-haired lad of low pedigree and limited accomplishments.

They both, though, regarded me with fleeting worry, and over a single grouchy remark. Perhaps I wasn't the only party made fretful when an investigation began.

"You have the book?" I asked.

Her Grace patted a quilted reticule. "I chose an unbound copy of

Mr. Douglas's *Eneados,* a translation of the *Aeneid* into Middle Scots. Hannah would already have Dryden's version."

"That manuscript has to be quite valuable."

"It's a copy, Julian. You and Harry were doubtless set to replicating great swaths of wisdom as punishment for your various boyish transgressions. Arthur might have made this copy simply out of boredom on a summer holiday. The hand looks to be his. The Stadlers are Scottish on the dam side, though you will never hear a hint of a burr in the viscountess's diction."

My mother had chosen shrewdly, in other words. The pretext for the call was to pass along to a bluestocking a tome Miss Stadler would delight in. Exactly the sort of generosity characteristic of my mother. Thoughtful, personal, and unfussy.

"We're here," Atticus said. "Captain MacNamara said to look for brick gateposts with rearing horses atop."

The coach slowed to take the turn, and we passed through a tidy park—too tidy. Somebody had landscaped the trees and pastures into submission, an expensive hobby wealthy families had fallen prey to in the last century. No towering sentinel oaks punctuated the horizons, no tangles of bracken sheltered in the dip and swell of the terrain. The carefully proportioned ornamental lake lay precisely where such a feature was expected to be.

Wooly white lambs grazed beside their mamas, not a black sheep to be seen.

When I'd rambled about the wilds of Spain, a verdant, tamed English expanse such as this would have figured in my dreams as the definition of rural beauty. For reasons I could not determine, the precisely placed spinneys and smoothly curving lane bothered me now.

If the landscape itself could be manipulated into a symmetric set piece for the Stadlers' convenience, how much more likely was it that our call would amount to a day wasted for the sake of tea and cakes served with liberal helpings of useless platitudes?

CHAPTER TWO

The cakes were tiny, the welcome genteel, if a trifle strained. Her Grace could have that effect on people, though her inherent graciousness usually soon set one and all at ease.

Still, she was a duchess, and our hostess was a mere viscountess who likely hadn't had a use for her formal parlor since she'd hosted a passing bishop at Yuletide—if then.

The space was cold, despite the mild day, and bore a hollow quality. No fresh flowers, no soft breeze from a French door propped ajar. The delicate furniture with its blue pastel upholstery sat in a symmetrical grouping before an empty hearth. The carpet wasn't dirty, but I was certain a good beating would have released a cloud of dust.

The formality was meant to impress, but instead it depressed. Staid, stiff, chilly... somewhat like our hostess.

Lady Standish was aging well in that her figure was trim, her complexion enviably smooth. She wore her dark hair swept up in fancy ringlets, which struck me as an odd choice for a mature female in her country abode. I also found it peculiar that her ladyship had not one strand of gray in her locks.

She might have been attractive in her youth, but at present she qualified as handsome, and that was not necessarily a compliment. The jaw was firm, the gaze impassive. She made no wasted or even spontaneous movements. The silver tea service arrived on trays arranged just so in every particular. No fussy linen or clanking spoons, and no object placed closer than one inch to the edge of the tray.

"If Miss Stadler is in," the duchess said, "I thought I might give the manuscript to her in person. We have an original in the library at Caldicott Hall, though it's fragile. Miss Stadler might like to see it when the occasion suits."

My mother's capacity for strategy was one of the most surprising aspects of her character. She had just extended a personal invitation to a spinster of the parish, a singular honor, particularly given the distance between households. True, Miss Stadler was a viscount's daughter. Even so, the duchess's personal notice was yet an unlooked-for honor.

An *unignorable* honor, in fact. Rather like an active rook was an unignorable threat on a chessboard.

"So kind of you, Your Grace," the viscountess said, holding out the plate of tea cakes. "So very kind, but our Hannah has decamped to take the waters, and with the weather so fine, she might well wander on for weeks. Don't you find that young people grow bored in the country?"

My mother chose the raspberry cake I'd been eyeing. "Rather the opposite, at least with my children. They grew restless in the confines of Town and longed for the more robust activity to be enjoyed at the Hall. Has your Strother gone up to London for the annual whirl?"

Her Grace had advanced a knight with that question. Strother was a bachelor heir. He had a responsibility to marry and be fruitful, and thus far, he'd shirked it.

As had I, in the opinion of some.

The viscountess set the tray of sweets aside without offering any to me. "Strother is out with the steward. He did the pretty in Mayfair earlier this spring, but came home to attend to myriad duties here. He is such a conscientious fellow, very mindful of the legacy he must safeguard. We are so proud of him."

Though he refused to marry, he had not served in uniform, and he was probably at that moment downing a tankard of the posting inn's finest, boots up on the hearth, barmaid flirting with him madly...

I was truly in a bad humor.

"Children are such a source of joy," Her Grace said, beaming at me contentedly. "I might be in the mood for a jaunt to the spas myself, and Julian is a very attentive escort. In which town did Miss Stadler begin her progress?"

And out came the duchess's bishop.

"She, um..." The viscountess peered at the remaining sweets and selected a lemon-iced cake. "She had an itinerary. Hannah is the organized type. She thinks ahead, always has a plan, never forgets a detail. I believe she might have gone straight to Bath for the sea air. The hordes from Town will soon descend, so a start at Bath before the crowds arrive appealed to Hannah."

Her Grace took a dainty bite of her tea cake. "Sound reasoning. Julian, might you escort me to Bath? I, too, would like to avoid the crowds."

"It would be my pleasure." Though Her Grace was casting a lure, not making travel plans. "Perhaps we might take the manuscript with us and hand it along to Miss Stadler in person?"

The viscountess set her lemon cake on the saucer of her tea cup. "I'm sure that won't be necessary. We could not possibly put you to that trouble, Your Grace. Not when Hannah might well have dashed off to Lyme Regis by now, or heaven knows where. She can be impulsive."

When she wasn't planning an excursion down to the last never-forgotten detail?

"I suppose your mother has gone with her," the duchess mused. "Lady Dewar was so kind to me when I was new to the area. A formidable woman, in her day."

"Mama doesn't travel much of late. She's grown frail and a bit vague, I'm afraid. We treasure her, for her remaining days might well be short." Said with a bearing-up sort of gaze at a portrait of a powdered lady in fine brocade.

"Miss Stadler has her grandmother's blue eyes," I said, "if I recall the ladies correctly."

The viscountess regarded me as if I'd proposed springing Old Boney from his island prison. "I beg my lord's pardon?"

"Striking blue eyes," I said, gesturing to the portrait. "I've ridden to hounds with both Miss Stadler and her brother. Your daughter is quite the equestrienne." The recollection had come to me only as I'd seen the grandmother's portrait. Miss Stadler was the better rider of the two siblings, but Strother was competent in the saddle as well.

"I'm sure that was years ago," the viscountess replied. "We dissuaded Hannah from spending much time in the hunt field. Not the safest place for a young lady, no matter how skilled she might be on horseback."

The comment seemed to imply that brigands lurked behind every stile and gate when, in fact, most hunt fixtures were assiduously maintained free of badger holes, dangling limbs, and slick footing. Accidents happened, of course, but those same accidents could happen while hacking sedately to divine services.

My mother's gaze had taken on a gleam that boded ill for the prevaricating viscountess. "Julian was raised with sisters who favor vigorous riding. Isn't that right, Julian?"

What was she up to? "My sisters are the reason I acquit myself in the saddle as well as I do. Would not have served to have them win every race, you know. A boy has his pride."

The viscountess hefted the silver teapot. "Well, as I said, Hannah is no longer so enamored of a muddy day spent among malodorous hounds. More tea?"

We were overstaying our welcome and had no new information to show for the outing.

"None for me," I said, measuring the distance from my empty cup to the tea cakes. "A treat for the road wouldn't go amiss."

"None for me either," the duchess said, "though I would like to pay my respects to your dear mama. One never knows when one might have the opportunity again, if at all, and she was very considerate of me when I was a new bride."

The queen herself had joined the affray, though what was Her Grace about?

"Mother often naps at this time of day," the viscountess said, without passing me the sweets. "The elderly need so much rest."

"Nonsense," the duchess opined, rising. "The elderly want for company and stimulation, and I insist on paying my respects. I'll be brief. Your butler can show me up to your dear mother's quarters. Julian can relieve you of those tea cakes in my absence. He's like any other bachelor, a threat to undefended comestibles of any variety. You there…" The duchess waved a hand at the hovering footman. "I'll look in on Lady Dewar if you'd kindly show me the way."

The viscountess would have had to invoke the authority of her husband to stop the duchess from her errand, and the viscount—the king on Lady Standish's side of the chessboard—was playing least in sight.

That in itself was odd when a duchess came to call, but we hadn't sent word ahead of our intention to visit, so perhaps his lordship was also out counting piglets with the steward.

"Have all the tea cakes you please," the viscountess said when the duchess had taken her leave, "but if I may be blunt, do not think to look upon my Hannah with a matrimonial eye."

Ah. Hence my mother's reference to my bachelorhood.

"Your ladyship, I am engaged to be married, though I'm sure Miss Stadler is in every way an estimable young lady."

The viscountess looked insultingly relieved, but she did pass me the tray of cakes. I took three. Two for me, one to slip into a pocket for Atticus when next I saw that worthy.

The viscountess entertained me with recollections of her

previous encounters with my parents. I reciprocated with news regarding neighbors from the Hall's corner of the shire. The duchess returned a very long quarter hour later, her usual cordial reserve giving away nothing.

As a reconnaissance officer, one learned to conduct arrivals and departures from camp with a studied show of nonchalance. If the French army had been spotted two miles away, one climbed from the saddle with the same weary indifference as if rumors were spreading of a stunning defeat for the Corsican at Russian hands.

The rank and file watched for the reconnaissance officers, noted when their absences were prolonged, and noted when they rode into camp on a different horse from the one they had ridden out on.

Or when they walked into camp with a pronounced limp and a bloody sleeve.

Her Grace had news to report. In her perfectly correct leave-taking, her good wishes for Miss Stadler's safe travels, and her reminder to pass her regards to the viscount and Mr. Stadler, she was every inch the duchess.

When it came to the smile she bestowed upon me, however, and the little squeeze she gave my arm as I escorted her to the coach, she was a Caldicott who'd come across information in the field that was relevant to the mission.

I gave John Coachman leave to spring the horses and waited for Her Grace's report.

∼

"Lady Dewar has the same lady's maid and companion she had twenty years ago," the duchess said as the coach turned through the rearing-horse gateposts.

Atticus, once again on the backward-facing seat, was devouring the tea cake I'd purloined for him. He, too, would have a report, but Her Grace had the floor for the present.

"They are loyal to her," Her Grace went on, "and would likely raise a hue and cry if any attempt were made to send Lady Dewar back to Scotland. The viscountess has apparently suggested it. Lady Dewar would rather remain near her grandchildren."

"A Scottish winter isn't for the faint of heart."

"Scottish winters are long, dark, and cold, true, while at Pleasant View, Lady Dewar has ample heat, a kitchen capable of producing feasts, and little need for funds. Banish the old dear to Scotland, and she'd likely be consigned to living on crusts in a garret."

I did not understand how one could treat a parent thus. The duchess and I had had our differences and misunderstandings, but she was *my mother*.

"Has Lady Dewar no independent means?"

"She should have, but, Julian, she's a bit dotty. Had to be reminded to address me in English, and while I'm sure she knew who I was, she had no idea what to say to me."

So far, Her Grace described a typical interview with an elder of declining faculties. "You asked after Miss Stadler?"

"I did, and the companion informed me Miss was off to take the waters. I asked who had the pleasure of chaperoning such an excursion and got an awkward silence, followed by a waved hand and mutterings about one of the viscountess's friends who was available for the journey…"

The coach picked up speed, and Atticus began sending the hamper on the seat beside him longing glances.

"That struck you as odd, that the companion would not know who Miss Hannah's chaperone was?"

Her Grace took the pin from her bonnet and removed her hat. "Very odd, Julian. A companion has little to do all day but step, fetch, and gossip with the other servants. She's an upper servant, but she has little authority over the rest of the staff. She must make alliances, and Miss Rumsperger has been in that household for decades, as has Claypole, Lady Dewar's lady's maid."

"Them two would know everything," Atticus said. "All the

secrets and who got a post with a cit and who was hired away by the neighbors. Ex-specially the old companion."

Her Grace should have stared the boy into silence, but this was a council of war. All were permitted to speak.

"Correct," Her Grace said. "A senior servant, almost family, of very long standing would know who chaperoned Miss Hannah, where the ladies went, what sort of retinue they took, and when they'd return."

I put the hamper on the floor and opened the top. "Would Your Grace care for a sandwich?"

"Anything without watercress, please. Atticus, you are not to eat the biscuits first. His lordship was forever attempting that misdemeanor in his misspent youth, and I saw what happened to your tea cake. I'm forced into proximity with a pair of scoundrels."

Atticus beamed. I passed Her Grace a cheese-and-butter sandwich. Bread from white flour, no crusts. Atticus contented himself with the same on rye bread, as did I.

"Do we conclude that Miss Hannah has eloped with the undergardener?" I asked when my first sandwich had been dispatched.

"We conclude that something scandalous is afoot," the duchess replied. "The looks, Julian, between the companion and the lady's maid were bursting with disapproval and doom. They were careful to keep their volleys from Lady Dewar's notice, but slipping memory is not synonymous with stupidity."

How well I knew that. "Then MacNamara's concerns might well be justified. What do we know of Miss Hannah's settlements?"

Atticus had finished his sandwich and was back to sending the hamper covetous looks. "Wot's that got to do wiv anything?"

"She's not an heiress," the duchess said. "Not famously well dowered, if that's what you're wondering."

"My question,"—I gave Atticus one-half of a second cheese sandwich on rye and took the other half for myself—"bears on the possibility of a forced elopement. If a fortune hunter without conscience grows too desperate, then hauling a young lady over the border to Scotland against her wishes can still result in matrimony."

"He kidnaps her, then marries her? That don't sound like a recipe for happiness." Into his little maw went one corner of the sandwich, but he knew not to talk with his mouth full.

"Such a ploy," I replied, "can result in solvency for the fortune hunter, which in some cases is a necessary prerequisite for continued existence. The lady is quietly sent to live abroad until the scandal dies down, but even if she's not married to the scoundrel, she has been ruined by his scheme. If she does marry him, he gains control of at least a portion of her funds."

"Yeah," Atticus said, "but then she can make his life a misery too. Might be some satisfaction in that."

A wife could not rain down violence and malevolence on a husband of anywhere near the intensity that a husband could inflict on a wife. Atticus would learn that verity too soon.

"Who would know the details of her settlements?" I asked, offering the duchess a jar of sliced pickles.

She waved the food away. "We'll ask the solicitors. They keep abreast of the possibilities in case Waltham decides to take a bride. Miss Stadler is a neighbor, of marriageable age, and wellborn. She will be on the list."

I paused mid-dive into the pickle jar. "If they've looked into her situation, they must have similar information on hundreds of young ladies."

"Also young widows. If a fellow is presented with a hundred options, he's more likely to find one to his liking than if he's presented with three. For the duke's men of business to make discreet inquiries into a young lady's situation is considered an honor."

Then half of Mayfair and the home counties had been so honored, and all for nought. The apple of Arthur's eye was his traveling companion, confidant, friend, and lover, Osgood Banter. The duke had made it plain to me that, for him, marriage to a woman would be an exercise in pointless appearances.

The burden of the succession rested on my own shoulders, which made the viscountess's rejection of me as a suitor for her Hannah somewhat puzzling. True, my military record was held in dubious regard by many, and I'd come home from the war the worse for my experiences. All of that notwithstanding, I'd still be considered above Miss Hannah Stadler's touch.

Speaking of touching... "Atticus, one takes a single pickle at a time."

He looked at the fistful he'd taken. "Sorry, guv. Should I put 'em back?"

"You should eat them," the duchess said. "Then we'll hear what you gleaned belowstairs, after which, if your belly has any room, and the swaying of the coach hasn't disturbed your digestion, you will be permitted one apple tart."

"They're small," Atticus said.

"One now," the duchess replied, looking exceedingly formidable. "A second later, conditioned upon good behavior and time spent on the box learning the coachman's art from the resident expert."

Atticus held up a slice of pickle. "Got you a bargain, ma'am. John Coachman has all the best stories. Like that time Lord Harry—"

"Your report," I said, jamming the cork lid on the pickle jar and giving it a solid pound with my fist.

Atticus munched his pickle like a squirrel dispatching a nut. "Nobody was saying a word in the kitchen or the servants' hall. I mean not nuffink, not a peep. One of the footmen came in from the footmen's stairway hollering about his lordship and the young master going at it again over the ledgers. He got scowled to silence worse than if he'd farted at a funeral service."

"Knowledge belowstairs," the duchess said with a perfectly composed countenance, but then, she had reared seven children and put up with our dear papa as well.

"What did you *see*?" I asked as Atticus finished his pickles.

"Kitchen is spotless. Servants' hall is clean too. A bit chilly, though. No fire in the hearth and, being like a half basement, not exactly cozy."

"Were you offered tea?" the duchess asked.

"Ale, and watered ale at that. Not so much as a biscuit to eat or a slice of cheese."

"No food on the servants' sideboard?" I asked. Our cook at the Hall, Mrs. Gwinnett, believed that hungry staff worked neither happily nor efficiently. She kept fruit, cheese, bread, and libation on the servants' hall sideboard at all hours.

"The servants' hall didn't have no sideboard, now that you mention it."

I passed Atticus the smallest apple tart of the lot. "What of the livery? Was it new, clean, mended, ill-fitting?"

He took a bite. "The footman what got stared to death was missing a button on his coat." Atticus patted his belly. "Here. The cook's apron was stained. Never seen Mrs. G in a stained apron."

The duchess listened to this recitation without comment, though she was likely drawing the same conclusion I was.

"You think they're skint?" Atticus asked, tearing off another bite of tart. "Cold hearths, watered ale, short rations, and such?"

"It's a possibility," I said. "Or the viscount's household might simply operate more frugally than what you're accustomed to." Though that interpretation was contradicted by the head of the family remonstrating loudly with his heir over the ledgers.

"I been frugal," Atticus said, chewing rapidly. "Don't care for it. Got frugaled nigh to flinders by the charity of the parish. My brother got farmed out, but the matrons said I should be grateful I'd not been sent to the country with him. Frugal is bad enough, but sent off to the baby farms was worse yet."

Had the boy begun quoting Caesar's Gallic letters in perfect Latin, I could not have been any more thunderstruck.

"You have a brother?"

Atticus finished his tart and dusted his hands together. "Had. Headmaster couldn't tell us apart most of the time. Tom went to somewheres in Chelsea. He were naughty, were Tom, and stubborn. Full of mischief. I got in trouble less when he were sent away. Can I ride up on the box now?"

Neither I nor the duchess were capable of a reply.

"May I, I mean?"

"You may," Her Grace said, rapping twice on the roof.

The coach slowed, and I opened the slot beneath the coachman's bench. "Atticus will be taking the air with you, John Coachman."

"Send the lad up, my lord. The team is settled, and I could do with the company."

When the coach had halted, Atticus monkeyed onto the bench with some assistance from myself and coachman. I returned to the forward-facing seat and took the place beside my mother.

She helped herself to an apple tart. "He has a brother."

"Or had. A possible twin. Full of mischief."

My mother offered me a tart, which I declined.

"Julian... I know what you're thinking. A brother lost to uncertain circumstances. Dead, we must presume, but still shrouded in mystery. Atticus doesn't see it like that. His brother was naughty, his brother went away. For a small boy, that makes sense."

No, no, and no. "It made sense to him at age five, or four, or whenever this atrocity was committed. They had only each other and were torn asunder because of a few pranks, or because nobody thought to put one in a brown jacket and the other in a black one. Such cruelty will make no sense to him at age twelve."

I was half barmy over Atticus's casual revelation. I wanted to cry, to bellow to John Coachman to turn the horses for Chelsea, to inform MacNamara that circumstances prevented any further investment of my time on Miss Stadler's situation.

I had answers to find and, very likely, as the duchess noted, a grave to locate. Probably unmarked and unremarked, though if a boy survived infancy in the hands of the parish, he was a tough little specimen, or very lucky.

"Julian, before you dash off in search of a child who likely breathed his last several years ago, you need to know the final detail of my visit with Lady Dewar."

I hauled my focus back to the matter at hand. "This is not a detail at all, is it?"

She shook her head. "As I was leaving, Lady Dewar lapsed back into her native tongue. My Gaelic is rusty, and she said only a few words. I can't be certain of what she said, but I had been asking very pointedly about Miss Hannah."

"And the companion had done all the answering."

"Correct, though Lady Dewar heard the exchange and was alert throughout. As I took my leave, I offered her a hug, and she muttered something very quietly."

Muttering beldames became my least favorite people in creation. "What did she say?"

"It sounded like: 'Thug iad i. Dà fhear.' Or something close to that."

I wasn't all that astute reading the Erse, but so much of Wellington's infantry had been Irish and Scottish that commands had to be given in both English and Gaelic. I'd picked up a fair amount of spoken Gaelic in camp and had studied what grammars I could find to pass the time.

"Say that again."

"*Thug iad i. Dà fhear*. We both know what it means, *if* I heard correctly."

We did, and the news was bad: *They took her. Two men.*

What on earth was I to tell MacNamara, and how soon could I tear up to Chelsea and begin the search for Atticus's twin brother?

CHAPTER THREE

"Tell me about Miss Stadler's family," I said, taking the place across the reading table from MacNamara. Late afternoon sunshine caught fatigue and forbearance in my guest's features, though the library was situated such that he'd heard the carriage return. He had awaited my report, but I hardly knew what to tell him.

"What would you like to know?" he asked.

"They don't care for you, but other than that, what sort of people are they?"

Beneath the table, my foot encountered a hassock. MacNamara had elevated his leg, but had done so in a manner not easily detected by any passing footmen.

"They are... decent," he said, setting aside *Gulliver's Travels*. "Decent and narrow in the manner of minor aristocracy. They haven't the graciousness of their betters nor the kindly spirit of the usual squire."

"You describe an unhappy group, though I know many a viscount or baron whose family is quite jolly."

He nodded. "The Stadlers are pinched, I guess you'd say. They must keep up appearances with the likes of you lot here at the Hall, but the older daughters were lucky to marry baronets or Honorables. Hannah feels sorry for her family, even though she doesn't like them much."

"She's the youngest?"

"The failed spare, to hear her tell it. Of all the girls, she is closest to Strother, who came immediately before her, though he's not exactly a scintillating intellect. His father hasn't taken the management of the estate seriously, and yet, the estate is about all they have left. Just short of ten thousand acres and maybe three-quarters of it under cultivation."

That was enough acreage to generate considerable revenue as rent, or should have been.

"One saw signs of economies about the domicile," I said. "Nothing too severe, but pervasive nonetheless."

"Cold hearths. Servants work fifteen hours a day. No new livery for three years. Hannah claims her mother's Scottish soul rebelled at lavish spending, but the Stadler town house is routinely rented out, their coach is at least twenty years old, and Hannah's mare is just as venerable. Had the family been well-off, I would have been less sanguine about approaching Hannah as a suitor."

"What of her settlements?"

MacNamara shifted in his seat, winced, and sat up straighter. "Our discussions never reached that topic. From a few of Strother's casual comments, I concluded that Hannah's settlements were modest in the extreme. Launching her sisters and then her brother took considerable coin."

The chairs at the reading table weren't padded. Surely that was an oversight? "Was Strother trying to warn you off?"

"You mean, was he lying about Hannah's situation in order to discourage me? Possibly, but that occasion was one of very few when I've seen Strother tipsy at home. I tend to think he was being honest and uncharacteristically forthright."

"*In vino veritas.*"

MacNamara's smile was sad. "In wine, there is truth. Cited originally by Pliny the Elder in the first century Anno Domini, as a proverb common at the time, though I believe Strother's preference is for brandy."

"How does the Honorable Strother fill his days?" I asked about Miss Hannah's sibling because he was the only one still dwelling under the same roof with her.

"I don't know much more. Strother has always been cordial to me in an offhand way. Hannah maintains he's easily distracted. He does the pretty up in Town each year—a bachelor in expectation of a title —but takes rented rooms rather than biding at the family's London property. I haven't heard of mistresses, cockfights, or curricle races, but I never did travel in fashionable circles. Hannah would have me believe Strother is a harmless fribble. A passable staff officer, though don't expect any ingenuity from him on the battlefield."

I had known many passable staff officers and had never aspired to join their numbers. "A neat, quick hand copying or deciphering a dispatch, not one to buck protocol." A son to be proud of, not necessarily a fellow to befriend or lend a substantial sum.

"Strother seems fond of Hannah, for all his self-absorbed inclinations, and she is quite fond of him. They all are. He was much doted upon, being the only boy with four sisters."

I had been fond of Harry, too, and yet, at times I'd wanted to pound him flat. "I need to speak to Strother privately. How might that be engineered? The viscountess gave us the same story you were handed. Miss Hannah is off taking the waters, possibly in Bath, but she isn't likely to bide there for long. If funds are short, that is an expensive excursion. Strother might have something to add to the picture. He and the viscount are prone to arguments over the ledgers, apparently."

"Strother rides his acres, or his father's acres. The viscount claims gout keeps him from long hours in the saddle, but my limp is far worse than his, when he remembers to affect one, and I can sit a horse well enough. Somebody in that household knows more than they're saying, Caldicott. A lot more."

I rummaged mentally for how to convey what Miss Hannah's granny might have said—*if* she was capable of accurate recollection, *if* my mother had heard her correctly, and *if* Lady Dewar had seen what she thought she saw, and not Miss Hannah strolling across the churchyard with her brother and the vicar's eldest boy...

"Excuse me, my lord." The first footman hovered by the open library door. "You're wanted in the nursery."

This again. "Am I wanted urgently?"

"Seems so, my lord. Urgently and loudly."

"Warn the rebel that I'm on my way, please."

The footman withdrew, smirking.

"MacNamara, excuse me. The infantry regularly grows rumgumptious, and my mother has deemed me the best resource for reading the Riot Act."

Blue eyes crinkled with amusement. "Best see to the king's peace, then."

"In my absence, please make me a list of Hannah's siblings and friends, their directions, and any noteworthy aspects of the relationship."

"Noteworthy?"

"Disappointed suitors. Frustrated creditors or debtors. Rivals cast into the shade because Miss Stadler caught your eye. The whole situation wants a motive."

MacNamara went through the laborious process of getting to his feet, or to his foot, because he put little weight on the left one. "You believe Hannah was kidnapped?"

"That's one theory. She might well have eloped. She might also have gone for a repairing lease to twit you into making an offer. We don't know, and I hope to replace ignorance with information. I must be off lest Miss Hunter's charge take another notion to admire the view of the property from the roof."

I bowed and withdrew at a pace intended to convey impatience rather than panic. When I reached the steps, I nonetheless took them two at a time, and I arrived to the schoolroom panting.

"Where is he?" I asked the governess, who stood by the open window.

"Out again, my lord. I am so sorry. I just cracked the window a little bit, and when I went down the corridor to retrieve some chalk from my room, out he went."

My soul rebelled at the notion of putting bars on the windows of any schoolroom, but my nephew was showing a nigh criminal genius for eluding his studies. I hoisted myself through the window, waiting out the predictable stab of agony in both eyeballs, and spotted my quarry up by the nearest grouping of chimneys.

Leander Caldicott, aged seven, hadn't a care in the world, by the looks of him, while I could barely breathe for the fear choking me.

"Young man, get down here this instant. You have been warned about this behavior."

"I warned you first, Uncle Julian. I like it up here."

His little chin jutted with righteous conviction, and I knew with a sinking certainty that I would have to make the ascent, because no power on earth could induce that stubborn boy to come down before he jolly well pleased to.

I had been at least ten before I'd ventured onto the roof—and then only in Harry's older and stronger company.

The view from the standing seam tin ridge was familiar to me from those boyhood adventures and just as spectacular now as it had been years ago. I was still taken aback by the magnificence of the park, the home wood, the church spire poking above the hedgerow, the tiny sheep and cattle dotting the landscape.

The whole verdant, peaceful, lovely lot of it belonged to the Caldicotts, or to the dukedom and family. That made it partly, indirectly mine, and I took pride in what I saw.

I wasn't at all sure what to make of my nephew, though. I settled beside him, a somewhat undignified process.

"Explain yourself, young man. In what regard did you warn me?"

He was the right size for his age, but quite small compared to me. He had Harry's dark hair and Harry's smile. I could only pray he hadn't also inherited Harry's penchant for reckless mischief, though the early signs were discouraging.

"You went to Hampshire, Uncle Julian, and you did not take me with you."

"I went to Hampshire briefly, and I came back when I said I would. The duchess bided with you here." Though in fairness to the boy, Her Grace might have looked in on him for twenty minutes once or twice a day.

"Then you went to Berkshire, but you did not take me with you there either."

"The invitations I accepted did not include you, Leander. I had serious business to attend to on both outings, and you have serious responsibilities in the schoolroom."

Let it be said that grown men do not find perching on rooftops comfortable, and the bright vista I so loved was tormenting my eyes. That I had somehow betrayed Leander's respect for me was also no damned comfort.

Leander muttered something snatched away on the breeze.

"I beg your pardon?" I leaned closer, getting a whiff of his lavender-and-little-boy scent.

"You took Atticus," he said, each syllable laden with injured dignity. "You took him with you today. You took him to Berkshire and Hampshire. Was he invited?"

Abruptly, I was in deep, hostile waters. I had, in fact, ordered Atticus *not* to accompany me to Hampshire, but he'd stowed away with the luggage and proven useful to that investigation. The more recent outing to Berkshire had called for eyes and ears in mine host's stable, and again, Atticus had been the logical resource.

"Invitations don't generally extend to servants." An excuse, and we both knew it.

"I want to go with you when you go away," Leander said. "You are gone for days and days and days. Miss Hunter makes me a calendar when you go, and we strike an X through a square each night, but you are gone *forever,* and I have told you and told you that *I want to go with you.*"

He had, and I had changed the subject, assured him of my speedy return, and promptly disappeared for at least a fortnight in each case.

"None of this excuses you putting yourself in danger on the roof, young man."

"Yes, it does, and we're not in danger. You don't listen to me, and I told you—I *warned* you, Uncle Julian—that if you won't listen to me, I won't listen to you. It's not fair for you to always go away. I am a good boy. I do what Miss Hunter tells me, and she says I am very bright. My sums are correct, and I can say the Lord's Prayer in Latin and almost in French. You still just *go away* and don't even wave when you canter down the drive. I'm not listening to you until you listen to me."

The little beast delivered these verbal blows calmly, even patiently.

I considered simply plucking him up into my arms, negotiating the downward slope, and chucking him (gently) back through the schoolroom window.

Too dangerous, especially if he squirmed, and Leander Caldicott would squirm mightily.

I considered a solemn promise to wave upon every future departure, but that gambit would likely get me kicked off the roof. Leander was a Caldicott male suffering repeated affronts to his dignity.

"I am traveling up to Town tomorrow," I said. "Would you like to come with me?"

"*Town?*"

"London, where you used to live. We will stay at Caldicott House and bide for only a couple days, but you are welcome to come with me, *if you behave.*"

I expected gleeful crowing, some gloating, or perhaps—I am a pathetic excuse for an uncle—grudging thanks for having finally listened.

"I cannot climb out any windows?"

"Not a single one. No howling like a ghost to frighten the maids and footmen. No running away to the home farm. No scampering naked through the house and claiming you're playing Garden of Eden."

"I only did that once. You won't leave me in London?"

Some of my frustration eased, because the boy's fears were well founded. He was Harry's by-blow, the same Lord Harry Caldicott who'd not stuck around long enough to marry Leander's mother, much less make Leander's acquaintance.

When the child's existence had been brought to the attention of the present duke, we'd collected the boy and his mother, intending to provide a home for both. The mother, Millicent, had sized up the situation at Caldicott Hall and promptly decided that Leander would be better off without her underfoot.

She'd gathered up the sum Arthur had already settled on her, given her good name a convenient repolishing, and retired to her home shire, where, last I'd heard, she was walking out with a childhood sweetheart.

Adults, in Leander's experience, were a dodgy lot. One had to rely on them when they were forever disappearing and forever leaving him behind.

"I will not leave you in London. You will return with me to the Hall. Understand, Leander, that climbing out on the roof when you simply want to have a talk with me will not be tolerated. You are frustrated because I undertake frequent travel, however briefly, and I doubt I will stop traveling any time soon. My hope is that you will come along with me to Town, be bored witless, and learn to trust me when I say I will always come home."

"His Grace hasn't come home."

Touché. Another abandonment, and Leander and his ducal uncle got along swimmingly. "Uncle Arthur is touring the South of France. Can you show me where that is on a map?"

Leander snorted and scampered down the roof. "I can show you every capital on the map, even Hell-stinky, though Finland is just a Grand Duchy, not a country."

I navigated the slope much more carefully. "Then your punishment for going absent without leave again will be to list all the European capitals with their countries or duchies. Mind you spell them correctly."

He climbed through the window as nimbly as a housebreaker's apprentice. "And you will take me with you to Town, right?"

"I have given you my word, Leander. When have I ever broken my word to you?"

My nephew looked up at me with a solemn little countenance that put me strongly in mind of his father in a serious moment.

He wrapped a skinny arm around my waist, mashed his face against my middle, then twirled away. "Never. You never have broken your word to me, Uncle Julian, and we are going to Town."

I explained to Miss Hunter that she would be coming along with us, which considerably doused Leander's enthusiasm, and then set the boy to work listing capitals.

I did not know what to do with him, but trying his nerves with my repeated absences was surely the wrong course. He might, eventually, learn to trust that absence was not inchoate abandonment, but he was a small boy, and that lesson would take time.

∼

"I'll consult the solicitors as briefly as possible. Certain information should not be entrusted to the mail." I offered that explanation to MacNamara as a footman handed Miss Hunter into the traveling coach.

MacNamara eyed the team stomping and swishing their tails. "I thought you'd confront Strother before you did anything else."

"I've set one of our gamekeepers to quietly nosing about the surrounds of Pleasant View. If I'm to cross paths with Strother on his morning hack, I need to know his usual routes. Ten thousand acres is a lot of ground. Meanwhile, the London solicitors can arm me with specific information regarding Miss Hannah's, the Stadlers', and Strother's personal finances."

My excuses were growing more credible, though in this case, I was also telling the truth. A gamekeeper could also discern whether the Stadlers were discreetly tolerating some lucrative poaching and if the help was grumbling about late wages or vacancies going unfilled.

"Then Godspeed to you," MacNamara said, stepping back and leaning heavily on a cane. "I will contain my frustration for a few more days."

"Regale the duchess with the usual reminiscences about Spain. She will appreciate your gift with a yarn."

"I'll tell her all the tales I know about you and Lord Harry."

"Not all the tales, please. Her good opinion matters to me. As for Harry, *nil nisi bonum* is the best course."

"*De mortuis nil nisi bonum dicendum est.* Of the dead, only good is to be spoken. Attributed by Diogenes to Chilon of Sparta."

"In Harry's case, a bit of a challenge, I grant you." We shook hands, and I climbed in, feeling more than a little guilty.

I could be making the same inquiries the gamekeeper was about. Even fifteen miles' distance between the properties meant that in disguise, I would not be recognized by the sort frequenting the local coaching inn's rathskeller. Pleasant View patronized a different market town from Caldicott Hall, and only the largest gatherings—a formal ball, for example—would see Caldicotts and Stadlers socializing.

I hadn't been through one of those ordeals since before I'd bought my colors. I'd be expected to wear my regimentals, and such a prospect sat very ill with me indeed.

We made good time up to Town, and Miss Hunter had packed a number of books in Leander's traveling satchel. She and the boy read to each other, while I pondered Miss Stadler's situation.

According to every Gothic novel ever written and more than a few Mayfair scandals, money, revenge, and passion were the usual reasons for a young lady's disappearance. MacNamara had not described Miss Hannah as given to wild romantic impulses, which left money and revenge. The Stadlers apparently lacked means, as measured by aristocratic standards, so upon whom...

Well, damn. I nearly told John Coachman to turn right back around. I needed to ask MacNamara who *his* enemies were. Remiss of me not to do so sooner, but I could send a pigeon to the Hall with the requisite inquiry once we arrived in Town.

"Are you forgetting your name, Uncle Julian?"

Leander asked his question quietly, his governess having drifted off against the bench's cushioned squab. I had yielded the forward-facing seat to the woman and child, and Miss Hunter had accepted with undue relief. Many people found the backward-facing perch a recipe for nausea, but I wasn't usually among them.

"Forgetting my name?"

"Atticus says you have forgetting spells, when you don't know who you are or where you are or who Good King George is, but you always remember after a rest."

Thank you, Atticus, for giving a little boy one more thing to worry about. "He speaks the truth. I am prone to short spells of memory lapse, and thus far they have always passed." The possibility of another outcome—memories that never returned—haunted me.

"Will you forget me?"

This was why children were to be confined to the nursery. They asked the most confounding questions under circumstances that allowed little to no prevarication.

"Temporarily, I have forgotten who my own mother is, but even when that happened, Leander, I still knew Her Grace cared very much for me and deserved my loyalty and trust." To be embarrassingly honest, when I'd been stripped of my prejudices and preconceptions, I had been *better* able to see Her Grace's regard for me than when I'd been in full possession of my entrenched biases.

Leander flopped back against the seat cushions and stared at a spot above my head. "I forget Mama sometimes. I don't forget her in my prayers, but I forget she's gone. I forget *her*."

"That is to be expected. You are growing up and filling your little head with all manner of facts and new abilities. Memories have to sometimes step aside to make room for freshly acquired information, but as long as you recall your mother in your prayers, you have nothing to fret about."

I wanted nothing so much as to haul the boy into my lap and hug the stuffing out of him. He was on reconnaissance in unfamiliar territory. His lifelong ally had deserted him, and in her place was this rackety Uncle Julian fellow, who frequently disappeared for days on end and who from time to time had the memory of a halfwit.

"Does Mama recall me in her prayers?" he asked, glancing at Miss Hunter. "Miss says yes, but Miss isn't a mother."

"My dear boy, I have it from an unassailable authority that Her Grace implores the Almighty every night to look after not only you, but also me and your late father and your uncle Arthur."

"My papa is dead."

"And yet, his mother still prays for him, though he's doubtless larking about from cloud to cloud, teasing all the pretty angels and playing Garden of Eden when he's feeling particularly frisky."

Leander smiled. A wan effort, but better than the solemn gaze of a melancholy boy. "Mama said Papa was jolly."

A bit too jolly for his own good, frequently. "He was jolly, handsome, charming, and a very good brother." Most of the time. "You can be sure that he's putting in a good word for you with the celestial authorities when the occasion permits and that your mother never, ever forgets to include you in her prayers."

"Will we reach London soon, Uncle Julian?"

Miss Hunter discreetly scratched her nose, though her eyes remained closed.

"We have reached London, or the outskirts thereof. The tolls come closer together, the traffic becomes ridiculous, but the middle of the day is a good time to make an inbound assault. The only better time is the middle of the night, which is why a lot of the mail coaches leave from and arrive to London after dark."

Leander was a very different boy from Atticus. He'd not once asked to ride up with John Coachman. He hadn't wheedled for food from the hamper, and he wasn't prone to fidgeting, though he was younger than Atticus.

During the years Atticus had spent learning to avoid a cuff on the head for a dropped tray, Leander had enjoyed a mother's guiding influence. Leander already read well and did simple sums. Atticus struggled with vocabulary and spelling and had little patience for history unless the topic was some sanguinary battle.

And I knew not what to do with either one of them.

"It smells different here," Leander said. "Like coal. The Hall doesn't smell like coal."

"What does the Hall smell like?"

"Grass when the groundsmen are scything, manure when the loafing sheds are cleaned out, lavender when I'm in my bed. Bread when Mrs. Gwinnett is baking. All sorts of smells, but not coal."

I hoped those mundane aromas would become the scents of home to him, the scents of safety and family and security.

The coach lurched through the streets of Knightsbridge, then around Hyde Park to the duke's Mayfair residence. I'd sent word ahead of our arrival, and the property was known to Leander from his first encounters with his Caldicott relations.

When the vehicle rocked to a halt in the mews, he leaped down, tore across the alley, and bolted into the back garden like a child liberated from catechism on a fine summer day. I handed Miss Hunter down, and she paused before pursuing her charge.

"You handled his questions well, my lord. I am not a mother, nor even an auntie, the boy is right about that. Leander pays attention to what you say, and your words were both honest and comforting. A letter to his mother might be in order."

She bustled on her way, a small, quiet, sweet woman with more patience than I could claim on my most saintly day.

I had much to do in London. I would inquire of our solicitors regarding Miss Stadler and inquire of the parish authorities regarding Atticus's brother. But my first errand, the one that had sealed my determination to come to London, was a call on my intended.

I had no sooner ordered a tray and a bath—one did not call upon one's prospective bride wearing the dust of the road—than I was informed that I had a caller awaiting me in the family parlor.

An odd choice in the ducal abode, which boasted an informal and a formal parlor, as well as His Grace's public sitting room and personal sitting room, to which few save family were admitted. All I could think was that my godmother, Lady Ophelia Oliphant, had got wind of my appearance in Town. Her Grace might have sent word, or Godmama's spies here at Caldicott House might have alerted her.

When I arrived at the family parlor, I found not my godmother, but Hyperia West, looking cool, tidy, and lovely. The scent of roses enveloped me as I made my bow, and then, without conscious thought, my arms were around her, my nose was buried against her hair, and I was so thankful to have her in my embrace that my composure was imperiled.

CHAPTER FOUR

"Jules, are you well?" Hyperia whispered those words near my ear, and I made the monumental effort to turn loose of her, but kept hold of her hand.

"I am infinitely improved for being able to behold you, Perry. I take it my note arrived?"

"Delivered this morning. The weather is fine, and I knew you'd make good time up from the Hall. God bless a trustworthy pigeon. Shall we sit?"

The sound of her voice, the quiet of her presence, that soft rosy scent... They soothed me, and only then did I admit that my nerves were more ragged than I'd realized, which made little sense. MacNamara's investigation might turn out to be nothing more than a young lady seeking diversion. Nobody at the Hall or in the greater Caldicott family was ill, and my intended was in charity with me.

"The weather is fine, but growing hot," I said as I seated Hyperia on the sofa and took the place beside her, "as it does with the approach of June. Leander is a good traveler, and traffic wasn't too awful."

"Haying keeps people in the country at this time of year. Have you begun at the Hall?"

I linked my fingers with hers. We were engaged, hence the blessed absence of a chaperone.

"We aren't quite ready for haying, but might we please not talk of things agrarian? The topic is as inexhaustible as it is dull. How are you? Is your brother behaving?"

Healy West was a young man who had yet to find his feet, as the saying went. He nonetheless considered himself the head of his family and exerted authority over Hyperia's funds. This was unfortunate, because Healy was a stranger to financial discipline. He'd been a poor steward of his family's resources, and luck alone had kept some of his wilder schemes from landing him in debtors' prison—thus far.

Well, luck and Hyperia's unceasing vigilance, abetted on occasion by my own humble efforts.

"Healy has finished drafting his second play, and he's begun a third. They are related, like an anthology of books, which he believes will make them more popular. The rake will be redeemed in the third play and so forth. I don't want to talk about Healy."

"Right. Inexhaustible and dull. How are you?"

She had taken off her bonnet. Bonnets in the usual course were designed to keep a man from seeing a lady's face if she didn't want him looking at her. I could watch Hyperia by the hour and still not guess all the thoughts whirling behind her calm green eyes.

"I am bored," she said. "I accept the appropriate invitations and sit among the dowagers and gouty uncles. I like them, for the most part. They enjoy wickedly naughty humor and don't put on airs, but I would rather be at home reading a good book or, better still, beating you at cribbage."

She was up a mere two games in our ongoing tournament. "Perhaps I can alleviate your boredom to a minor degree. I've become involved in another investigation, Perry, and that is my nominal excuse for coming to Town."

"You did not come just to show Leander the sights?"

"I came to see you, first, and to investigate a revelation that has me reeling." Her Grace had seen the truth—I was morally and constitutionally incapable of ignoring a brother missing in action. "Atticus let slip that he has, or had, a male sibling. They were put on the parish together, but the brother was farmed out to some establishment in Chelsea. They might well be twins. Atticus says the headmaster could not tell them apart."

Hyperia paused while fixing my tea. "Baby farming does not often end well for the baby, Jules."

Baby farming—sending infants from urban poorhouses to foster in the cleaner air of the countryside—was notoriously dangerous for the infants involved.

"Tom was three or four when he went to the country, which should have given him a better chance of survival than a smaller child would have had. Atticus describes him as mischievous, which I will interpret as resourceful. Atticus is certainly quick-witted."

A footman rapped on the jamb of the open door.

"I ordered a tray," Hyperia said. "I hope you don't mind?"

"I ordered one too. I am hungry, now that you mention it." Famished and thirsty. I'd partaken sparingly of the hamper in the coach, mindful that both Leander and Miss Hunter needed sustenance. I'd also been mentally preoccupied for the entire distance.

"Dodds, isn't it?" I asked the fellow as he pushed a tea cart into the parlor. He was blond, ruddy, and six feet if he was an inch.

"Aye, milord. I answer to Yorkshire belowstairs, but Dodds is my surname."

He was well spoken for a footman, though the Dales accent was undeniable. "Please thank Cook for this lavish spread and let her know that supper will be early. We'll keep country hours while we bide here, and a simple menu will do."

"I'll tell her, milord, but she was off to market the instant the pigeon landed. She went muttering about fricassee of this and *à la française* that. Will there be anything else, sir?"

"No, thank you. Well, yes. If you could pay a call on the nursery.

Miss Hunter and her charge might need a snack. Let her know that your escort is available if she and Master Leander would like to visit the park."

He brightened considerably. "I'll do that, milord. I will be happy to do just that, and on such a fine day too." He departed with a bow and a jaunty step.

"Somebody wants a bit of fresh air," Hyperia said, passing over my tea. "From Yorkshire to London must be quite an adjustment. You pour out for me. I'll make up the plates."

I adored this sort of informality as much as I adored Hyperia's bottomless store of common sense. She steadied me and occasionally brought me up short. I hoped I provided her the same sort of ballast against life's challenges.

She passed me a heaping plate while I drizzled honey into her cup.

"I know what you're about, Julian. You are trying to tell yourself that hope where Tom is concerned is justified, but hope doesn't really come into it, does it? This goes back to Harry."

Her tone said that the whole subject of Harry was a bit tiresome, and that was all too true.

"I have to try, Hyperia. If I can't find the boy, I can at least find the truth." The tea was strong, hot, and sweet, but the best tonic was Hyperia's company.

"Because you never saw Harry's body, never saw his grave. Has it occurred to you to look for his final resting place?"

"Not if I have to return to France to do it." I did not like to hear French spoken, though French was as much my native tongue as English. I did not like to read in French, or to recollect my travels in France. That Arthur might one day bide there made me uneasy, but his liaison with Banter was not a crime in France, while it was a hanging felony in England.

One deceased brother was one too many.

"If you did decide to return to France," Hyperia said, "I'd go with you, assuming Lady Ophelia was willing to join the expedition."

Why not assume we'd be married before embarking on such a journey? "Let's consign France to the conversational midden, along with haying and Healy. Let me tell you about this investigation, though it might turn out to be so much foolishness."

We demolished sandwiches, tarts, cherries, and slices of buttered gingerbread—truly, I had been famished—and I gave Hyperia my report on the situation with Miss Hannah Stadler.

"I'm casting around for a motive," I said, finishing my second slice of gingerbread. "The Stadlers are not magnificently wealthy, Miss Hannah never interfered with another young lady's marital aspirations, and MacNamara describes her as a paragon of good sense. Why would somebody snatch her away? Mightn't she simply be enjoying the sea air?"

"You have eliminated ransom, revenge, and romance as motives, but where are your facts, Julian? How many times have you told me that a reconnaissance officer first assembled observations without spinning any theories, and when he had a heap of evidence, only then did he begin to conjecture about its significance."

I stopped in mid-reach for a third slice of gingerbread. "You are absolutely, humblingly correct. I know little of Miss Stadler's true situation."

"And you've forgotten about the Stadler hoard."

"Good heavens. Do tell."

"A trove of ancient Irish gold came into the family at some point, shrouded in antiquity. The pieces might have been originally acquired by some old Roman, or they might have dated much earlier. Little is known of their provenance. Less is known about how the Stadlers acquired them. 'By marriage' is the tale of record. The few pieces I've seen are gorgeous, Jules. The gold glows. It's said other pieces were melted down to reset precious gems, and still others are beautiful but barbaric. They would be worth a fortune, if you knew a discreet goldsmith."

"Are we certain this treasure still exists? The Stadlers have fired off three daughters already."

Hyperia poured me more tea. "And none of them married all that well, did she? A baron or a knight, possibly a baronet or a pair of Honorables, or..." She set down the pot. "A mercer's son? The details are vague, but those are not the sort of matches that require ancient torques and golden bracelets."

"Perhaps they were love matches. I am a great fan of the love match, myself."

She peered into her empty tea cup. "Now you flirt. Now that you've put this puzzle before me. I know the heir, Strother, in passing. He is singularly forgettable. Perhaps the jewels are being held in reserve to attract him a suitable wife."

"These jewels shed a very different light on the entire business. I suspect MacNamara has no knowledge of them. Tell me more about Strother."

We ended up strolling in the garden, where the duchess's roses were in glorious bloom. Hyperia's report filled in some blanks, raised new questions, and gave me an excuse to walk arm in arm with her in the afternoon sunshine.

The creeping sense of anxiety and melancholy that had been dogging me at the Hall receded, and my interest in MacNamara's problem caught hold.

We had a motive, or a possible motive. An ancient treasure added possibilities both intriguing and alarming to the options before us.

Hyperia and I mapped out a busy plan for the coming day—call upon the Caldicott solicitors and call upon the parish authorities who'd been responsible for Atticus and his brother. Call upon Lady Ophelia, who was in Town apparently, rather than ruralizing.

I resented the entire agenda, but for the fact that Hyperia would attend to it with me. Perhaps the malaise creeping over me at the Hall had been nothing more than a symptom of separation from Hyperia, and that at least was easily remedied.

"These matters are always shrouded in innuendo and indirection, my lord, but our figures tend to be reliable." Mr. Postlethwaite passed a tidily written list of names across the polished mahogany table.

Down the left margin marched all the diamonds and heiresses, infantry in full evening parade dress.

Lady Julianna Pottinger (£3,700 per annum, 2,500 acres, Gloucestershire) – Daughter to Earl Pevensy, mat. grandsire Marquess of Owings. Comely, accomplished in all the domestic arts, said to favor hill walking and is partial to irises. Fond of reading novels.

Lady Sophia Hillmont (£6,000 per annum, 4,200 acres, incl. two islands, Kirkcudbright) – Daughter of the Marquess of Colminster, pat. grandsire Earl of Percyfield. Polyglot, handsome, and a fine archer. Quite robust.

Miss Evangeline Ratcliffe (£15,000 per annum, an additional £200,000 in trust upon marriage. Dower estate Montemaison, Berks, 8,000 acres). Daughter of the Honorable Thomas Fortescue (heir to Earl Dingford), mother born in Philadelphia but of acceptable British heritage. Further details on file.

"The, um, prospects closer to Caldicott Hall are on the next page, my lord."

Postlethwaite carefully avoided Hyperia's eye. He was every inch the genial, prosperous solicitor. Immaculately groomed, a full head of white hair worn swept back into an old-fashioned queue. His twinkling blue eyes were nonetheless watchful.

"It's three islands," Hyperia said, reading beside me. "In addition to her Scottish properties, Lady Sophia also claims a small island off the Irish coast, courtesy of her late aunt. Good for goats, I'm told."

Bushy white eyebrows rose and subsided as Postlethwaite scribbled a few words on the sheet of foolscap before him.

"I will make a note of that, Miss West. One can fairly easily determine what sums have been set aside for a young lady. The real estate involved in her settlements can be harder to discern. Those assets can be tied up in bequests, covenants running with the land, and personal trusts."

If Postlethwaite thought it odd that Hyperia had accompanied me, he was too good at his profession to show it.

So much wealth riding on the perfect dynastic matches. I turned the page. "You have an asterisk beside Miss Stadler's name." The lady was thought to bring a mere £500 to the union, along with Irish "acreages" and "assorted domestic commodities." Her trousseau, likely comprised of linens, porcelain, silver, a wardrobe, possibly a riding horse and a small conveyance for her personal use. The Irish acreages were probably a couple of modest tenant farms.

Not much, but then, the family's wealth had to be spread over four daughters, with enough left over to keep Pleasant View in trim and Strother in cravat pins and new boots.

"'Sensible,'" Hyperia murmured, reading the few words allotted to Miss Stadler's finer qualities. "'Given to direct speech, though well-liked in the parish. Would run a household with efficiency.' Why the asterisk?"

"That indicates a possible match for the lady in the offing, though perhaps we were too hasty in reaching that conclusion." Postlethwaite jotted another note to himself. "A little less than two years ago, just after the great victory over the Corsican, we heard that Miss Stadler had caught the eye of the Honorable Sylvester Downing. He's heir to Viscount Muldoon. Irish, but still... a viscount is a viscount, if you will pardon a pragmatic observation.

"She apparently dropped him flat," Postlethwaite went on, "sometime last year. Not a broken engagement, but a decision that they would not suit before matters progressed. Downing went back to Ireland with less than gentlemanly grace."

"I heard something about this." Hyperia's gaze went to the law books in row upon row on the library's bookshelves. The whole small chamber smelled of books and silence, a soothing scent. "Wasn't there a rumor that Downing was honestly smitten with Miss Stadler? He went down to Pleasant View on a repairing lease with Strother Stadler and fell top over tail for Strother's sister."

"Miss West, you are indeed well informed. I heard something

to the same effect, but the source was less than reliable given the late hour and empty decanter. Downing has since returned to Town, last I heard, though I am not *au courant* with the lesser lights of the Mayfair whirl. The Irish have such charm, don't they?"

"Downing can be charming," Hyperia said, and she was not offering the man a compliment. "He's generally regarded as a decent catch."

"Not a fortune hunter?" I suggested the translation, but that begged the question: Why would a viscount's heir pursue plain, *sensible*, Hannah Stadler at all?

"Not a fortune hunter," Hyperia said, "but prone to drink and wagers and the usual vices."

I did not parse that euphemism in present company. Hyperia indicated that Downing was a womanizer, and if he was enjoying his bachelorhood that enthusiastically, why marry at all?

"Does he have brothers?" I asked.

The solicitor remained silent.

"Three," Hyperia said. "All in good health, and three younger sisters, who are pretty and pleasant, though the youngest made her come out only this year. The youngest son is said to have left for America."

Like my mother and like Lady Ophelia, Hyperia was a walking appendix to *Debrett's Peerage*, though I hadn't realized quite how much detail her knowledge encompassed.

"If my lord would like to take the list with him, we have copies," Postlethwaite said. "This time of year, the asterisks appear with great frequency, and new names must be added as young ladies leave the schoolroom and prepare for next year's festivities."

Another Season was winding down, in other words. New matches were made, new faces graced the dance floor at Almack's, and perennial bachelors fell to Cupid's arrows—or to the necessity of paying the trades.

"You might be interested to know that Miss Stadler's asterisk could still apply," I said. "She and Captain James MacNamara have grown quite cordial."

"Captain MacNamara of the Royal Artillery?" Postlethwaite asked.

"The very one."

"She's a lucky young lady, then. General Dickson himself speaks highly of the captain. Highly indeed, and well he should. MacNamara's antecedents are well above reproach, and like many a younger son, the war advanced his prospects. He served in Dickson's very battalion, you know."

General Andrew Dickson had been Wellington's choice to manage the entire Peninsular Army's artillery resources, and he'd been pressed into service again at Waterloo. A fine soldier and a shrewd tactician, though I doubted he would recall me, or acknowledge me, if our paths crossed.

"I had some idea that MacNamara served with distinction," I said, "but wasn't aware of Dickson's praise. Quite an honor. You've given me and Miss West much to think about, and we thank you for your time."

"Delighted to be of service, my lord, Miss West." Postlethwaite ushered us out into the sunny morning, though I did find a moment to pull him aside and offer some pointed instructions on a topic dear to my heart.

I handed Hyperia up into the Town coach, grateful for its shadowed interior. A tap on the roof with my walking stick had John Coachman giving the horses leave to walk on.

"Interesting," Hyperia said. "First, we realize the Stadler family does have some wealth, now we learn of Downing, a rejected suitor who might bear a grudge against Miss Stadler."

"If so, he's waited some time to play the scorned lover."

"The sequence of events suggests Hannah threw Downing over for the captain, Jules. She could be in Dublin by now if Downing is our man."

This kind of conversation—matching conjectures to facts and

theories—was usually among my favorites, and Hyperia my favorite partner in them. My usual enthusiasm eluded me, probably because the questions were multiplying apace.

"Why would Downing pursue a woman of such limited means, Hyperia? He's in line for a title, a bachelor with no need to settle down as yet—or ever if his brothers are dutiful."

Hyperia turned her head as if to gaze out the window, and because she was properly bonneted, her face was completely obscured.

"I am a woman of limited means, Julian. What motive do you suppose people attribute to you for our engagement?"

"Utter besottedness explains the whole business—at least on my end. What's your excuse for taking up with a forgetful fellow who is no longer received in the best homes and dependent on his collection of blue spectacles on days as bright as this one?"

The question was meant to invite flirtation, but my intended merely sighed. "I don't like the facts we have in hand, Julian. I want to believe that Hannah Stadler dodged off with an auntie to get a break from the stultifying existence of a rural spinster. Perhaps the auntie insisted, though to the best of my knowledge, Miss Stadler hasn't any aunties."

"She has a worthy suitor in MacNamara, worthier than I knew and perhaps worthier than he himself understands."

The coach swayed around a corner, which should have sent Hyperia's weight more snugly against my hip. She grabbed the strap hanging by the window and resumed watching the street.

"He's in line to inherit a lordship," she said. "The next brother up fell in some battle or other. The oldest has consumption. The heir bides in Scotland rather than jaunting about London, which suggests the disease is progressing."

I wanted to take her hand, ask what besides the investigation was preoccupying her. "How do you know these things, Perry? If I pointed to a passing Town swell, you'd likely know his particulars at a glance. I am in awe."

She spared me another half glance. "How well would you know the mountains of Spain if you'd grown up there and spent your whole life navigating the valleys and heights? The glorified gentry such as myself spend most of the social Season chatting, and we chat about other people. It's not even gossip so much as it's comparing maps and assessing terrain. A rockslide here, a flood there, a great crop of hops on the way over in that direction." She rubbed her temple with gloved fingers. "You are right. The heat is becoming a bit much."

The heat and the pervasive stink of London in summer, especially close to that increasingly ineffective open sewer referred to as the River Thames.

"Are you up to a call on the poorhouse, Hyperia? I can manage that sortie by myself if you'd rather I take you home."

I did not want to set foot in that establishment on my own, but I would if I must.

"I'll come with you, and we can share lunch in the garden when we're through. A note to Lady Ophelia is in order, isn't it?"

A fine suggestion, though the prospect of lunch in the garden earned my heartier approval.

"I did not like that list," I said, taking Hyperia's hand. "I didn't care for it at all." The tidy assessment of young women, their wealth, their personal preferences... I loathed the whole notion, though conscientious solicitors all over Town were likely keeping similar lists of bachelors for the consideration of the heiresses.

Hyperia squeezed my fingers. "Neither did I, and my name wasn't even on it."

We remained like that, holding hands, sharing a vaguely unhappy mood, and, at the same time, separated by a silence neither of us was inclined to break.

CHAPTER FIVE

"How did you explain this trip to Town to Atticus?" Hyperia asked as the coach inched through a crowded intersection.

"I did not explain. I announced." That strategy had taken some thought on my part. "I told him I'd be making a quick journey. That Leander is ready for some properly tailored company attire, his first pair of tall boots, and so forth. The seamstresses at the Hall can mend the wardrobe the boy's mother made for him, but he's growing like topsy and could do with some fresh garments."

"Atticus accepted that?"

The coach picked up speed, though the horses were still walking. "I don't know. He remains quite enamored of the stable, Perry, and in my absence, he will exercise Atlas every day. That's his idea of a fine way to spend a morning. He's dead set against spending time in the schoolroom with Leander. Atticus's reading has nonetheless improved, and I hold out hope for his spelling."

Hope was a far cry from *optimism*.

Hyperia bumped me with her shoulder. "You'll have to take Leander along to Bond Street, then."

Well, drat. "Suppose I will." The tailors wouldn't simply record the boy's measurements. They would insist on showing me dozens of fabric samples and explaining various cuts and styles until I wanted to run howling across London Bridge.

"And Hoby's," Hyperia went on, "if he's truly to have his first pair of tall boots."

Double drat. "I can do that after lunch."

Harry would have loved attending to these little rites of passage, would have loved showing his son London from Lord Harry Caldicott's singular point of view. Harry had been keen on fashion. I was utterly indifferent to it, provided my linen was clean and my clothing fit. I'd been the better hand at disguises, though, while Harry had made it a point to know which gemstones symbolized what virtues.

An asinine little hobby.

Dwelling on Harry was seldom cause for joy. I swiveled my mental cannon to what the interview with Postlethwaite had told us.

"We aren't ahead by much, are we?" Hyperia asked. "Mr. Downing falls under suspicion, but only as a vague possibility."

One suspect was better than none, and Downing was back in England. "We know the gold wasn't part of Hannah's dowry. Does that matter?" What looked like just another pebble of information could turn out to be the essential pea under the mattress. Hard to know the difference except in hindsight.

"You're right that the gold wasn't *listed* as part of Hannah's dowry," Hyperia said, "but that might mean it was already liquidated to launch Hannah's sisters or to secure Strother's inheritance. I have renewed appreciation for why you do so much to-ing and fro-ing at the beginning of an investigation, Jules. It's all an ever-widening darkness."

"Perhaps the good headmaster will have some answers for us regarding our Atticus."

Mr. Devilbiss could have been Postlethwaite's shorter cousin, right down to the merry, shrewd blue eyes. Devilbiss had a heartier manner and a slightly more generous paunch.

The way his eyes slid over Hyperia made me want to backhand him into the Thames. He subjected her to a flicking appraisal that took in her person—healthy, female—and her station. My sense was, he was at once assessing her as a male animal evaluated a female—and being obvious about it—and considering her possibilities as a charitable donor or committee member.

I was inclined to hate him, but then, if he sought resources to provide for the poor, his ruthlessness must be excused. His rudeness was beyond forgiveness.

"My lord, miss, this is an unexpected pleasure. What brings you to our humble establishment?"

Humble the poorhouse might be, but its façade was majestic. The edifice no doubt dated from the last century, before London began to gobble up the surrounding countryside, and Bloomsbury was nearly rural. Devilbiss's charitable operation rose to three full stories plus an attic and spanned half the length between street corners. Tall windows graced the two upper stories, each one topped with a tidy Adams pediment. The building material was granite, the blue front door adorned with symmetrical pots of red geraniums.

The sashes and shutters were painted white—an extravagance given London's foul air—and the whole presented with an understated air of civic virtue. A wealthy family had likely built this establishment as their quasi-London abode, and heating it properly would require a small fortune.

"We're seeking information about a child," Hyperia said, taking off her gloves and stashing them in her reticule. "A small boy, first name Thomas, possibly a twin and definitely a sibling to another boy, Atticus. They would have been here about five years ago."

Devilbiss affected a thoughtful expression. "Thomas is a very common name, miss."

"Atticus," she replied, "is unusual. Moreover, we know that Atticus was sent to work at Makepeace, home of the Viscount Longacre, in Kent, upon the occasion of his fifth birthday."

"Now that gives us something to work with. Please do have a seat, and I will provide these details to the matron best suited to consulting our records. Shall I ring for tea?"

His office was as well appointed as Postlethwaite's, if a bit less scholarly. Fresh hydrangeas occupied a brass bowl on the windowsill, the andirons in the swept hearth had been recently blackened, and the carpet was thick Axminster of understated floral design. His furniture tended to solid lines and generous upholstery, and the walls were hung in dark green silk.

"No tea for me," Hyperia said. "My lord?"

"I'll pass as well."

"Then excuse me for a moment." Postlethwaite bustled out, a man determined to accommodate his guests.

"He would tell you," Hyperia said, perching on a wing chair, her back very straight, "that when his donors call upon him and when potential donors are good enough to meet with him, he must provide a setting in which they are comfortable. Wealthy widows cannot be expected to entrust sums to an establishment that offers them hard benches and stale bread."

"Silk on the walls, Perry?"

"He'll claim it was donated. Perhaps it was."

She was angry, and for that, I loved her. "Did you notice that the windows are all closed on the upper floors? A day growing hotter by the hour, and not a single window cracked."

The only thing worse than a schoolroom full of reluctant scholars was a sweltering or freezing schoolroom full of reluctant scholars.

Devilbiss's office had a French door that opened onto a small brick patio ringed by privet hedges. A hint of a breeze came through the partly opened door, and more geraniums added a splash of color between wrought-iron chairs.

"You would notice the windows," Hyperia said, smiling slightly. "Devilbiss will claim the high ceilings ensure the children are quite comfortable on warmer days. Moreover, closed windows are safer than the open variety. Unless, of course, you'd like to donate a sum sufficient to bar the windows?"

I prowled along the bookcase behind Devilbiss's desk, which was sparsely decorated with improving tomes. *Fordyce's Sermons*, Marcus Aurelius's *Meditations*, Bunyan's *The Pilgrim's Progress*. The books were propped to face out, a display for the benefit of guests. I wanted to pitch the lot through the French door.

"Julian, a poorhouse is better than nothing. For some, it's enough. For others, it's a step up from debtors' prison."

"For children... I hate to think of Atticus here."

"He would probably have died but for this place. Try to think of it that way." Hyperia spoke from an informed, even jaded perspective.

"Do you and Devilbiss have a prior acquaintance, Perry?"

"I know his type. He will see to it that the children are adequately provided for, and his definition of 'adequate' will be parsimonious but defensible, given how many children are in his care. He doesn't want them getting too comfortable, you see, because hardship inspires them to overcome obstacles."

"So we starve children for their own benefit. How enlightened of us. I want to kick something."

Her smile became a grin. "You want to beat the stuffing out of Devilbiss. So do I, provided I could wear gloves lest I actually touch him. They do keep records, though, Julian. We can be encouraged by that."

I felt instead *dis*couraged. "I can't hear any children, Perry. This building is supposedly full of well-kept, thriving children, and I hear no thunder of unruly feet, no laughter, no protests presaging the need for a nap."

"Julian, don't."

She was right. The poor laws were outdated, everyone agreed on that much, and the poor were growing in number. Given the passage of the Corn Laws, with their relentless import tariffs, those numbers would doubtless grow yet faster in years to come, and the people most likely to face starvation had no voice in Parliament to guard their interests.

I was estimating the value of Devilbiss's ornate cherrywood desk when he finally returned.

"Success, miss, my lord. Success of a sort!" He held a file bound in a blue ribbon. "The child Atticus bided with us for less than a year before we were able to find him a post suited to his tender years and limited abilities. The notes I consulted say the boy was slow of speech and wit and only moderately disobedient, but easily led by his sibling."

"We are most interested in the sibling," Hyperia said. "Tom or Thomas."

"A twin, you are right about that, miss. The boys were identical, and the matrons despaired of telling them apart. For the sake of the general peace and because Thomas was a bad influence on Atticus, we arranged for Thomas to go to a private situation in Chelsea."

He beamed as if he'd found a piece of the true cross just for us.

"We were aware of that much as well." I ran a finger along the edge of the bookshelf and rubbed the dust off with my thumb. "We need to know which establishment, when, and any other particulars regarding the child's current whereabouts."

Devilbiss dimmed the beacon of his self-congratulation. "Might I inquire as to why, my lord?"

"Because in the normal course, siblings care for each other and should not be turned into strangers for the convenience of those charged with their protection."

I took a turn on the receiving end of one of those flicking appraisals.

"Just so, my lord, and you are absolutely right. The poorhouse, however, is not the normal course. You will surely agree that the lad Atticus would have suffered, would have continued to suffer, had his naughty brother been permitted to go on leading the slower sibling astray. That would have been an injustice, my lord, and might have blighted the slower boy's prospects for his entire life. One must be logical about these things, because sentiment can invite one down many a bewildering path. The best interests of the child must always prevail."

I could hardly breathe for the impulse to do violence. At four years old, Thomas had been labeled incorrigible and Atticus considered a dunce. No family, cast into an unfamiliar and terrifying world, then ripped apart because of a childish prank or two.

I'd fisted both hands. I opened those fists and found myself staring at the hydrangeas.

The floral symbol for bad luck in love.

Hyperia rose and linked her arm through mine. "If you will tell us the specific situation into which Thomas was sent, we'll take no more of your time."

"Thomas was placed with a Mrs. Merryweather on Burden Lane, Chelsea. I am sorry to report that her establishment is listed in the notes as having burned to the ground shortly thereafter. You might inquire locally for details, but our files relate to our charges, and once Thomas was given the benefit of a new placement, our obligation to him was fulfilled." He looked from me to Hyperia. "I am sorry."

He wasn't sorry enough, not nearly.

"Mrs. Merryweather, Burden Lane, Chelsea," Hyperia murmured. "Thank you. We shall continue our inquiries elsewhere. My lord, I am in need of fresh air."

"Of course." I offered Devilbiss half a bow and let Perry lead me out into the bright sunshine, and for once, I was glad for it.

"You could leave the matter there," she said as we waited for the coach to come plodding around the corner. "Atticus can take up the investigation when he's older. No one would blame you for delegating further inquiries to him if he's so inclined."

And let the cold trail become entirely obliterated? "I would blame myself."

"Julian..."

"I thought Atticus should be spared uncertainty regarding his brother's fate, Perry, and that was before I learned that Thomas has likely perished in a fire. It's bad enough to think you have a sibling in an obscure location, living a life you have no part of, but to conclude that he's dead and not know for certain how and why he expired? I can tell you, emphatically, that is a hell nobody should have to dwell in."

The coach appeared. I wanted to cover the distance to the ducal town house on foot, to walk off my upset, but Hyperia was deserving of my escort and the comfort of the coach.

"You'd rather not sit in that vehicle and brood," she said. "I'd rather not sit in there and watch you brood. Tell John Coachman we'll walk, but promise me you will set a modest pace, Jules. My legs are shorter than yours, and I'm wearing stays."

"You are also carrying my heart." Which at the moment was a weighty burden indeed. "I could not love you more, Hyperia West."

She discreetly hugged me by the arm, and in due course, we made a dignified progress to the leafy surrounds of Mayfair.

*

My brother Arthur, His Grace of Waltham, was six years my senior and worlds ahead of me in the art of living a life that was both responsible and comfortable. In Spain, I'd excelled at surviving on short rations with little shelter. Arthur excelled at carrying the weight of a duchy upon his shoulders, while yet allowing himself excellent tucker, fine art, and a back garden that soothed and delighted the senses.

The roses were in a blooming riot, the irises still making a show, and the spices thriving in their pots and borders. The effect was a magical feast for the nose, eyes, and subtler senses. I wished, for the hundred thousandth time, that Arthur were home and not kicking his heels in France with Banter.

"His Grace moved the roses," I said, peeling the rind from a succulent orange. "They were along the back wall—a deterrent to invaders—but he moved them into the sun, where they appear to be thriving."

Hyperia and I were finishing our meal at a wrought-iron grouping that caught morning sun and afternoon shade. The perfect place to sit and read the newspapers or simply sit and think.

"Your mother might have done that," Hyperia said, sipping her meadow tea.

"She had decades to rearrange this garden if that was her preference. Arthur moved the roses. Had them moved. He should put raspberries along the back wall if he needs to deter housebreakers. Raspberries need less sun and have more thorns." Though less sun meant fewer berries.

Hyperia regarded me over her tankard. "Julian, this is a Mayfair residence, not a fortress. I must conclude the heat truly disagrees with you."

"While present company agrees with me very much. Thank you, Perry."

She put aside her drink. "For?"

"For keeping me from putting out Devilbiss's lights, for prodding Postlethwaite to usefulness, for knowing more about MacNamara's situation than I do. In the usual course, an investigation grips my imagination, and I can't wait to be kicking over rocks and peering under figurative beds. The doubts and reluctance come later. I almost expect them now. In this case... I know Miss Stadler might be in peril or at least enduring uncomfortable circumstances. I know she could have been abducted for nefarious purposes. My interest in resolving her difficulties has yet to catch fire."

The situation was worse even than that. I knew Miss Stadler might be enduring *captivity*, a fate in some cases worse than death. I wanted to free her if that was the reality, truly I did. And yet, she might also be strolling the seashore at Lyme Regis, so here I was, dodging off to London on the trail of answers that in all probability led to a pauper's grave.

Bad of me. My priorities were not as they should be, and I knew it.

"Has melancholia come to call, Julian?" Hyperia put the question gently, which both touched and annoyed me.

I wanted to protest, but this was Perry. My dear, dear Perry, and like me, she preferred the truth to pretty nonsense.

"Some of the elements of melancholia are present. A sense of detachment, of what's-the-use, of watching myself move about and speak and function, and wondering why that Caldicott fellow must ceaselessly stir around. Part of me would rather sit in a dim room with a book open on my lap while I stare at nothing."

"And the rest of you?"

"Is grateful to share a meal with you, to be *able* to stir around. So many who served with me cannot. Harry…"

"Harry?" Hyperia conveyed a touch of asperity even saying his name.

"Harry should be taking Leander to the bootmaker's and the tailor's, shouldn't he?"

She patted my wrist. "If I had one wish for you, Julian, *for us*, it would be to lay to rest Harry's ghost once and for all. He got himself killed, and now it's up to you to see to his son. I dearly hope, wherever Harry is—and I do not automatically consign him to the celestial realm—that he has the plain decency to be grateful to you for taking his offspring in hand. Not all uncles would."

I grasped her fingers and kissed her knuckles. "Come back to the Hall with us. Please. We can be there by sunset tomorrow."

The lady and I were engaged to be married. The highest sticklers would still insist that we not travel a long distance unchaperoned, but Miss Hunter and Leander would be underfoot the whole time, and good roads would see us home in a matter of hours.

"I would love to, Julian, but I am reluctant to leave Healy to his own devices in Town."

"We'll bring him along." I detested the notion of having the great, as yet undiscovered, playwright underfoot at the Hall. Nonetheless, Hyperia was being her usual indispensable self when a matter needed investigating. Then too, whatever malaise stalked me, it kept a greater distance when I was with Hyperia.

I added selfishness to my growing inventory of shortcomings.

"I can discuss it with him," Hyperia said as a rapid patter of feet sounded on the terrace above us. "Your nephew approaches."

"Uncle Julian!" Leander stopped at the top of the terrace steps and spun like a top. "Miss says we're off to Hoby's, and then the tailors', and then Gunter's. Gunter's has ices and cakes and sweets and everything."

His whirling caused him to miss a step, and down the stairs he toppled.

I rushed over to where he lay, sprawled half on the bottom steps, half on the flagstones. "For God's sake, boy, be more careful. You could have cracked your fool head on the stones."

He sat up and pushed aside the hands I was using to check for blood in his hair. "I'm fine, Uncle Julian. You needn't shout. Can we still go to Gunter's?"

Both Hyperia and Miss Hunter were looking at me curiously, and I realized I had raised my voice and spoken quite sharply, while they appeared entirely composed.

Little boys took tumbles. Little boys got up and dusted themselves off in the majority of cases, particularly when the staircases figuring in their misadventures were comprised of exactly six shallow steps.

I hauled him to his feet by the expedient of grasping both of his wrists. "We can still go to Gunter's, provided you are well behaved as we complete our errands. Perhaps you'd fetch my brown top hat from the foyer, and we can be on our way."

He was off like a swift on the wing.

"You'll take the coach?" Hyperia asked.

"We'll go on horseback." I made the decision in the moment. "I have pleasant memories of being up before my father on some of our London jaunts, and wheeled traffic is still miserable." A month hence, fashionable Society would have abandoned the heat and stink of

London for the house parties, rural respites, and Scottish hillwalking expeditions.

"First," I went on, "I will escort you home. Leander can assist the grooms to get a horse ready, preferably the biggest hack in the stable."

The boy returned at his usual gallop, I explained the sequence of events, and Miss Hunter gratefully yielded her charge into the keeping of the grooms. Hyperia and I kept to the shaded alleys, and I soon had her in her own back garden.

"You're struggling a bit, aren't you?" she said. "You've had a busy year, Julian. Perhaps you should tell Captain MacNamara that you haven't the time to take on his problems."

"Now you are being a bad influence. I like the investigations, Perry. They are invariably challenging." Though the challenge was usually how to locate the villains, not finding the gumption to catch them. "MacNamara is a fellow soldier, the last person whose troubles I could ignore, even if I wanted to, though I don't want to. Not truly."

She hugged me among the straggly rhododendrons. "I worry about you, Julian, and I also miss you terribly. Town will soon be dull indeed, and I will try to talk Healy into a repairing lease at the Hall." She kissed my cheek. "Don't brood. Think of Miss Stadler being kept in a stuffy garret somewhere and surviving on crusts of bread and watered ale with only a tattered copy of *Cecilia* to sustain her spirits. She needs you, and I do too."

Hyperia stepped back, and my heart felt bereft.

I waited in the garden until she'd disappeared into the house, and said a small prayer that I was worthy of her esteem. She could be difficult, in a polite, intransigent way, and she could be wrongheaded, but we were learning to be patient with each other and to put differences behind us.

I left the garden and set a fast pace back to headquarters. Leander would be doubting my return—a bequest from his parents, that doubt —and I wanted the afternoon's tasks behind us. In the morning, Hyperia and I would make a sortie to Chelsea and learn what we could about Mrs. Merryweather, late of Burden Lane.

As I mentally reviewed the day's activities, I heard again my exchange with Hyperia in the garden. She had made one of her rare errors in the discussion, though with the best of intentions. According to her, Harry had *got himself* killed.

Strictly speaking, I had *got myself* captured—I walked right up to the French patrol that had taken Harry into custody and presented myself for the same treatment. I had thus arguably been responsible for getting Harry killed.

Not a new thought, but one that sat ill with me, especially when I spent time in proximity to Harry's only surviving child.

CHAPTER SIX

"Leander even chose a cinnamon ice," I said, guiding the phaeton around a pair of swells on horseback who were conferring right in the middle of the street. "Cinnamon was Harry's favorite."

Hyperia made a pretty picture in the early morning Town bustle. We'd reached Knightsbridge, at present thronged with young fellows returning from either a dawn hack in Hyde Park or a night of dissipation. Most would wander through Tatts's stable yard, as much for the company to be found there as for any interest in buying another equine.

"How was Leander for the tailor and the cobbler?" Hyperia asked as we made our way south toward the Thames.

"A model of good behavior. Polite. Patient. Respectful. He's a good boy."

"When he wants to be?"

Leander was always on good behavior around Hyperia, much like Atticus and myself. "You know, Perry, I would have said that about Harry—he was a good fellow when he wanted to be, though he could also be sarcastic, bitter, and self-indulgent. I need to stop comparing Leander to his father. The two have never met, more's the pity.

Leander is his own person, and I must see him as such rather than exclusively as Harry's son."

I halted the gelding pulling our conveyance while a farm wagon heaped with steaming manure lumbered through the intersection.

"Leander likes you, Julian. He looks up to you, and he's on his best behavior so you will take him with you the next time you leave the Hall. How was he at Gunter's?"

"Ecstatic but biddable." I clucked to the horse, who toddled on like the London veteran he was. "The boy deliberated at length over the choice of flavors and informed me that next time, he will try the vanilla." Harry's second-favorite flavor. "Have you considered returning to the Hall with me?"

"If you can give me until noon to pack, I will accompany you. Healy will come down within the week, or so he claims."

My hands were on the ribbons. Otherwise, I would have hugged her for all of London to see. "Well done, Miss West. We will pick you up shortly after noon." My relief at her decision was enormous, and if the celestial powers were merciful, Healy would never bestir himself to leave Town for the Hall.

Hyperia would winkle details from MacNamara that he'd no idea he knew, she'd charm Mrs. Gwinnett into irresistibly delicious menus, and she'd brighten my mother's otherwise placid summer days.

To say nothing of the effect her presence had on my own spirits.

"Was Gunter's an ordeal for you, Jules?"

I was so happy to contemplate her company at the Hall that I didn't even try to prevaricate. "A minor ordeal, but yes. Fashionable Society is still congregating beneath Berkeley Square's maples, and I wasn't prepared for that."

We navigated a narrow path between two cursing fishmongers, and then I told Hyperia the rest of it.

"Two men I served with, a pair of captains who I thought held me in some regard, pretended not to recognize me. A lady who danced a quadrille with me at her come-out ball whispered to her companion and then crossed the street three yards away from where I would have tipped my hat to her. Leander was oblivious, but I didn't anticipate that sort of reception. The rudeness grows tedious."

And some year soon, Leander would notice the whispers and sidelong glances and think he had caused them.

"Do you suppose they thought Leander was your son?"

"In which case, their behavior was beyond ill-bred. He's just a boy, and the circumstances of his birth are certainly no fault of his."

Hyperia treated me to a silence for the length of three streets.

"Perry, I'm sorry. I know how polite society is, and perhaps an outing to Gunter's was badly done on my part, but the boy earned his treat." Then too, illegitimate aristocratic offspring, boys in particular, were politely tolerated by Mayfair Society, so long as their fathers provided for and acknowledged them.

Leander wasn't the issue.

"London is sprawling," Hyperia said as we tooled on toward Chelsea. "The fields are disappearing, the houses sprouting like weeds."

We passed a fancy stone mason's emporium with granite monuments displayed along the roadside. Any number of livery establishments sat cheek by jowl with taverns, a cheesemonger's, butcher's... The houses were mostly new, with an occasional denizen of the previous century standing taller and grander than its younger neighbors.

So much change, and yet, I remained in disgrace with some.

"Where will you start our inquiries?" Hyperia asked as we reached the village of Chelsea proper. The stink of the river was stronger here, though the air was free of coal smoke.

"We begin at the livery. I'll try the nearest parson next, or his wife. Tavern owners hear a lot of gossip that becomes local history."

"You could ask him," Hyperia said, tipping her chin.

An old fellow sat upon a bench outside a busy livery stable. Well, not old, exactly, but no longer young. He wore a battered infantry cap, and his jacket might once have been part of a uniform, though so much dust and mending had befallen the garment that its provenance was dubious.

He whittled without watching the progress of his knife against the chunk of wood in his hands. Blind, perhaps, or an expert whittler.

I handed the phaeton off to a groom and inquired as to the whereabouts of Burden Lane. In accents indicative of a Cornish patrimony, the groom indicated that our destination was up two streets and down a lane to the left. *Turn at the oak, can't miss it.*

We found the lane easily enough. Finding somebody who'd resided in the vicinity for more than five years proved nearly impossible.

A dairymaid with empty milk cans dangling from the yoke on her shoulders told us that the biggest house on the lane had been destroyed by fire some years past, and three other dwellings now occupied the space where the former abode had been. She indicated a lot with three cottages spaced precisely along a curved drive. No great looming oaks, but a trio of young cherry trees already past bearing for the year shaded the front yards.

The dairymaid could not describe the house that had burned down and knew nothing of the fate of its occupants.

Neither did a pair of passing beldames who had just retired to the area with their spouses. Neither did a crossing sweeper or a sprightly gent on his way to the watchmaker's shop.

Too much change, too quickly, and not enough in the way of reliable informants.

"We have made a start," Hyperia said, twirling her parasol. "The neighborhood is genteel. That's something."

Genteel. Well, yes. Retired-sea-captain genteel and spinster-auntie genteel. A boy could land in worse situations.

"We're for the vicarage," I said, winging my arm.

But that, too, turned out to be an excursion of limited value, despite the fame of the local church. The vicar and his missus were at the seaside on holiday. The curate, a spotty young fellow with a bobbing Adam's apple, was very recently arrived to his post at All Saints.

He knew nothing of a fire five years ago on Burden Lane, and such was his neophyte status that he could not refer us to any village elders who might be better informed. Perhaps if I called again in a month?

I allowed as how I just might do that. We declined his offer of a tour of his most venerable church, though I hated to disappoint him. Hyperia and I instead retreated to the livery, where I retrieved a hamper kindly packed by Arthur's cook.

I wasn't particularly hungry. "We ought to be getting back if you're to have time to pack for a visit to the Hall."

"Nonsense, Jules. When you are on the hunt, you forget to eat and sleep. We will have a quick picnic and discuss next steps."

My commanding officer had issued my orders. I scanned the surrounds and spotted an empty bench near where the whittler sat. My choice was a few yards from the livery entrance, bordering a patch of grass that had doubtless provided many a snack for the hard-working equines on the property.

"We'll have shade," I said, "and you are right. We should discuss next steps now, while the morning's disappointments are fresh in our minds."

My blue spectacles had attracted a few curious glances, but I detected no hostility. Chelsea was awash in new faces and new shops, but still had the basic friendliness of an English village.

For now.

"I am hungry," Hyperia said, taking the bench. "We need not tarry long. You can write to the vicar, and I'm sure he'll reply. A Mr. Quiston."

"At Chelsea Old Church, also known as All Saints, dating from the twelfth century. Did you want to see Sir Thomas More's chapel?"

I took the place beside her, and she opened the hamper. "Not especially. The poor man came to a very difficult end. You?"

"The views from that bell tower are likely impressive." Also odoriferous, the church being immediately proximate to the River Thames.

"You mean, a reconnaissance officer could see a lot from that tower?" She handed me a cheese-and-tomato sandwich and started on one for herself.

"Yes, as could a small boy or a passing traveler. The sun on the river is a challenge for my eyes, but artists would appreciate that view."

The whittler had ceased wielding his knife. He was, in fact, staring at me. I was not in the mood for some old gunnery sergeant to dress me down in front of Hyperia for whatever wrong I had done him, his regiment, his cousin's uncle's grandson, or that worthy's favorite dog. I'd had unreasonably high hopes for this outing, I knew that, but to turn up nothing in the way of information was still disappointing.

The whittler heaved himself off his bench and crossed to stand directly before me. I'd put his age at about forty. Not old, but not wearing well either. One eye was rheumy, the other a piercing blue. His air was truculent, and he walked with a limp.

"I knew it was you," he said. "The blue specs, and then the bell tower caught your eye. You were a great one for church towers, way I heard it."

His voice, a particularly grating bass, did not suit his spare frame, but it did tickle a chord in memory.

"You had that trick donkey," I said. "You taught that creature to count. He earned you a packet. MacInnes, is it?"

He grinned, showing remarkably good teeth. "I taught the beast to paw until I took my hand off my belt buckle, and yes, he was worth his weight in grog and bread. A pleasure to see you, sir."

I rose and extended a hand, which seemed to fluster him, but we got through the handshake. "Miss West," I said, "may I make known to you Corporal Hunter MacInnes, late of the Royal Artillery. He had the best bass voice in Wellington's entire army and entertained the whole camp with his magic donkey."

"I left wee Killian with the nuns. They needed him, and he'd be pampered like the smelly little prince he is. I miss him, though. What brings you to Chelsea?"

For a moment, I was not a ducal heir or even a disgraced former prisoner of the hated French. I was one soldier passing the time with another on a muggy summer morning. The river was growing riper, I was still disappointed, and I'd failed to uncover a single additional detail about Tom, but I beheld a friendly face and recalled some reasons to smile about my military ventures.

"What happened to the eye?" I asked.

"Shrapnel. Can't see outta that one. The other'un works just fine, but for the carving, I hardly need my eyes." He fished in his pocket and produced a spectacularly detailed wren.

"She's lovely," Hyperia said, touching the wood with a gentle finger. "I could almost believe those feathers are real."

"She is yours." MacInnes bowed with a flourish and put the bird into Hyperia's hand.

"Oh, I cannot. She's too... Julian, please explain. She's too lovely, and you made her with your own hands." Hyperia was truly moved and, doubtless, truly at a loss.

MacInnes was likely subsisting on what his carvings could earn him, and nobody needed a little wooden wren, no matter how exquisitely she was carved, so his income would be sparse indeed. Hyperia did not want to be the reason a former soldier—a wounded former soldier—went hungry.

"Join us," I said, gesturing to the hamper. "We've come to Chelsea seeking some answers. If you can help us empty the larder, so to speak, Cook will be pleased, and I can use the time to explain our quest to you."

MacInnes arched a brow that would have had recruits backing slowly toward their tents.

"Oh, do," Hyperia said. "The woman packed enough to feed the whole village, and in this heat, the food won't last. His lordship eats less than your little wren, and I can only do so much."

MacInnes succumbed to Hyperia's importuning, and while he dispatched three sandwiches, all of the shortbread, the remaining meadow tea, and two oranges, I explained the reason for our presence in Chelsea.

"I wasn't here five years ago," he said. "Otherwise detained, don't you know? But I am here now, and when I'm not scaring small children with my evil eye, I do pass the time with the stable lads and crossing sweepers. Somebody will know something, eventually."

"Take these," I said, passing him one of the spare pairs of blue spectacles that I always kept about my person. "Your eye might heal if you protect it from the sun." I lowered my spectacles and peered at him directly for a moment. "Word of an officer."

He snorted. "You'll keep my little wren?"

Hyperia cradled the bird in her hands. "For all the rest of my days. She's beautiful. Thank you."

We parted cordially, the hamper empty and the morning well advanced.

Considering that the outing had been a complete failure, I had little excuse for my improved spirits. But then, Hyperia was accompanying me to the Hall, we'd made some progress with MacNamara's problem, and I now had a reconnaissance officer on the job in Chelsea.

Not a battle won, but modest advances on my objectives, and enough to content me for a time.

～

The gamekeeper's inquiries regarding Strother Stadler's routines had borne fruit. The Standish heir followed a series of bridle paths and lanes that in the course of five outings would take him past every tenant farm, stand of hardwoods, trout pond, pasture, and hayfield on Pleasant View land.

His pattern never varied, save for delays for inclement weather or the lung fevers to which he was prone. I chose a stretch of bridle path that ran beside a shaded stream, a location unlikely to be frequented by foot traffic.

"Stadler, good day." I nodded rather than put Atlas's reins in one hand. "A fine morning for a hack."

He sidled his bay closer. "Lord Julian Caldicott. It's been an age. Salutations, and my best to your dear mother. What brings you and that fine beast to our corner of the shire?"

The greeting was friendly, the gaze he turned on Atlas appreciative. Stadler was not strikingly handsome, but his looks were genial. Brown hair neatly curled against his collar. His field boots were polished to a shine, his doeskin breeches were spotless, and his dark green riding jacket emphasized eyes of the same hue.

His features were regular, though his brows were a bit heavy and asymmetric. The left arched higher than the right, giving him an air of friendly inquisitiveness rather than hauteur.

And yet, Hyperia had called him forgettable.

"I've been in Town for the past few days," I replied, though I'd in truth spent less than forty-eight hours in the metropolis. "Atlas here was ready to cover some ground upon my return. One must atone for one's absences. My mother and I paid a call on Pleasant View recently, and I was reminded of how pretty your neighborhood is."

"We are fortunate in our situation," he said. "Might we amble along together for a patch? I try to keep to a schedule, and that way, the tenants always know where and how to find me. What they would never bring up in the churchyard, they somehow find a way to mention when we're chatting by the stream."

I urged Atlas forward in the direction Stadler had been traveling. "Leaking roofs, a broodmare who won't catch, that sort of thing?"

"Yes, though the steward is expected to stay on top of those developments. Never hurts to have a means of keeping that worthy on his toes, though. One also hears about who is walking out with whom, or getting up his nerve to ask to walk out with a certain young lady. My mother takes an interest in those matters. You would never think it, but her hand is everywhere."

Was the viscountess's hand involved in Miss Stadler's absence? Good heavens, that was a possibility to be discussed with Hyperia and Her Grace.

"The duchess is similarly effective without seeming to do more than tend to her correspondence. All very mysterious. Tell me, has your sister returned from her travels?"

Stadler's bay caught a toe on a root and took an uneven step. He patted the horse and adjusted the reins.

"Steady, Lars. Hannah is off taking the waters or something of the sort. A fellow doesn't inquire too closely lest he be pressed into service as an escort. I cannot imagine anything less stimulating than swilling water that tastes of rotten eggs in order to hasten one's progress to the privy. If that's what old age holds, my lord, may I be forever young. What do you hear from the duke?"

Harry had been a genius at winkling information by indirection and verbal stealth. Between his charm and his cunning, even his foes had spilled secrets to him when the topic was nothing more compelling than the weather.

I was not so gifted. "His Grace is enjoying the South of France. I fear he's enamored of the milder climate and in no hurry to return home."

"We cannot begrudge him some fashionable travel. Then too, the Continent is said to be very affordable. I'd love to go, but Papa puts too much faith in the steward, and Mama is prone to the outlook of the proverbial dour Scot. I don't dare leave them unsupervised for very long, or both the household and the larger property would fall into squabbling and disarray."

He regarded the situation with patient humor rather than long-suffering. Hard not to like a man who took on life's challenges with such equanimity.

"Stadler, if I might speak in confidence, and somewhat awkwardly, I was hoping to cross paths with you because of something your granny said to Her Grace on our last visit."

"Oh dear. If Gran is involved, I must brace myself for the fanciful. Poor thing is growing vague, but I refuse to let Mama ship her off to Scotland. Not unless Mama goes with her, and Papa won't hear of that. Hannah managed to remain above the affray—keeping her nose in a book has advantages—but I haven't the luxury of obliviousness."

"Her ladyship seemed quite lucid when the duchess called on her. When Her Grace asked about Hannah, your grandmother claimed that two men took Hannah away. Your grandmother whispered this to Her Grace in the Erse, clearly trying to avoid notice by the lady's maid and companion. Your mother, by contrast, offered no details about Hannah's whereabouts, her expected return, and even her itinerary and the company she's traveling in."

The path curved away from the stream to run along a stone wall that bordered a field ready for haying. Stadler halted his horse before we left the shade.

"This is an extraordinary tale, my lord. Do you imply that Hannah was abducted?"

"I don't know what to think. My mother's Gaelic is rusty. Your granny is venerable. I wasn't present for the exchange, but a fellow soldier of my acquaintance, Captain James MacNamara, says a sudden disappearance is out of character for Miss Stadler. I thought it best to bring the matter to your attention, you being the apparent adult on the premises."

He sat a little taller in the saddle. "You and MacNamara are acquainted?"

"We served together for a time." I had a distinct memory of MacNamara's hand applying a hearty shove to my backside, boosting me out of a muddy trench in which the French would have found us, and doubtless buried us, had I spent another moment noisily scrambling around.

He'd saved my life. I'd saved his on another occasion. What else did serving together imply?

"MacNamara is a hopeful suitor, my lord. One must regard his concern with sympathy rather than alarm. Mama doesn't care for him, though I regard him as a decent fellow, all told. Not to put too fine a point on it, he's a decent, somewhat impecunious fellow." Stadler urged his horse into the walk. "You see how that might put Hannah's absence in a different light?"

I positioned Atlas beside Stadler's bay. "You believe she was trying to let him down gently by simply leaving the stage without an explanation?" What I knew of Hannah Stadler did not comport with that theory, but then, I wasn't her brother.

"My darling baby sister has done this before," Stadler said. "I hope you will keep that in confidence. She had an Irish lordling trailing after her a year or two ago, and believe me, Mama approved of him. Dowling... or, no, Downing. He and I were chums of a sort at the time. An heir, albeit an Irish heir, and his interest in Hannah struck me as one of those this-cannot-last affairs. Perhaps her literary bent was a novelty to him. Who knows with the Irish? Half daft, half fey, half inebriated, according to Papa."

And how would the Irish characterize rackety English viscounts? "Hannah did not share Downing's enthusiasm for matrimony?"

"She humored him for a time, but he was all sweet words and no substance. Hannah does not suffer fools. She can't help herself. I adore her, but my opinion of her represents the minority of polite society."

Stadler's admiration bore a curious resemblance to faint praise. "And when she'd had enough of humoring him, she simply quit the scene?"

Stadler glanced over his shoulder, though we were quite alone on the path. "She gave no notice. Simply summoned the coach early one morning, and the next thing we knew, we were reading a note she'd sent from the local posting inn, telling us not to worry. She planned to stay with a school friend for a few days and had her lady's maid with her. Not a proper chaperone, of course, but better than nothing. She gave us the direction, which lay a mere ten miles away in Kent. To Downing, she was to be emphatically not at home."

A simple, expedient plan. "He desisted?"

"After about two weeks of Hannah not being in when he called, and a few pointed words from me, he went back to Ireland. Mama fumed for weeks, but Han would never have been happy married to him. One hears things at the clubs and so forth. Downing lacks the gift of temperance."

Diplomatically put, but also true of most young lordlings. "You believe Hannah is treating MacNamara to the same tactic?"

Stadler, while remaining in the saddle, deftly opened a gate, his gelding apparently well-versed in that particular country maneuver. Atlas and I passed through, and Stadler closed the gate with equal ease.

"She well could be. To be honest, my lord, this is a busy time of year. Our steward is getting on, and I try to stay out of the skirmishes between Hannah and Mama. Hannah is cleverer than Mama, but Mama has determination that makes Wellington look like a lollygagging schoolboy."

We were once again riding beneath a stand of stately hardwoods. "Has Hannah sent you the same sort of note? *Off to visit a school chum, tell MacNamara I'm not in?*"

Stadler patted his horse for no particular reason I could see. "Not as yet. In the alternative, such a note was entrusted to the potboy at the inn, and he has long since forgotten it, or the laundress turned out his pockets, and the note has been burned with the rubbish. One doesn't dare inquire, does one?"

Inquiring was the best way to find answers, in my experience. "Certainly, discretion is in order. MacNamara is still very worried, and the duchess is also concerned. I don't suppose you could tell me the name of the school friend in Kent?"

"Heavens, Caldicott. The whole business was some time ago. I can inquire of Hannah's lady's maid, if I can pry her loose from Claypole and Rumsperger. Thick as thieves, those three. She might recall the name of Hannah's former hostess and even the direction. I'll send you a note if I have any luck."

"My thanks. I don't envy you the challenges you face, Stadler, but you do have a lovely property. If you should become concerned for your sister, please feel free to call upon me in any capacity. My years in Spain honed an ability to reconnoiter discreetly in enemy territory, and you might find my skills useful should trouble arise."

Had a fortune in Irish gold gone into maintaining his acres, or was his conscientious management responsible for the greening fields, tidy stone walls, and majestic oaks? He certainly wanted me to think that, and to think he maintained order among the eccentrics biding under Pleasant View's stately roof.

I did not see a way to raise the issue of the gold and its potential use should a ransom note arrive, so I took my leave of Stadler and began sorting through our discussion.

I had learned that Hannah was capable of taking French leave. Knew how to do it, had done it before, and had places to go where Society wouldn't necessarily look for her. I had learned that the viscountess and her sole unmarried daughter were out of charity with each other. I had learned that Downing had shown some persistence in the face of Hannah's absence. A fribble he might be, but he had not quit the field until his defeat had been made embarrassingly obvious.

I'd learned that Stadler had matured into a well-spoken, pleasant young man of whom I ought to think well.

Instinct told me that I was overlooking some fact, some disclosure that Stadler had made without realizing it. I was missing something...

As Atlas and I approached the local posting inn, a young man stood in the stable yard and watched me. He was in the lanky phase between youth and manhood, his dusty trouser cuffs hovering two inches above the tops of his worn boots.

To my astonishment, he'd knotted a red and white checkered kerchief about his skinny neck in a perfectly tied mathematical.

"Good morning."

He touched his cap. "Sir. Will you be wanting your gelding rubbed down and stabled?"

"A thorough grooming, please. Offer him hay if you have it, or grass if that's available, and certainly give him a go at the water trough. No grain. I'll break my fast and be back on my way."

"You come from Pleasant View?" A note of hope lay disguised in that simple question.

I put that together with his vigilance and the kerchief. "I did, and in answer to your question, Miss Hannah has yet to return."

Young ears turned cherry red. "She lends me books. I always finish 'em and give 'em back, and we talk about 'em. Miss Han is ever so smart and twice as kind. She says I could amount to something."

He was worried about her. The supposedly prickly, difficult spinster had supporters in unlikely places. "Captain MacNamara is concerned for Miss Stadler, as am I."

"If she'd meant to be gone this long, sir, she would have asked my cousin Petey to exercise her mare. He's at Pleasant View, working in the stables. Petey is taking the mare out, but Miss Stadler never let him know she was travelin'."

"The last time she went away, she gave you a note to take back to her family, didn't she?"

His ears were still red, but his stance became more upright. "She did, and I took it. This time, no note, no warning. I gotta bad feelin', mister."

"Then keep your eyes and ears open." I passed him my card. "I'll leave coin with the innkeeper so you can send me a note if you see anything interesting. I intend to locate Miss Stadler and return her to her family, if she's agreeable."

He stashed the card in his pocket. "I'm good at keeping my eyes and ears open, see if I'm not. You get word from Jem Bussard, that's me. We like the captain around here, and if you're a friend of his, you might be hearin' from me."

"My thanks to you, Jem Bussard." I passed him two shillings, a generous tip by any standard.

He nodded gravely, saluted with two fingers, took Atlas's reins, and disappeared with the horse into the shadows of the stable.

I was enjoying a tall tankard of lemonade when I realized what exactly Strother Stadler had revealed in the course of our conversation. He'd offered to consult with Hannah's lady's maid regarding her previous sojourn to Kent.

Meaning that the lady's maid yet bided at Pleasant View and was not traveling with her employer.

The whole situation had just become much more worrisome.

CHAPTER SEVEN

"We need to speak with the grandmother," Hyperia said. "If Hannah went willingly with her escorts, that's a very different situation from a forced abduction."

She and MacNamara had been watching for my return, enjoying the shaded bench under the enormous oak at the center of the stable yard. I had barely stepped down from the saddle before Atticus had absconded with Atlas, giving the beast a thorough visual inspection and apparently finding him in acceptable condition.

Did the boy but know it, Atlas had stamina sufficient to put most English mounts to shame. His Iberian sire had passed that on to him, along with nimbleness of body and brain. From a dam born to the plow, Atlas had inherited a calm temperament and significant strength. The horse had saved my life numerous times, and I would never intentionally put him in harm's way.

"Hannah might have gone willingly at first," MacNamara said, "only to realize too late that she'd been hoodwinked. She tends to believe the whole world is as forthright as she is."

He sat with his bad leg almost straight before him, a walking stick propped at his side. Even in the fresh air of the stable yard, a faint vanilla hint of pipe smoke clung to him.

I lowered myself to the dusty ground and sat cross-legged opposite the bench. My eyes ached, despite my blue specs, and while Atlas might be up to long hacks, my recent horseback excursions had all been shorter than the morning's outing. I was saddlesore and reaching the frustrated portion of the investigatory program.

"Strother was exceedingly pleasant," I said, "almost ingratiatingly so, but he had little in the way of information. He explained to me that Hannah has disappeared previously. She shook off the Irish viscount's heir by making an unannounced visit to a school friend in Kent, though Strother did not recall the friend's name."

"I cannot contradict him," MacNamara said, "not in the generalities. Hannah did visit an acquaintance to the east. She mentioned to me in passing her intention to travel, though we were little more than cordial at the time. We were just getting to the point where I'd call us something more than literary friends, hacking-out friends. I credit the viscount's heir for aiding my cause as a suitor."

I gathered up a handful of pebbles and amused myself as I often had around campfires in Spain by trying to toss them in a perfect circle.

"Let me guess," Hyperia said. "Downing was the fate that awaited Hannah if she didn't find herself a more agreeable spouse, and there you were, all bookish and bashful?"

MacNamara smiled. "And that strategy finally worked, or I thought it did. The school friend is Mrs. Dabney Witherspoon, of Little Pomset. The village is actually in Surrey, though the next village to the east lies in Kent."

"A brother might not know such things," Hyperia said, watching my pebbles fall. "If I asked Healy who my best friends were at school, he'd recall one or two of the prettiest, but he'd not know to whom I was closest or with whom I still correspond."

My circle was lopsided. I gathered up my pebbles and tried again. "Even so, if you undertook to visit one of those chums, wouldn't you have to pack a few dresses, choose some reading for the journey, decide upon which hats and how many pairs of slippers, and so forth? I recall my sisters preparing for house parties less than a two-hour ride from here, and it seemed like days of extra work for the laundry, the seamstresses, the cobbler... Can a lady truly sneak off to pay a visit of two weeks' duration without a sibling taking notice?"

Hyperia peered at me. "You have a point. Everything must be packed just so, or the wrinkles are endless. One wants to take at least three shawls—formal, informal, and practical for warmth—and that's just the beginning. Which jewelry to bring along. Whether to include a riding habit, which means tall boots, a cloche, riding gloves... The preparations are complicated."

Rather like moving around a general. The business wanted forethought, and stealth was nearly impossible.

"Do we conclude Strother was lying?" MacNamara asked, using both hands to raise his knee enough to allow the sole of his foot to rest flat on the ground. The shift caused him a fleeting wince, and Hyperia, noting his expression, sent me visual orders.

Enough pondering. Let's get him back to the house.

I rose and dusted off my backside. "My nether parts are no longer inured to using Mother Earth for my wing chair. Let's find more comfortable surrounds, shall we? We can continue this discussion over luncheon, but as to Strother's mendacity... He doesn't strike me as dishonest by nature. He is, though, forgettable, as Miss West noted. He gives no offense, he takes none. He leaves almost no impression at all."

Though I did have the lingering sense that Strother had wanted my good opinion, perhaps simply because I was the local ducal heir?

MacNamara used his cane to stand upright on his good foot. I assisted Hyperia to rise, or we used that pretext to avoid watching MacNamara's struggles. That he'd come all the way to the stable to await my return was a measure of his anxiety, because clearly the man was in pain.

"Once more unto the breach, dear friends," he muttered, straightening.

"Shakespeare's *Henry V*," Hyperia countered. "Not one of my favorites."

Nor mine, but soldiers quoted that speech back and forth the night before a battle, so I pitched in with the closing lines, as MacNamara must have known I would.

"'The game's afoot: Follow your spirit, and upon this charge, Cry "God for Harry, England, and Saint George!"'" My dear brother had particularly liked that last part, the wretch.

Hyperia frowned at the mention of Harry—and Harry—while MacNamara grasped his cane and shuffled forth.

"We tentatively conclude," he said, "that Strother failed to note Hannah's travel preparations on this occasion and that he forgot the name of her school friend. We hold open the possibility that he's instead simply trying to minimize the risk of scandal by weaving a convenient little sampler of facts, recollections, and omissions. He does care for Hannah, and the rest of it—Hannah and her mother being on the outs, the viscount sniffing at her hems—is all accurate."

"Strother brushed aside the confidence Lady Dewar reposed in Her Grace," I said, keeping to the very moderate pace MacNamara set. I did not offer Hyperia my arm, nor did she take it. She was doubtless waiting, as I was, for the moment when MacNamara stumbled or tired to the point of needing assistance.

"Said the old girl was growing daft, no doubt," MacNamara replied. "If she's daft, I'm the next patroness of Almack's. Lady Dewar might well forget what was on last Tuesday's supper menu, but her hearing and vision are as sharp as mine."

"Then we need to arrange a discreet conversation with her," I said. "Hyperia, what do you think of attending divine services this Sunday at St. Rumwold's?" I cited the house of worship in Pleasant View's market town.

"Worth a try." She paused to snap off a blooming spear of purple iris. "We can call upon my Fortnam cousins for Sunday supper. They worship at St. Rumwold's, or collect their local gossip in St. Rum's churchyard. They might know something of Miss Stadler."

"You are related to the Misses Fortnam?" MacNamara asked.

"They are aunts to my late mother, but we've always called them cousins. Formidable dames, or they were in my childhood. I have no Gaelic, Julian. You will have to be my escort if we're to interview Lady Dewar."

"MacNamara, are you up to a churchyard conversation with Miss Stadler's granny?"

He stopped and rested heavily on his walking stick. "If I must. What will you be doing?"

"Have you a miniature of Miss Stadler?"

The lady's home, oddly enough, had had no likenesses of her that I'd seen. Of her brother, I'd noted sketches aplenty and even a portrait in the music room that I'd glanced at in passing. Her sisters had been rendered in oils over the formal landing, a trio of young feminine pulchritude, but of Hannah, not so much as a pencil drawing.

"I have this." MacNamara produced a small oval folding case and opened it to display the painting inside. A lock of dark hair occupied one half, a smiling visage the other.

"She's pretty," Hyperia said. "Why do people insist that a woman who isn't gorgeous must be plain, when she may yet be very attractive despite a wide mouth or definite chin? Hannah is quite comely."

MacNamara snapped the miniature closed. "Hannah does not emphasize her beauty, and she's no Venus, but I am no Adonis. Her most impressive qualities are of the heart and mind. We suit."

Did they, or had Hannah arranged a departure that suggested MacNamara had a wishful grasp of her true sentiments? The latter possibility seemed less and less likely.

"If you will accompany Miss West to services and supper with her cousins, I will find the school friend with whom Hannah stayed previously and learn what I can. I will make discreet inquiries at the coaching inns within a one-or-two change radius of Pleasant View, though that trail is growing cold. Then too, kidnappers would not allow Miss Stadler to take the air unsupervised, if it's kidnappers we're dealing with."

What I did not say was that even kidnappers would have to allow the young lady the use of the facilities. Murderers, of course, would not face that problem, but then, what possible motive would justify the extreme measure of homicide?

MacNamara returned the miniature to his breast pocket. "You have hard riding ahead of you, my lord, if you seek to inquire at two dozen coaching inns."

"If Miss Stadler has been abducted, she is likely still in the vicinity." Assuming she was alive. I put a hand under MacNamara's elbow and resumed our halting progress toward the house. "The greater the distance an unwilling traveler is transported, the greater the likelihood they will slip a note to a chambermaid, draw the notice of an inn's proprietress, and so forth.

"Then too," I went on, "if Hannah was abducted by two men, she could not be removed from the surrounds without some sort of female companion. The entire shire knows what her brother and father look like and that the strange men accompanying her would answer to neither description. Either they've secreted her somewhere locally, or they had to recruit a decent-appearing female accomplice."

MacNamara stopped again and studied me. "Your mind, Caldicott, is like no other I've encountered. You can think like a kidnapper. You did not pick up that skill at public school."

He tottered on, and my hand stayed under his elbow.

"Let's not forget to also think like a disappointed suitor. I want to make Downing's acquaintance, get his version of events, and assess the extent to which his disappointment might motivate him to ruin the lady who turned him down."

MacNamara stiffened.

"That sort of revenge happens," Hyperia murmured, getting her hand under the captain's other elbow. "Elopements that begin as kidnappings are not strictly the province of lurid novels."

"Hannah could have been kidnapped," MacNamara said slowly. "I doubt she could be forced to speak vows against her will. Her sisters are married and beyond the touch of scandal."

"But," I replied, "her brother is not, and unless I miss my guess, Strother would be well advised to marry wealth."

MacNamara muttered something ungentlemanly in his native tongue.

We shepherded him into the house, though the terrace steps were an insult to his dignity. He accepted the assistance of the first footman and decided on a tray for lunch.

"How are your eyes, Julian?" Hyperia asked as we stood in the Hall's bright foyer. Midday sunlight flooded through the skylight, and white marble and gleaming parquet floors bounced the illumination against sparkling windows.

"My eyes are tired, as is the part of me that occupies the saddle, if you must know. Miss Stadler's prospects are not improving, Perry. I could now kick myself for nipping into Town."

"Julian, no matter what order of battle you follow, you cannot be everywhere at once, and in this case, you would not have learned the extent of the Stadlers' wealth without consulting me. That information bears critically on potential motives, does it not?"

I took Hyperia's hand and led her down the corridor to the cool, quiet confines of the estate office.

"The gold is complicated," I said. "Downing might have kidnapped Hannah to get his hands on the gold. Very straightforward, simple, criminal thinking."

Hyperia took the seat behind Arthur's majestic desk. I settled into one of the wing chairs opposite.

"Anybody might have kidnapped Hannah to get that gold"—she picked up a stick of Arthur's signature purple sealing wax and sniffed—"provided they knew of the gold. Go on."

"Kidnapping can result in ransom paid, but whether the ransom is paid or the victim frees herself, scandal must inevitably follow *her* all the rest of her days."

Hyperia set aside the wax, propped her chin on her hand, and tapped a nail against the blotter. I mentally sketched her thus, looking pretty, serious, and fierce. If she'd disappeared from my life without notice, I'd be turning the whole of England upside down until I knew she was safe.

MacNamara, poor, limping devil, needed me to do his turning upside down for him.

"You are saying," Hyperia murmured, "that if somebody wanted only to ruin Hannah, kidnapping is the end in itself, and the gold has nothing to do with it. We're back to Downing."

"There's another possibility. Two more, actually."

"You don't care for the viscountess. I grant you she's something of a prig, but her lot hasn't been easy. Why would she arrange for Hannah to disappear?"

"To ensure that Hannah does not marry the penniless, plain-spoken captain."

"He isn't penniless," Hyperia said, "and his prospects have improved since the war."

"You know that, but this battle of wills between Hannah and her mother predates the war." Predated civilization, perhaps. "If the viscountess is truly wroth with her daughter, then sending Hannah to live in disgrace in some Scottish croft is victory for the viscountess."

Hyperia sat up. "Gracious saints, Julian. That is… credible. Convoluted, but credible."

The lunch bell rang, reminding me that I was famished. "I have another theory that isn't nearly so convoluted."

Hyperia rose. "MacNamara has no reason to subject the woman he loves to an ordeal, Julian. He's a good man, bearing up under difficulties. I refuse to include him on a list of suspected felons."

"Not MacNamara—or I can't see a way to incriminate him yet—but look at the situation from Hannah's perspective. She wants to marry the captain, her mother objects, and her father is unwilling to contradict his wife. Strother has no authority, despite posturing to the contrary, and tries to keep out of it. What would make the viscountess view even the captain as a suitable parti?"

"Oh dear. If the captain was the only option left, he'd become a suitable parti by default. Hannah is an intelligent woman, and she might well appear to ruin herself to get what she wants. Julian, I don't like this."

"I am less enamored of the situation by the hour." Though I adored having Hyperia on hand to sort through theories and evidence.

"But your theory, that Hannah had herself kidnapped, isn't supported by facts, Jules. If Hannah had herself kidnapped, why hasn't she stumbled out of the hedgerow, breathless, disheveled, and ruined in name? A week in the company of kidnappers is long enough to wreck a reputation for all time."

I left the comfort of the chair. "Precisely. Somebody's best laid plan is going quite agley."

But whose, and how?

Hyperia paused with me behind the closed door. "'The best laid schemes o' mice an' men… Gang aft agley…' Robert Burns, 'To a Mouse.'" She hugged me around the middle. "Be careful, Julian. Matters are taking a nasty turn, and you are but one man."

One tired, hungry man. I hugged her back. "But I am not without substantial allies, and neither am I a mouse. We'll find her, Perry, and soon."

Assuming she wanted to be found.

∽

I acquainted myself with every hostler, potboy, cook's assistant, and groom in a twenty-five-mile radius of Pleasant View, and all for nought.

Almost for nought, rather. After three days in the saddle, some of my stamina was coming back to me. I was pushing past the bounds of exhaustion, relearning the need to drink from my canteen *before* I was thirsty. Perfecting again the art of snacking on horseback.

My marathon interviewing innkeepers' wives and stable boys also took the edge off the ostinato of anxiety underlying my days and nights. The trick to managing the fear that kept a reconnaissance officer alive was to stay just tired enough that fatigue raised a barrier to panic without inviting carelessness.

For two nights, I camped with Atlas, as I had so many times in Spain, the summer night sky providing a reassuring display of nocturnal grandeur. I sent regular reports of failure to the Hall, and that kept me humble and determined.

Nobody had seen a lady answering to Hannah's description leaving the area in a vehicle of any kind.

I returned to the Hall on Sunday evening and sank into a bath with the relief of a soul restored to heaven's graces. Once I was thoroughly clean, I demolished most of a tray of beef and brie sandwiches, an entire bowl of fried pickles, two slices of gingerbread, and two tankards of Mrs. Gwinnett's meadow tea.

"Nectar and ambrosia," I said, leaving the last half a sandwich for Atticus. While Atticus clucked and fussed about the state of my boots, I changed into comfortable attire, tied a cravat loosely about my neck, unearthed a lapel vase from my jewelry box, and appropriated a pink rosebud from the bouquet on my sitting room sideboard.

The flowers were fresh, doubtless a welcome-home gesture from Her Grace.

"You should join the discussion in the library," I said, surveying my appearance in the mirror.

Atticus glowered up at me from the hearth, where he was swatting at the dusty toes of my riding boots with a badly wrinkled handkerchief.

"I shoulda *joined* your little jaunt all over the shire."

I'd covered an average of fifty miles on each of three very long days. Few horses would have been up to that test, and Atlas deserved several days' respite to recover from his exertions. Granted, we'd moved slowly and used every hour of the daylight. I knew to look after my horse on forced marches, but how to explain to Atticus the decision to leave him behind?

"What is more memorable, Atticus—a toff passing through on his tired horse, or a toff passing through with a boy up on a cob beside him? Neither has any luggage to speak of, and they do not appear to be father and son. The man might be recognized as a lordling from one of the shire's great houses, but nobody is quite sure who the boy is."

"You're just saying that because you think I'da slowed you down. I wouldn't. I rode practice gallops in Berkshire. I can stick on a horse, and you know it."

What I knew was that clinging on for ten minutes of a fast canter wasn't at all the same as enduring hours in the saddle, despite heat, dust, flies, and unrelenting sun.

"I would have preferred to take you with me," I said, pulling on a pair of comfortably worn Hessians. "Your ability to wrest information from those in service and in the stables far exceeds what I can accomplish. But tell me, Atticus, which horse in our stables could have kept up with the punishing pace that was a mere romp across the countryside for your boy Atlas? Mare, gelding, colt… Name me the horse who is his equal."

Atticus ceased abusing the dusty boots. "He ain't got an equal. Atlas is the best in the shire, maybe the best in England. I keep him fit for you, and there's none coulda matched his pace."

"Precisely, and time is increasingly of the essence regarding Miss Stadler's disappearance. Prudence and practicalities demanded that you guarded the fort while I covered as much terrain as possible. The exigencies of war must take precedence over our petty conceits. It's damned hard to tend the fire at headquarters when the patrols are out and the enemy approaches. That said, without somebody keeping watch behind the lines and ensuring every map and report is current, battles would be chaos."

Battles generally became chaos after the first quarter hour or so. I prayed Atticus would never learn that lesson.

"I don't like it when you leave without me. Miss West don't like it neither."

My tiger was developing a natural talent for strategy and discretion. What he left unsaid was that one of my memory lapses could have befallen me while I'd been on my solo mission, a truly disquieting thought.

Which I pushed aside. "I don't like leaving the Hall without you here to ensure Miss West has an ally, but you explain that to the lady at your peril, young man."

He studied the boots. "That brother of hers is a turbulent sort. Has a fine opinion of hisself, does Mr. Healy West, though mayhem follows him everywhere."

"He wants you to think he has a fine opinion of himself, but watch him closely, Atticus. He's a new recruit obsessed with putting in a perfect appearance at parade inspections. He hasn't found a path forward in life, and many worries press upon him."

"He's skint. Lady Ophelia told me that. She said gents hate being skint, and they hate anybody knowing they're skint, so they dress like lords, and ride lordly horses, and buy lordly snuffboxes, and generally waste what little blunt they have pretending they ain't skint. Foolishness, if you ask me."

I wanted to tousle his unruly hair. "Nothing but, and the tactic generally works in reverse. A fellow making wild wagers at the card table while his boots are down at the heel is letting all of Mayfair know he's short of coin."

I considered my reflection in the cheval mirror. My eyes were tired, and that showed, as did a certain planed-down quality to the way my clothing fit me. I'd shaken off the creeping dismals, though, at least for the present, and I'd completed the largest task on the list of items that might help locate Miss Stadler.

"Onward," I whispered. "For true love, Miss Stadler, and truth."

"What you muttering about, guv?"

"A gentleman does not mutter. You will please take Atlas out in the morning for a very quiet hack. A mere toddle to ensure he doesn't stiffen up. You may hop two logs at the trot if he's willing, but no more, and I do mean logs on the ground, Atticus. No stiles, streams, or standing wagons. No mad gallops and very little cantering. That horse has earned his rest."

Atticus grinned and saluted with a boot over his right hand and forearm. "Two little bitty logs, guv. I'm yer man."

"Don't wait up for me, though I will be early to bed myself. My thanks for manning the parapets."

He huffed out the door ahead of me, boots in hand. They would reappear in my dressing closet without a speck of dust upon them.

Some of my good cheer ebbed as I made my way to the estate office. I could put Atticus off with excuses about Atlas's prodigious stamina, but in truth, I could have hired a fresh hack for the boy at any and every coaching inn. I simply hadn't wanted him to slow me down or intrude on a solitary mission.

I should be flattered that both Atticus and Leander sought my company—and I was—but they were also both complications in my life, and in my present condition, I did not feel up to the challenges they represented.

Though perhaps I might also lay some of that feeling of inadequacy at Miss Stadler's elusive feet.

CHAPTER EIGHT

"The good news is, I turned up not even a hint of a sighting of the young lady. I tried every posting inn, many more than once."

Hyperia and MacNamara occupied the wing chairs. I sat on a hassock before the estate office's cold hearth. The window was open, letting in an early evening breeze perfumed with the grassy scent of haying. A much-creased likeness of Miss Stadler stared at the library ceiling from the middle of the reading table.

Her steady, intelligent gaze reproached me. I ought to have been on hand to ride around the fields with the steward and encourage the hard labor of bringing in the hay crop. I should not have jaunted off to London. Why hadn't I found the young lady by now and seen her restored to the captain's loving arms?

Time was running out, and the mission was not advancing, though the creeping dismals were making a return.

"Competent kidnappers might have spirited Hannah past the inns," MacNamara said. "She might have been bound, gagged, and drugged."

"If the objective is to haul her to Scotland for an anvil wedding," Hyperia said, "that approach makes sense. If the objective is to hold her for ransom, then keeping her at a distant location only complicates matters. A *discreet* location is necessary. A *distant* location would make communicating with the Stadler family more time-consuming and difficult."

"And every day," I added, "is another day when the curate visiting an invalid might see smoke from the chimney of an abandoned cottage, or a yeoman coming home from darts could see a light in a window that's been otherwise dark for months. A successful kidnapper wants his ransom, the sooner the better."

We were assuming Hannah was alive, when the other explanation for having found no sign of her at the posting inns was that she'd taken up permanent residence among the angels.

Murder and kidnapping both earned their perpetrators a trip to the scaffold, if caught.

"Then we assume Hannah is being held locally," MacNamara said, "and Miss West and I can add little to our meager store of facts. Lady Dewar declined to attend divine services this morning."

"Or she was prevented from attending by her family." Hyperia longed to toe off her slippers and tuck her feet up under her. I knew the look.

I longed to sit beside her on a comfy sofa, holding her hand while we faced facts and sorted theories. Hyperia likely grasped as much, and I adored that we knew each other so well.

"How was Sunday supper with the venerable cousins?" I asked.

"Excellent food," MacNamara replied, something a former soldier would never take for granted. "The ladies confirmed that Lady Dewar is neither a Papist nor a Dissenter, and she does attend services in the ordinary course. I was surprised at how highly both women spoke of Hannah."

"Miss Reenie Fortnam has a passion for lending libraries," Hyperia said. "Miss Harolda Fortnam is a walking lexicon of British poetry. Can quote Burns by the mile and isn't above a line or two of Wilmot along with the requisite references to the Bard. I gather she spurred Hannah to memorizing quotes, while Miss

Reenie takes credit for Hannah's sponsorship of the local lending library."

"They are proud of her," MacNamara said, eyeing my hassock. "I am proud of Hannah as well, but I hadn't realized… That is to say…"

"Her family does not appreciate her," Hyperia suggested. "A woman who is not appreciated for her many obvious gifts can go to great lengths to earn notice from those who should never ignore her."

MacNamara stared at Hyperia. "You think Hannah has staged this disappearance to annoy not only her mother, but also her brother and father?"

"No." Hyperia toed off one slipper. "No, I do not, though Hannah is essentially a woman scorned by her family. According to the Fortnam cousins, Lady Dewar shares Hannah's interest in books, and the two of them had a standing appointment to visit the lending library on Tuesdays. Hannah might be exasperated with her mother, despair of her father, and view her brother with fond impatience, but she would not purposely upset Lady Dewar."

"She would *not* upset me either." MacNamara banged a fist on the arm of his chair. "She hasn't a devious, sly, bitter bone in her body. I know my Hannah."

I rose and shoved the hassock in his direction. "Would anybody like a drink? The offerings include Armagnac, hock, lemonade, and Mrs. Gwinnett's signature meadow tea."

"Lemonade for me," Hyperia replied. "Captain?"

"Brandy."

I poured out. More meadow tea for me. In summer, I drank it by the gallon. Part mint, plus spent black tea leaves and a dash of honey along with some magic blend of spices known only to the queen of the ducal kitchen.

I saw to Hyperia's lemonade and passed the captain his brandy. "If you know Miss Stadler so well, MacNamara, then where would you keep such a lady if you had kidnapped her and wanted to return her to her family in good condition?"

He eased his foot up onto the hassock and sipped his brandy. "Interesting question. Hannah isn't a sybarite, but she's a lady."

"A lady who loves books," Hyperia said, "which is why we paid a call on the local librarian, a Mrs. Ellington."

"Rhymes with Wellington," MacNamara added tiredly. "She guards those books like a dragon protecting golden eggs. Woe unto anybody who fails to return a borrowed volume on time. I once passed her a volume of Burns in the churchyard that by rights I should have turned in a day earlier at the library. She dressed me down like a gunnery sergeant going after a tipsy recruit with his cap on backward. The whole village enjoyed a good laugh at my expense."

"Where would Mrs. Ellington's patroness be most easily stashed in the local surrounds?" I asked, sipping and sending up a silent prayer of gratitude for Mrs. G. "Whose pensioner cottage is perennially empty. Whose hunting lodge has fallen into disuse? For that matter, MacNamara, who would want to ruin the lady you esteem?"

He rubbed his knee. "I've given that question a lot of thought, my lord, and the answer is... nobody I can think of. I pay my bills early or on time. I tithe and then some. I will lend any equipment or staff to my neighbors upon request, and I am neither bibulous nor quarrelsome. I might not be knee-deep in friends, but I don't seem to have accumulated enemies either."

Hannah Stadler was his friend, and for a man like MacNamara, that alone made her precious to him. I did not need to have that explained to me.

He was regarded poorly by the viscountess, though, so allies would be thin on the ground in any circles that felt her influence.

"If I were kidnapped," Hyperia said, "I'd need to be isolated. I am not above yelling my head off, climbing down a drainpipe, or using a coat stand to wave a flag out the chimney from a hearth in the garret. You'd want me off the beaten path, no roads in sight where passersby could see me waving frantically from a window."

"Remind me never to kidnap you," I replied. "A coat stand?"

"I'd need a stool to climb on in the empty hearth. I'm not very tall, in case you failed to notice. Waving a pillowcase out a window would not attract as much notice."

"She's right," MacNamara said. "You'd want a location where Hannah could be locked in, not seen by those who'd recognize her, and kept in enough comfort that she'd not be desperate to escape. If I'd kidnapped Hannah, I'd explain to her that she was being ransomed, or held pending a threat—merely a threat—to her family of a forced elopement. I would eschew the bullying that might inspire the lady to leap into the branches of the garden oak."

"She might enjoy the thought of her family stewing a bit," Hyperia murmured, discreetly tucking her stockinged foot under her. "She wouldn't like tormenting her beau, but to think of her mother worrying about scandal and gossip might gratify Hannah."

"And," I added, "she'd know the Irish gold was available to pay the ransom. Would she tell her captors that? Did they already know of the gold—neither I nor the ducal solicitors had been aware of it—and was the gold why she'd been taken? In the alternative, did the kidnappers assume every viscount has sufficient means to ransom a purloined daughter?"

My questions met with silence. Too many unknowns, too much room for conjecture.

I went on nonetheless, voicing thoughts half-formed. "Telling the kidnappers of the gold would ensure they exercised patience," I said. "Any distinctive items would have to be liquidated or turned into bearer notes."

"There you go," MacNamara muttered, "thinking like a crook again."

"Trying to. And all that said, if the hoard *wasn't* a factor in Hannah's kidnapping, revealing its existence to the malefactors would cost the Stadlers what might be the last of their fortune. Any half-way loyal daughter or sister would be reluctant to ruin her family's finances, if so."

"I will make a list of possible locations." MacNamara set aside his brandy. "We don't tend to pensioner cottages around Pleasant View, but we have hunting lodges, empty tenant cottages, a few old gatehouses, and the like. I fear you'll soon be back in the saddle, my lord."

"I like being in the saddle. Give me a good night's sleep, some tucker, and a map, and I'm ready to mount up again." A slight exaggeration that MacNamara would forgive as a soldier's bravado.

"We'll find her," Hyperia said, getting to her feet. "I'll have a tray sent up to your rooms in an hour or so. You might also try a hot, soaking bath for your foot and knee. Mrs. Gwinnett's comfrey compresses work wonders. I've asked her to make some up, and you are to use them first and last thing of the day, Captain."

He shoved himself upright. "Yes, miss." He winked at me and departed, probably grateful to have something to do.

Hyperia had her arms around me the instant the door was closed. "I worried about you."

"I worried about Miss Stadler. She's well-liked, though, Perry. If anybody had seen anything—a lady wearing a bonnet similar to the ones Miss Stadler favors, a parasol in her favorite colors—they would have mentioned it. Her absence at services was doubtless noticed as well."

To hold Hyperia was the true moment of homecoming for me. I loved the Hall. Some part of my heart was claimed by my home and always would be, but Hyperia had become a part of my soul. I thought better when I was with her, I felt stronger, and I could look more easily forward and less compulsively dwell on the past.

"Mrs. Ellington is worried about Hannah too." Hyperia straightened in my arms and looked up at me.

"Out with it." Clearly, she had sensitive information to pass along.

"As the captain was fetching his hat and coat, Mrs. Ellington told me that it was unlike Hannah to keep a book past its due date, but she failed to turn in *The Wanderer*, Mrs. Burney's latest. Mrs. Ellington didn't plan to chide Hannah because Hannah technically owns the whole collection, but for Hannah to keep the book *and* miss services was worrying."

"And Mrs. Ellington informed you of this out of the captain's hearing. Have you told him?"

"Not yet."

"I'll mention it," I said, breathing in roses and fortitude. "Does this development scotch any notion that Hannah had herself kidnapped?"

"It... does." Hyperia slipped free of my embrace. "Hannah Stadler would never have borrowed a book she hadn't any intention of returning. She simply would not."

"Not even to make her abduction more credible?"

"Ask the captain. He knows her best, but we can both guess what he might say."

We could.

A tap on the door heralded my mother's arrival.

"Your Grace." I bowed, though we'd greeted each other upon my return to the Hall a few hours earlier.

"An express for you, Julian. From Lady Ophelia." Her Grace handed me a single sheet of paper, folded and sealed. "I recognize her handwriting. Is the captain's limp worse, or am I imagining things?"

"He's worse," Hyperia said. "I recommended comfrey compresses, but he needs that French physician Julian consults."

"Monsieur St. Sevier." The duchess closed the door. "He is cordially received and always a credit to the guest list. Julian, have you received bad news?"

I scanned the letter, which was written in tidy, flowing script. "Not good news. I do believe it's time for another interview with the Honorable Strother Stadler."

∼

By return express, I asked Lady Ophelia to acquaint herself with Sylvester Downing's whereabouts and recent movements. The

London Season would soon be ending, but for now, her networks of informants should still be in operation.

I also sent a note to Pleasant View begging the favor of an appointment with Strother Stadler on Tuesday afternoon at two of the clock. If he penned me a demurral, I could credibly claim to have missed it, given that I would spend tomorrow—Monday—locating Dabney Witherspoon. I wanted to rule out a repeat of Hannah's previous disappearing act, and if Mrs. Witherspoon could offer more information besides, so much the better.

An investigation often turned on details easily overlooked but significant in hindsight. Mrs. Witherspoon might be in possession of such details.

Monday morning, I set out on Beowulf, my brother Arthur's majestic gelding. Bey was an altogether grander creature than Atlas. His coat gleamed in the morning sun, his reflexes were lightning-fast, and he stood an inch or so taller than Atlas.

The grooms considered keeping Beowulf in good condition a sacred trust. Before I left the stable yard, I was admonished to have a care with the footing, to mind the beast didn't toss me off, and to recall that horses needed plenty of water in warm weather.

Leander on his pony was never given so much well-intended, annoying advice.

The trip to Mrs. Witherspoon's took a couple of hours and found Beowulf barely settled for having exerted himself to that degree. He missed Arthur, clearly, and tolerated my company as a duty rather than a pleasure.

One sympathized with the horse. I missed His Grace as well.

I reached Mrs. Witherspoon's cottage, a lovely stone edifice of two and a half stories, eight windows across, and a wide front porch freshly coated with white paint. A wizened stable lad took Beowulf's reins from me and ran an appreciative eye over the horse.

"That be the Dook of Waltham's personal mount." His tone said I would be strung up for horse thievery unless I produced an immediate explanation.

"I am the duke's personal brother. Lord Julian Caldicott, at your service. Beowulf will appreciate having his gear off for the next hour or so, assuming that Mrs. Witherspoon is in. Grass and water wouldn't go amiss either. His ground manners are impeccable."

The old man grinned. "Unless he don't like 'ee. Then he'll pinch yer sleeve and mash yer toes, all accidental-like. Come along, Yer Grace. Old Deevers knows a patch of clover fit for a king."

They walked off quite in charity with each other, leaving me weary and a little envious.

I rapped the lion's head knocker on Mrs. Witherspoon's bright red front door. Potted geraniums of the same hue adorned the edge of her porch, and window boxes on the first floor continued the theme.

All very tidy and attractive. I was preparing to rap yet again—the hour was not quite late enough that anybody should be sitting down to lunch—when a lady came around the side of the house. She wore a wide-brimmed floppy straw hat, a walking dress that had seen better days, and a positively disreputable pair of large York tan gloves.

"Sir, might I help you?" She had a pleasant alto voice, and if she was intimidated by six-feet-plus of a strange fellow wearing blue specs, her voice did not betray her worry. Her features were obscured by a light gray veil dropped from the hat brim.

I came down the steps, tipped my hat, and bowed. "Lord Julian Caldicott, paying a call on Mrs. Dabney Witherspoon."

"I am Mrs. Witherspoon. What possible interest could a duke's brother have in me?" The question held only mild curiosity.

"Might we converse somewhere not so bright? The sun is hard on my eyes, and my tale might take some telling. I realize I'm presuming when we haven't been properly introduced, but I can explain the lapse in manners." Moreover, a certain part of my anatomy would not object to making the close acquaintance of a deeply cushioned chair.

"Of course. I daresay you could do with a spot of sustenance as well, and Cook always prepares enough for the whole choir. The staff lets nothing go to waste, and thus they have the same fare as is served abovestairs. A fine system."

To which she objected not at all, though some ladies would consider that system wasteful and indulgent.

We reached the blessedly shadowed foyer of her little castle, and she removed her gloves, then held out a hand for my hat and spurs.

To remove my spurs, I sat on a rush-bottomed chair in the foyer, one likely put there for the purpose. The space was perhaps eight feet square, with a sideboard, a row of pegs for hats, parasols, and the like, and the chair I occupied. The floor was gleaming polished oak, and light came in through two windows flanking the door.

I was in a farmhouse. A grand, lovely farmhouse, but not the sort of surrounds one would expect a viscount's daughter to consider a commodious retreat.

When I passed my spurs to the lady, I got a shock.

Mrs. Witherspoon had removed her veiled hat and revealed herself to be beautiful. Dark hair was knotted in a heavy chignon at her nape. Her features were classically lovely. Pale complexion, perfectly arched brows, high forehead, delicate jaw, and high cheekbones. The only discordant note in the whole portrait was a wide mouth and full lips that might have once been prone to smiles.

She was beautiful *and* lovely. That she racketed about in old clothes and a worn pair of men's gloves suggested she'd escaped the curse of vanity.

"Come this way," Mrs. Witherspoon said, starting down the corridor. "We'll dine in the breakfast parlor, though I'm afraid it's designed to be bright. If you'd like to freshen up, the guest room at the top of the steps is kept in readiness for company."

I took her up on that gracious offer. I washed my face and hands, held a cold cloth to the back of my neck, and longed to get out of my boots. I settled for giving them a light dusting with the damp cloth, dragged a pocket comb through my hair, and hoped I qualified as presentable.

When I returned to my hostess, she was closing the drapes along the row of east-facing windows typical of most breakfast parlors.

"My eyes thank you." I'd removed my spectacles and wasn't in a hurry to put them back on. "I would not want to put your kitchen to any trouble. If a guest is an imposition, I can simply keep you company at the table."

"You are famished, or you should be. If you've ridden the distance from Caldicott Hall, a fellow your size could put period to the whole buffet and consider it a snack." She finished with the drapes. "My husband was nearly as tall as you and carried more muscle. He ate prodigious amounts before he fell ill."

"You have me at a loss, ma'am. Are condolences in order?" *Why hadn't anybody told me she was a widow? But then, if Hannah Stadler had sought refuge with a school friend, a widow's home would be the ideal retreat.*

"Condolences are in order. We were a love match, which is the polite term for a mésalliance. You probably know the particulars but are too well-mannered to allude to them."

"I hope my manners are a credit to my upbringing. I am a keen supporter of the love match, provided the sentiments are equal all around. The specifics of your past have not been made known to me, nor are they relevant to the purpose for my call."

She smiled, a breathtaking beam of warmth in the shadowed room. "Oh, how you talk, my lord. I was told you were the quiet brother, but I would hazard 'quiet' hides an abundance of independence in your case, and no small store of contrariness. Andrew would have liked you. Help yourself to the food. I can fill my own plate."

She proceeded to do so, taking healthy portions of sliced ham, mashed potatoes, buttered peas, and braised carrots. I did likewise and supplemented my feast with two thick slices of buttered bread. Our beverage was cool, hard cider.

I held the lady's chair, we bowed our heads in silence for a moment, then she whisked her table napkin onto her lap.

"What brings you here, my lord?"

She would have no patience with dithering or roundaboutation. "Hannah Stadler has gone missing, and her friend Captain MacNamara fears for her safety. The family is being evasive and went so far as to suggest Miss Stadler might once again be biding with you. I am here to find out if that's the case, or if you know anything regarding the lady's disappearance."

Mrs. Witherspoon put her knife and fork down, her ham untasted. "That mother of hers... The viscountess has threatened Hannah with banishment to Scotland, my lord, and nothing would suit the viscountess better than to commend Hannah and Lady Dewar both to some bleak croft in the Western Isles. If Hannah has become least in sight, ask the viscountess what she knows."

"I tried. She's keeping mum."

"The viscount?"

"Haven't had the recent pleasure." I would have crossed paths with Lord Standish occasionally in my youth and during my Oxford years, but other than recalling him as a jovial bustler, he'd made no impression on me.

"Surely you've interrogated the Honorable Strother?" She imbued his name with distaste. "Hannah despairs of him, and she is a tolerant woman as a rule. Strother was spoiled rotten by his older sisters and his parents. He can do the pretty when anybody's watching, and he'd say he's fond of Hannah. What he means is, she lends him money without dunning him for repayment. Hannah keeps him afloat knowing he'll never make good on the loans. Eat something. Surely my assessment of Strother's character isn't any sort of revelation?"

I sliced off a bite of tender ham. "It is, in fact. Everybody else speaks well of him. Not glowingly, but well."

"Because the folk around Pleasant View are fairly isolated, my lord. No smattering of baronets married to bankers' daughters to ensure the intelligence flows from Town to Country. Not all of my friends dropped me when I accepted Andrew's proposal, and more than a few have tried to pick me back up now that it's plain he wasn't an impoverished farmer after all."

The ham was delicious. Not too salty, delicately redolent of clove.

"You imply that Strother's reputation in Town differs from his reputation in the shire?"

"One expects that to happen with young men, to some degree. I had three Seasons, my lord, and the occasional offer. The fortune hunters were easy to spot because they always left Town abruptly well before the Season was over. The excuse was ever the same: Must help Papa see to his acres. Plowing, planting, haying, always so much to do! Most of them went to Paris to avoid creditors until their next quarterly allowance came through. The truly desperate went to Rome on remittance. Pass the pickles, please. They are a guilty pleasure this time of year."

I passed the pickles. "Strother is a fortune hunter?"

"He certainly should be, and nobody would blame him for that. One tries to marry well, or that's the received wisdom, meaning one ought to marry money, money, always money. My family washed their hands of me when I chose Andrew. Tossed me into his arms without a penny. He wasn't a scoundrel, but he wasn't *good ton*. A glorified farm boy, according to my father. Andrew was shrewd. Kept most of his wealth out of sight, and didn't put on airs."

She considered a pickle and then chewed it into oblivion. "I am a farm boy's widow in possession of ten thousand, highly lucrative, gorgeous acres. My family now makes it a point to look in on me for most of each winter. They can't afford to heat their houses, poor things, so they 'take pity on me' and impose themselves on me from November to March."

I felt sorry for her, having to pour out the tale of this Pyrrhic victory to a stranger. What response would Hyperia advise? Not pity, never that.

"Your family is fortunate that your kind heart prevails over your right to some vengeance. This is excellent ham."

"Cook knows her job. I will pass on the compliment." She selected another pickle. "Hannah said the same thing: I'm twisting the knife by being generous to my family. She's wrong. The thought of them shivering away in their fancy parlors gives me no joy. That won't bring Andrew back, and neither would Andrew approve of pettiness. He had no time for Strother Stadler, though."

"You've met Strother?"

"Any number of times. He was responsible for escorting Hannah to and from school, and he attended Andrew's funeral service with Hannah." She patted those full lips daintily with her table napkin. "Strother called on me three months later and propositioned me. One doesn't forget disrespect of that magnitude. I had the footmen see him to the door, but, my lord, I wanted to wallop the blighter. Hard."

"You never told Hannah?"

"Didn't dare. She would have taken him to task, and that might have earned her a tour of the Highlands. You'd better have some more pickles now, because I intend to finish whatever you leave me."

I took two more pickles and surrendered the plate.

CHAPTER NINE

"Mrs. Witherspoon was critical of Viscountess Standish," I said, passing MacNamara a brandy. I indulged in a cool glass of meadow tea, the hour not yet late enough for the decanter to have any appeal. "The widow is very fond of Hannah, but hasn't seen or heard from your intended for three weeks. The last letter was a routine lament about the viscountess's sour nature and Lady Dewar's increasing frailty."

"You read it?" MacNamara sipped his drink. His foot was propped on the estate office hassock. A sluggish afternoon breeze riffled his hair. He appeared tired and worried. If I'd been confined to quarters while somebody else tried to locate a missing Hyperia, I would have looked far worse.

"I read the letter. I detected no hidden codes or warnings of impending disaster." The meadow tea was a tonic to the body and soul, and I silently vowed that Mrs. G must write her recipe down for our London cook.

"What did you think of Dabney Witherspoon?"

MacNamara expected me to say that she was pretty, and she was. Very. "She's angry and grieving. She risked the rest of her life for true love, and even ten thousand acres and the tacit remorse of her family aren't comfort against her loss."

"I am not sure what killed her husband. Some sort of wasting disease, I gather. Andrew was big, bluff, and merry. He lacked polish but was nobody's fool. A husband worth missing."

I settled into the second wing chair. "Don't brood. Hannah is doubtless missing you. Mrs. Witherspoon claims the viscountess threatened Hannah with banishment."

"Banishment for walking out with me?"

"I wasn't given specifics. I suspect banishment was the threat of first resort for any transgression, from whistling to bookishness to laughing out loud on the Sabbath." I'd seen Dabney Witherspoon smile, I'd not heard her laugh, but a part of me had wanted to provoke her to mirth.

She would not have appreciated the effort, not when anger was her most reliable prop and stay. Laughter had a way of getting under grief and lifting it into mere sadness.

"Then we take a closer look at the viscountess," MacNamara said. "Did you learn anything else of significance?"

I could not tell the captain, but I'd learned that my manly humors were more in evidence than they'd been of late. I'd left my animal spirits somewhere on the battlefield at Waterloo, and while I could appreciate the ladies in an abstract sense, and I delighted in affection shared with Hyperia, real desire had gone absent without leave.

True, I was engaged to marry Hyperia, but she was unwilling to have children. The situation had had a sad sort of symmetry. One party unwilling to risk intimacies, the other unable though longing for offspring. A workable match, if not exactly blissful in every particular.

A crooked pot needs a crooked lid, and what marriage was blissful in every particular?

As distant thunder rumbled in the south, I realized that Dabney Witherspoon had *tempted* me. Not in any alarming way, but in the sense that I'd noticed her as a man notices a woman, and I'd liked what I'd seen, felt, and sensed.

"Caldicott, you look to be staring into a particularly puzzling set of tea leaves."

Trying to decode a dispatch not meant for my eyes, perhaps. "Strother Stadler deserves a closer look too. Mrs. Witherspoon claims he's in dun territory and he left Town with creditors nipping at his heels."

MacNamara finished his brandy. "Ah, youth. I suspect Hannah's pin money disappeared into Strother's pockets. She never said as much, but she also never went up to Town to shop for bonnets, never ordered bolts of velvet for a new fancy evening gown. She purchased books or nothing at all."

I pulled my focus away from the conundrum of the angry widow and my wayward manly humors.

"How did Hannah afford to stock an entire library with books, MacNamara? Bound volumes do not come cheap."

He considered his empty glass. "For Christmas tokens and birthday gifts, she always and only asked for books. She raided the family library—all without permission—and she is a careful manager of her funds." Clearly, MacNamara's answer didn't satisfy him any more than it satisfied me.

"Your Hannah bought books by the dozen, and she spared her brother the occasional coin, too, according to Mrs. Witherspoon. The family has doubtless allowed Hannah a mere pittance for her own use. That is careful management, indeed."

"You are thinking Hannah raided the family hoard of gold somehow?"

Hannah was intelligent, had every right to resent her family, and would have been expected to forgo a dowry if she intended to marry the captain.

She might well have raided the family coffers on the sly. The ramifications of that possibility wanted pondering at length.

"I am thinking," I said, "that Strother will be out when I call on him tomorrow, so I'd best show up at Pleasant View early." Another protracted horseback jaunt, unless I took the coach and asked Hyperia to join me.

But the exchange I hoped to have with Strother was not one he'd want any lady to hear.

"Why will Strother bestir himself to avoid you?"

"Mrs. Witherspoon claims he's not as upright as he appears to be. He not only racks up the usual debts when in Town, he comports himself irresponsibly. He comes back to the shires to avoid his duns." I considered telling MacNamara about Strother's grossly improper advance toward Mrs. Witherspoon when she was yet in first mourning, but I kept my own counsel.

Telling MacNamara of the incident might burden the captain with the decision of whether to share the information with Hannah. I had only Mrs. Witherspoon's word for the matter, and Strother might have been bungling an infatuation rather than intending any insult.

Might have been, but I did not believe so. Mrs. Witherspoon held Strother in contempt, and that sort of disdain was usually earned.

"You aren't disclosing all you learned," MacNamara said. "You did this with the generals too. If a family of Rom were camping in some valley, you'd warn them to move on and forget to mention their presence at headquarters."

"I neither admit nor deny the charge." MacNamara could know of that incident only if Harry had tattled on me, because I had mentioned it to no one other than him. "I am honestly confounded. We're told the viscountess wanted Hannah out from under Pleasant View's roof, but marriage to you was not seen as a solution in that regard. We can only speculate as to why a mother would turn on her sole remaining unmarried daughter in such a fashion."

I rose stiffly. Beowulf was a magnificent steed, and he had magnificently powerful gaits.

"We are also told," I went on, "that Strother is fond of Hannah, but we find out that he might have owed her a small fortune. That he might owe any number of parties small and large fortunes, so where does that leave him when it comes to stealing from the family coffers? Where does the viscount fit in all this as paterfamilias, and what does Lady Dewar know that we do not?"

MacNamara sat forward and put his head in his hands. "I just want Hannah found, safe and sound, none the worse for her ordeal. She doesn't have to marry me. I don't care if she spent the whole pile of gold on Gothic novels. I don't care if she staged the entire business. I just need to know that she's well."

A suitor worth missing—and marrying. "I hope to have more answers for you tomorrow," I said, taking our empty glasses to the sideboard. "Are you using the comfrey poultices?"

"I am. I will be fussed to death if I neglect them. Your ladies are fierce, Caldicott."

"That they are, by both breeding and necessity. I am off in search of Miss West and will see you at supper. Don't get up."

I left the captain staring out the open window, the sultry breeze bringing another rumble of thunder.

I needed to make my report to Hyperia, but when I found her in the conservatory, she was not alone.

"Godmama," I said, enfolding Lady Ophelia in a hug. "You are a dear and welcome sight. I assume you bring news from Town, and I have the day's report to offer in return. Perry, budge over."

Her ladyship felt frail to me, but then, she'd always been slender. The slenderness in my arms leaned not toward the grace of the sylph, but rather, toward the insubstantial frame of an elderly woman.

My imagination was growing as morose as the rest of me. In all other regards, Lady Ophelia was her usual self—softly redolent of gardenias, attired in the first stare of understated fashion, and blue eyes snapping with mischief and intelligence.

My beloved budged over, I joined her on the settee, and Lady Ophelia made a great production over stirring honey into her tea. Godmama also looked tired to me, but then, the Town whirl did that to people. Mixed up days and nights, until rest became a succession of unsatisfying naps.

Godmama was a veteran of that battlefield, though. She knew how to manage her time and energy. She was aging well, but she *was* aging.

A sad thought.

She sipped her tea with regal leisure. "You asked me to locate Sylvester Downing, heir to the Muldoon viscountcy. I am loath to report that he appears to have also gone missing. What on earth do we make of this development?"

∼

"They ran off together?" Hyperia suggested. "The captain will be devastated if that's the case."

"When did Downing leave Town?" I asked, freshening the ladies' cups of tea and pouring one for myself. We were enjoying the slightly close and humid surrounds of the conservatory, which this time of year should have been an airy, fragrant retreat. The primary scent on the breeze was aged manure, faint but distinctive, and an overcast sky resulted in a pervasive gloom.

We were surrounded by the ailing specimens that were not fit for display along the terraces or garden walks. A pair of anemic potted lemon trees. A peach tree with some spotty yellow leaves. A rosebush that looked to have more thorns than leaves.

The sole cheerful note was a pot of violets blooming like mad in the middle of the low table.

"Downing left London at least a month ago," Lady Ophelia replied. "He is received, but he is not sought out by the elite hostesses. The man is handsome in a Black Irish way and full of charm when he wants to be, but his father is not yet fifty and in roaring good health. Then too, the family's means have dwindled considerably in the last few decades. A younger brother is said to have emigrated to Boston."

"Taken ship ahead of creditors?" My tea was tepid, and I'd forgotten to sweeten it. I put the cup down after a single sip.

"Very likely. A younger son of an impoverished peer seldom travels to the hinterlands because he's tired of clean linen and Continental vintages. You don't care for the tea?"

"Tea should be hot or cold, not lukewarm, and why the silver service wasn't trotted out in honor of your arrival, I do not know. At least then the tea would have been kept hot."

Hyperia became fascinated with the pink roses climbing the trellis on the east-facing windows. Lady Ophelia narrowed her gaze on me.

"Have you been going short of sleep, Julian?"

"He's been riding all over creation," Hyperia said. "Up to Town and back, all around the shire, tiring even Atlas, and now he'll doubtless wear out Beowulf."

Her ladyship swiveled her gunsights to Hyperia. "Atlas is that great dark beast with the poetical eyes?"

"The very one," Hyperia said. "Julian, don't glower at me as if I've told tales out of school. Her ladyship knows when you neglect your rest just by looking at you."

"I will get a good night's sleep tonight, and my travels will take me only as far as Pleasant View tomorrow. When trying to find a young lady who has disappeared without explanation, a certain urgency attaches to the situation."

I sounded as peevish as I felt, and neither lady deserved my ill humor. "I'm sorry. I have doubtless exceeded my physical limits with this investigation. At first, I was not sufficiently motivated to do much on Miss Stadler's behalf, and now her circumstances worry me exceedingly. Godmama, tell us what else you've learned regarding Mr. Downing."

I owed Hyperia an extended apology when we were private. I had hauled her down from Town and promptly abandoned her to MacNamara's understated charms.

Not well done of me.

"Downing drinks to excess," Lady Ophelia said, apparently willing to grant me clemency. "He gambles, very likely to excess. He wagers at the horse races, and we may imply excess there as well. He did, though, part ways with his mistress earlier this year, and a young fellow generally does that only when he's seriously contemplating matrimony."

A gust of wind caught one of the French doors and banged it closed. Hyperia rose and fastened the door latch.

"Or," she said, regarding the darkening sky, "the couple part when the lady finds a fellow who is more regular about paying her expenses. The idea that the gentleman decides when the liaison is over doesn't always hold water."

How did she…? She just did, that's how. "The timing is suspicious," I said. "Downing leaves town, and a fortnight later, Hannah Stadler is escorted from the property by two men. Her family starts propounding falsehoods to explain her absence, and nobody has heard a word from Miss Stadler since."

"You think they eloped?" Lady Ophelia asked. "With what money, Julian? One doesn't get to Scotland in any kind of style without ready coin."

"Hannah Stadler might have plenty of ready coin. She could simply snatch a bracelet or brooch from the family stash of heirlooms, have Downing pawn it, and away they go."

Hyperia returned to my side on the settee. "You do think they eloped?"

"My instincts say no. MacNamara is an exceedingly shrewd man, and I cannot see Hannah duping him as to her feelings for either Downing or MacNamara himself. But if I were intent on kidnapping a young lady, the last thing I'd do is absent myself from public view, effect the crime, and remain out of sight when the young lady's disappearance was noted."

Thinking like a criminal was becoming a habit.

"You'd be seen lounging about your clubs," Lady Ophelia said. "Assuming you recall how to lounge and still patronize any London clubs. Failing that, you'd lurk at Tatts or at least hack out in Hyde

Park on fine mornings. Well, Downing isn't in Dublin, and he isn't in London. I will send a pigeon, so to speak, to Paris."

"Please do," I said. "My plan for tomorrow was to confront Strother Stadler about the inconsistencies in his stories. Hannah is not taking the waters with one of her mama's aging friends. Her Grace sent her figurative pigeons to Bath and Lyme Regis, and they confirm that Miss Stadler hasn't been sighted in either location.

"She is not on a repairing lease with Mrs. Witherspoon," I went on. "Strother left Town in disgrace, and his own mother threatened Hannah with regular banishment. If I beat those bushes hard enough, I might startle some answers from him."

Lady Ophelia made a face that suggested a whiff of bad fish had tainted the air. "Lady Standish is not a pleasant woman. The Town tabbies make a regular joke of referring to her residence as Unpleasant View, when they refer to her at all. She prefers to be queen of the shire rather than compete with the leading lights of London. They disparage her for that too."

"I don't care for these tabbies." How odd that Lady Standish and I both avoided Mayfair's so-called polite society, and for similar reasons.

Godmama smiled. "The tabbies don't care for you either, young man. All that havey-cavey business with the French, locking yourself in your town house week after week when you mustered out, your hair gone ghostly white. They dined on your poor bones until I put my dainty foot down."

They were still dining on my poor bones, though they had sense enough not to snack on my reputation where Lady Ophelia could get wind of it.

"What if Strother merely plays ignorant with you, Jules?"

A crack of thunder had me nearly jumping out of my boots. The ladies appeared unruffled—they excelled at appearing unruffled, bless their dear hearts.

I needed a moment to consider Hyperia's question. "Strother well might continue to prevaricate or claim he knows nothing. That is why

I'd like you ladies to drop around to Miss Stadler's favorite lending library tomorrow and catch Lady Dewar on her regular rounds."

"Lady Dewar is nobody's fool," Godmama opined. "Or she wasn't. Time steals the wits of so many."

Captivity in a French garrison could make off with one's wits too. "How is your Scots Gaelic?" I asked.

Another bad-fish face. "Passable. Lady Dewar is quite fluent in English."

"So is her companion and lady's maid. She resorted to Gaelic with Her Grace out of what I fear was desperation."

"Then Hyperia will have to distract the toll keeper while I slip past the turnpike. Honestly, Julian, not every mission is best accomplished alone and on foot." Her ladyship rose in the manner of the elderly or the injured, in stages, without pride, intent on getting the job done however undignified the appearances.

I knew how it felt to move like that. MacNamara probably prayed for the day when he could move in any other fashion.

"I am off to my quarters for a lie-down," Godmama said. "Travel is wearying, and that you, Julian, do so much of it pleaseth me not. Miss West will have her hands full with you."

She swanned forth, leaving me with Hyperia in the uninspiring confines of the conservatory. A slap of rain spattered against the panes, and I almost leaped behind the settee, so badly had the sound startled me.

"You should nap too," Hyperia said. "Atticus will scold you for overdoing, Julian."

I wanted to stay with her and wanted to get away from the dreary, malodorous half-outdoors space we occupied.

"See me to my door?" I asked, rising and extending my hand to her.

When she rose, I tugged her into a hug that shaded closer to clinging on my part. A welter of unpleasant sensations—dread, anger, resentment, sadness, grief, I could not name them all—threatened my composure from out of nowhere.

I felt as I had after a battle, knowing more battles were to come, knowing them all to be pointless and tragic and inevitable.

"The storm doesn't help," Hyperia said, stroking my back. "I hate that. We used to love storms when we were children. We'd play in the rain and vex our nannies, and they'd fix us nursery tea and scold us with shortbread."

I wasn't a child. I was a grown man who needed rest and answers, in that order. I let go of Hyperia.

"You don't mind a trip to Hannah Stadler's library with Lady Ophelia?"

Hyperia brushed my hair back from my brow, a caress I usually treasured. The same touch annoyed me now, and I had no idea why.

"You could send Her Grace," Hyperia said, stepping back. "She has passable Gaelic if anybody does."

"The duchess is too conspicuous, and she and Godmama are not the easiest companions."

"Ah. Former rivals, possibly, or your not-so-sainted papa made them so. We will probably never know, and thank goodness for that. Julian, is something wrong?"

Many things, but I had no specific answer for the question she was truly asking: Was something wrong *with me*? I was in a frustrating phase of an investigation, true, but we had many places yet to look for answers and no reason to believe the worst had befallen Miss Stadler.

"I have neglected you and snapped at you." I brushed a kiss to Hyperia's knuckles. "Badly done, and I am sorry for my behavior."

"You snapped at the tea tray. We should have sent for fresh." Hyperia treated me to a quick hug and made for the door. "Shall we share that nap you've mentioned?"

She did not often offer this degree of intimacy, though we'd passed a few nights in blissfully affectionate slumber, emphasis on the *slumber*.

What to say? I was out of sorts, genuinely tired, and suffering the inchoate signs of a roaring bout of melancholy. Then too, Dabney

Witherspoon had given me much to think about that wasn't exactly comfortable.

"I am unnerved by the approaching storm," I said, "and fear I would conduct myself more like a limpet than an affectionate lover, Perry. I also need a bath."

She smiled. "One refrained from mentioning the obvious, but I did suggest that the water be heated when we saw you trotting up the drive." She kissed my cheek, patted my arm, and left me in the conservatory, where another gust of wind sent brown-edged rose petals cascading to the flagstones.

My unsettled mood was a variety of battle nerves, I knew that much. The worry had nowhere to go once weapons were cleaned and gear had been inspected for the tenth time. Some men paced the night before battle, some drank, some wrote maudlin letters. I had tried to read, but mostly stared at the pages and wondered what Jacques or Pierre, my counterparts three miles to the west, were thinking on what might be the last night of our lives.

But was the coming conflict a difficult conversation with Hyperia? A reckoning with Atticus, who showed no inclination to resume book learning as summer approached, or a former captive's anxiety about Miss Stadler's fate? Was instinct telling me that my sole extant brother had come to grief in France?

These thoughts and worse accompanied me as the coach rumbled toward Pleasant View.

"Once we finish at the lending library, we'll await you in the ladies' parlor at the Pig and Pickle," Hyperia said as that worthy enterprise came into view. "Tread lightly, Jules. The viscountess is Hannah's mama. A daughter gone missing would make any parent fretful."

I squeezed her hand, while Lady Ophelia remained silent on the forward-facing bench beside Hyperia.

"I will tread as lightly as circumstances allow. My regards to Lady Dewar." I kissed Perry's cheek—*so there, Step-mama*—and left the coach for the sunshine of a bright, warm day. My spectacles helped, but even deep blue glass could not entirely protect me from the late-morning glare.

I hired a sturdy hack from the livery and was soon rapping on Pleasant View's front door.

An antediluvian butler admitted me, took my card, and asked me to wait in the same sterile formal parlor where I'd last been received. He went off to see if Mr. Stadler was *in*, setting a pace worthy of an inebriated turtle with a poor sense of direction.

I went on a brief reconnaissance tour, poking my head into a warming pantry now doing service as a linen closet, a formal dining room shrouded in dusty Holland covers, a music room that boasted a spinet, a harp, and one lone fiddle. The library, by contrast, looked lived in and housed a goodly collection of books.

The library furniture was comfortably worn, the chairs apparently placed to hide carpet stains rather than to catch the natural light. One pair of faded velvet curtains had been made to do duty for two windows. I was perusing some pamphlets on the desk—Eve's Advocate was among the more rational of the semi-seditious authors —when a gentleman bustled into the room.

He was of medium height, graying, a trifle paunchy, and carrying a top hat.

"Beg pardon, must not leave without my... Oh, I say. Has Beekins misplaced you? I do apologize. Formal parlor is two doors down across the corridor. You look familiar."

"Lord Standish, good day. Lord Julian Caldicott, at your service. I was more concerned that Beekins might have misplaced himself."

Standish smiled, showing a resemblance to his taller, trimmer son. "Beeky hasn't managed that yet, but the day is young. Please do excuse my rudeness. I wasn't aware we were to have callers, and I must dash. Just thought to grab the..." He strode to the desk, opened a drawer, and divested it of more pamphlets, letters, and odd bits of paper. From the bottom of the drawer, he produced a black velvet drawstring bag, upended a dozen coins into his palm, and replaced the bag in the drawer.

"I'm off to London to catch the last weeks of the annual bacchanal," he said. "If dear Strothie is determined to ruralize, no need for both of us to miss all the merriment in Town." He closed the drawer with a bang and shoved the coins into a pocket. "You will excuse me? I'm terribly sorry to run, but 'ever fleeth the time' and all that."

Chaucer, et alia. *Ay fleeth the tyme; it nyl no man abyde.* "If the viscountess should ask, do I deny any sighting of you?"

He exactly mirrored the expression of a guilty schoolboy deciding whether to wheedle the kindly old tutor or to brazen it out with an awkward lie.

"You never saw me," Standish said, eyeing the door. "I am not even a figment of your imagination, young Caldicott, and if fate is just, I will be in Town before her ladyship knows I'm gone. Kinder to all concerned that way. My womenfolk are feuding. Haven't seen my daughter for nigh on a fortnight, and dear Hannah is the only person capable of managing her darling mama. I esteem my wife greatly, of course. A fine woman, but one better appreciated from a safe distance when she's in certain moods. You were a soldier. You know all about a strategic retreat."

He winked heavily, patted his pocket, and quick-marched to the door.

"My lord, you have no idea where Miss Stadler might be?"

"I do not, and I am sure that is by design. Hannah is the brains of this operation, my lord. Ask your lovely mother, and she will confirm my words. Strothie is a good boy, but he's taking his time settling down. My other girls know to give Pleasant View a wide berth, and the viscountess is not a happy woman.

"Hannah loses patience with us," he went on, "and I don't blame her. One-eyed in the land of the blind and that sort of thing. Hannah grows weary. Probably eloped with a curate just to spite her mama, not that we have a curate these days. Strothie will go completely into the ditch without Hannah to rein him in."

In the land of the blind, the one-eyed man is king. Erasmus quoting some old proverb, as best I recalled. "She didn't elope with Captain MacNamara?"

White brows rose. "A solid fellow, but m'wife doesn't care for him. If he's eloped with Hannah, more power to him, and I commend the happy couple to a long and fruitful union *in Scotland*. I will visit often. Must dash, my lord. Mum's the word."

He dashed on particularly quiet feet, leaving the door open in his wake.

He would stay at his club in Town rather than go to the expense of opening up his London residence, and he'd spend his days semi-inebriated over cards and chess, taking the occasional constitutional around St. James's and accepting pity invitations to dine with his friends.

Raiding the household money to pay the turnpike tolls was not the behavior of a man in possession of a fortune. I gathered up the rest of the mess he'd left on the blotter—mostly duns, along with meeting notes from some charitable committee for the betterment of the deserving poor, and a trio of radical pamphlets raging against the Corn Laws—and stuffed the lot back on top of the half-empty black velvet bag.

CHAPTER TEN

I returned to the formal parlor and cracked a window that gave me a fine view of the viscount setting a brisk pace down the lane that led to the stables. A footman trailed behind him with a valise. Lord Standish had likely timed his escape for the part of the day when the viscountess regularly reviewed menus or tended to her correspondence. Not a stupid man, but prone to living to fight another day.

His circumstances saddened me, and I formed a resolve that if Hyperia and I ever found ourselves dodging around each other, sneaking into the hedgerows, and hiding in our figurative clubs, that I'd face the situation squarely and do all in my power to repair it.

"Rubbishing hell."

Strother Stadler emerged onto the path a dozen yards behind his father, another footman lugging another valise in his wake.

I pushed the window the rest of the way open, dropped to the ground, and trotted across the garden, keeping to the grass lest my quarry detect my pursuit. By the time I fell in step with Strother, we had passed the privet hedge that kept the stables and carriage house from the view of the manor proper.

"Suffering saints, Caldicott. Must you sneak up on a man?"

Farther up the path, the viscount forged onward, oblivious to my rear-guard action.

"You'll want to take that back to the house," I said to the footman holding Strother's valise. "The viscount might well be off to London, but Mr. Stadler has pressing business to attend to here at Pleasant View."

To his credit, the footman looked to Strother for confirmation. That worthy nodded, and then I was alone with the viscount's heir.

"I ask myself, has your sister followed the family tradition and taken flight on her own initiative? Losing a sister is not well done of you, Stadler, and Captain MacNamara is most concerned, as am I."

"Lost? Hannah? I say, that is... Well, on second thought. Oh dear. The very notion confounds... But this is Hannah... and..."

"And without her to bail you out of the River Tick, your creditors will soon descend on the family seat, and thus you thought to hide very discreetly in plain sight in London or to squat in the rooms of some chum who has left Town early. In either case, you are a very poor excuse for a brother."

An antique traveling coach, two bays in the lead, the wheelers a pair of sturdy chestnuts, lumbered around to the stable yard.

"You aren't going anywhere," I said, ready to make my point with my fists if necessary. "Your sister is missing in action. We either retrieve her from her captors, find her among the wounded, or locate her body. Every shred of evidence I've come across suggests Miss Stadler has been kidnapped, and you are deserting your post."

The militance of my words surprised even me, but a gently bred young lady, no matter how resourceful or well-heeled, wasn't safe for long on her own in the English countryside, much less in the hands of kidnappers.

"She's not dead," Strother said, though the words seemed to annoy him. "I can't see that it's any business of yours."

"I am making it my business. You either accept the aid I offer, or all of London will soon know of your troubles." Bruiting about Miss Stadler's difficulties figured nowhere on my agenda, but getting through to her blockheaded brother sat at the top of the new business list. The lady had been missing for nigh two weeks, and I could see no sign that her family had made an effort to find her.

"Mama won't hear of you becoming involved." A lament rather than an objection.

"I *am* involved. I've been searching for any word of your sister, any sighting of her, for days. She's disappeared, and before you send me on a goose chase, she is not biding with Mrs. Witherspoon. You've lost her or sent her away, and neither Captain MacNamara nor I will rest until we know she's well and happy."

MacNamara's motivations included love and loyalty. I was inspired by guilt. If I'd gone straight to work, and denied myself a jaunt to London, would Hannah Stadler be home, safe and sound?

Strother must have sensed that now that I'd accepted my orders, I would not abandon the mission. He regarded me with rare seriousness.

"We've had a ransom demand, and they sent us a lock of her hair. I compared it to the lock Han gave me when I went off to university, and it's hers, or as near as."

My relief was enormous. "Back to the house," I said. "*Now*. I assume your father remains in ignorance of the entire situation?"

"Blissfully so. I thought it best, and Mama concurred. Papa isn't stupid. He knows something's afoot, and as usual, it's not something that bodes well for the family. Let him have his furlough, Caldicott. The reprieve will doubtless be temporary."

We watched as the coach rattled off, using the lane that led directly to the village rather than taking the longer drive that swept graciously past the house.

"March," I said, gesturing in the direction of the manor, "and prepare to be very, very honest."

He marched. I prayed for patience. Tread lightly, Hyperia had said. I wanted to boot dear Strothie in the arse, hard, and speak to his mother as no gentleman ever addressed a lady.

∽

I dispatched one footman to fetch the viscountess, another to bring a tray of lemonade and sandwiches. Strother chose the library for our conference, which led me to believe that the informal parlor or family parlor had likely been retired from active duty.

So many families, gentry and aristocracy both, were hanging on by their fingernails and counting on the Corn Laws to prop up their situations. That the same laws were swelling the ranks of the wretched poor and providing a military-minded government an excuse to oppress the "unruly" masses was, to the likes of Lady Standish, an acceptable price for new curtains.

I did not envy Arthur his responsibilities in the Lords.

Lady Standish paused in the doorway. "Young man, that is a singularly ungracious expression. One does not greet a lady with less than his best manners, most especially when he is intruding into her home without an invitation."

As artillery barrages went, that one failed to impress. "Neither does a loving mother threaten her adult daughter with banishment simply because that lady hopes to marry for love as well as security."

Strother stared resolutely out the window. Her ladyship stepped into the library and closed the door quite firmly.

"Strother, either summon the footmen to eject his lordship bodily, or explain to me why he thinks he can disrespect your mother while you do nothing."

Strother turned, though he remained near the French doors. "Lord Julian *knows*, Mama. He knows we've lost track of Hannah and that she might be the victim of foul play."

For the merest instant, her ladyship's features showed consternation, then her impassive mask slipped back into place.

"We have no idea what has befallen Hannah. For all we know, she's tormenting us with a very nasty prank. She reads too many novels, and novels inflame the imagination. Pamphlets are even worse. I have told her and told her that a lady reads her *Book of Common Prayer*, improving tracts, or the Society pages. But no, not for Hannah. She must have poetry, and Shakespeare, radicals, and philosophers. Don't blame me if the girl has come down with a brain fever. I have done my best by her. More than most mothers would do."

"By threatening her with banishment to the Western Isles? By insisting that she marry an Irish lordling who bored her silly? By disapproving of a suitor who could make Hannah happy?"

Strother unlatched the French door, letting in a slight breeze.

"You impudent young man," Lady Standish said, fisting her hands. "You know nothing. You have no idea, not the first, earthly notion, of the suffering Hannah will endure if she persists in her wrongheaded, outspoken... I will not be made to listen to your insults when all I want is to see my daughter take her place in Society and derive contentment from it."

That Lady Standish would bicker with me was interesting. She revealed a degree of upset that felt somehow off. I could believe she was worried for her daughter, but the focus of her concern wasn't Hannah's immediate whereabouts.

"Contentment," I countered evenly, "as you are content?"

The viscountess advanced on me. "I comport myself as befits my station, which is more than one can say for you, my lord. The next thing to a traitor, perhaps worse than a traitor. Does your late brother haunt you? Some say you went mad after Waterloo, and that—"

"Mama, this gets us nowhere. We need to find Hannah."

The viscountess waved her hand. "She just wants the gold. Hannah is stupidly fixated on that gold, which we should have turned into coin years ago."

Too late, the viscountess realized what she'd admitted before my impudent self. The Stadler family had gold, and that gold was urgently needed. She gave the bell-pull a defiant jerk, probably hoping to have me tossed from the premises.

I had called Wellington's bluff when necessary, though I'd done so carefully and politely. Viscountess Virago wasn't half as formidable as the duke.

"Let's assume your groundless theory is correct," I said. "If Hannah is essentially blackmailing you into parting with the family treasure, then locating her is the simplest way to thwart her schemes. If she has been kidnapped by malefactors, the situation might well be life or death."

"I tell you, she has done this to us. You don't know my daughter, sir, and speaking as her mother—"

"We need to find her." Strother spoke gently. "Mama, we do. Putting it about that she's traveling will only work for so long. We can't say that she's in Paris, because half the aristocracy will soon be in Paris, and we'll be caught out in a lie. The other half will go north next month in anticipation of the shooting, so we cannot put Hannah on a fictitious coach for Scotland. We must find her or Lord Julian will raise the hue and cry."

"You may depend on me to do exactly that."

The viscountess twitched at the faded burgundy curtain and sent the books lining the shelves a glare. "Has your father left yet?"

"Not a quarter hour past."

She went to the desk and took out the black velvet bag, hefting it in her hand. "He left us at least half the wage money this time. He knows something has gone seriously amiss."

Thanks to Hannah. The words hung in the air, bitter and unspoken. That the viscountess held her husband in some affection, though, was also apparent.

"I have been tasked by Captain MacNamara with discovering Miss Stadler's whereabouts," I said. "Your interests and his are the same in this regard. Object to him as a suitor after he's asked for permission to court the lady, if you must. For now, he is concerned for a dear friend, and with good reason."

"He encourages her." The hint of softening her ladyship had shown at her husband's peculiar generosity fled. "The captain finds Hannah's literary obsession and political views *charming*. He will be the ruin of her."

"For him to ruin her, we must first find her. Might I see the ransom note?"

"Strother, do as the man asks."

Strother headed for the door, opened it, and found a footman holding a tray in the corridor. Neither one looked surprised to see the other, suggesting the staff well knew what had Lady Standish in such a temper.

The staff always knew, which put a different complexion on the butler's earlier dilatory tactics.

"Do come in," Lady Standish snapped. "Leave the door open when you depart. I rang only for a tea tray. Has Cook become confused?"

"The kitchen received more than one order, your ladyship. Tea will be along shortly." The footman set down the tray, which included sandwiches, cakes, and lemonade. He sent me a fulminating look on the way out.

That look bore undercurrents. Had I thought to bring Atticus, I might have some intelligence from belowstairs to show for the excursion. Badly done again, Caldicott.

When my hostess was alone with me, she neither invited me to sit at the reading table nor offered me a plate. I was hungry, and she was rude, but I nonetheless remained on my feet, nigh panting for a glass of lemonade.

"This is it," Strother said, returning with a single sheet of paper. "Short and to the point."

"'By whatever means necessary, gather up five thousand pounds in banknotes and gold. Further instructions within the fortnight. Do as you're instructed, and Miss Stadler will be returned to you unharmed.'"

"This is written in Miss Stadler's hand?" I asked.

Strother nodded. The viscountess wrapped herself in vindicated silence.

"You are dealing with an intelligent kidnapper, then. Handwriting can be distinctive, and making Hannah write the note leaves us with one less clue as to who might have taken her captive." I held the paper up to the window.

Generic foolscap such as any stationer in the realm might sell. Plain black ink, nothing in the way of a faded tearstain or smear of blood to lend the note drama, much less show a man's large thumbprint in the corner.

I laid the note on the reading table next to the tray. "Assuming Hannah is not engaged in a protracted, scandalous, expensive, and unkind prank that will result in her own social ruin, whom do you suspect of taking her?"

Strother threw himself into a wing chair. "That's the thing. We suspect everybody and nobody. Hannah is well-liked—don't sniff, Mama, she is—and yet, *we* are not well-liked. We've raised the rents a bit in recent years. We're a tad behind on repairs. Mama has trod on a few toes among the local ladies, and Vicar tires of importuning us to choose a curate. But none of that justifies a demand for five thousand pounds."

None of it justified kidnapping the one family member who was locally popular.

"What have you done to gather the money?" I did not so much as glance at the tray. Did not take the second wing chair either.

The viscountess fixed herself a plate and settled at the desk, then bit into a sandwich while looking straight at me. And yet, she accused her daughter of boldness.

"Gather what money?" Strother asked, taking a plate and sandwich for himself and two cherry tarts. "You probably know about the famous Roman gold, though the pieces predate the Romans. All very romantic, and most of it is quite pretty in a barbaric way, what I recall of it. The gold has gone missing, or Papa liquidated it and won't say so. Perhaps Grandpapa did. We don't know. It's not where it's supposed to be, and if word of that gets out, we are truly and forever ruined." He took a bite of his sandwich. "Cook stinted on the mustard."

Cook stinted on the mustard. A sister missing, her life perhaps in peril, her reputation hanging by a thread. A fortune stolen, though nobody knew by whom or when, and Strother Stadler focused on a minor oversight in the kitchen.

Like polishing spotless boots the night before battle. The mind was a curious thing.

"What do you know of Hannah's actual disappearance?" I asked.

Strother shrugged, his mouth full of sandwich.

"She went out to read in the belvedere," the viscountess said, sipping her lemonade. "She was always hiking to some obscure corner of the estate with a lap desk or book in hand. She'd be gone for hours. She went off to read and didn't come back."

The viscountess took another nibble of her sandwich and appeared to relish the food. "We didn't think anything of it," she went on, "until Hannah missed supper. Lord Standish was concerned she'd turned an ankle or something. Strother and the footmen went in search of her. I concluded she was off on another one of her ill-timed adventures. We waited to hear that she'd safely arrived at Mrs. Witherspoon's or some other location of Hannah's choosing. The morning before you and Her Grace called, we received that note."

"Then you have only a few days before your two weeks are up."

Strother reached for another sandwich. The viscountess sipped her lemonade.

I battled the impulse to upend the reading table, but instead took another look at the ransom note.

"I should have brought Atticus." I settled onto the backward-facing seat, entirely unhappy with the day's events so far. "I hope Lady Dewar had something useful to say?"

Hyperia and Lady Ophelia regarded me with similarly unreadable looks, both hinting at concern, disapproval, and something feminine and *knowing*.

I did not need a nap—not badly enough to signify—but I was thirsty and hungry. True enough. "Shall we raid the hamper?" I asked.

"Please do," Lady Ophelia said, untying her bonnet ribbons. "Peckish men can be difficult company."

"You were right about Lady Standish." I dragged the hamper from under my seat and hefted it onto the bench beside me. "She is deficient in charm, though she seems to like her son."

"That one male child, however unprepossessing, allows her to hold up her head," Lady Ophelia observed. "I gather Hannah was supposed to be a boy as well, which might account for the viscountess's antipathy toward her youngest daughter."

Hyperia had already taken off her bonnet, and we spent a moment organizing food, fashion accessories, and drink.

"Her ladyship resents Hannah," I said, biting into a meat pasty. "I cannot fathom why. At least not why the intensity of the resentment. A bit unnerving, to be honest." My mother and I had been distant to a degree and for a time, but I could never imagine Her Grace aiming true venom at me, nor I at her.

My mother and I were cut from different cloth, but a family of perfect replicas would have been a boring and unnatural group.

My own children...

I cut the thought off with a mental saber slash. "What did Lady Dewar have to say?"

"She is beside herself with worry." Hyperia passed me a cool, silver flask. "She tried to tell Lady Standish what she'd seen when Hannah did not come home for supper, but the viscountess would not hear a word. Told Lady Dewar to have a lie-down and then conferred closely with Lady Dewar's companions."

Godmama took a nibble of gingerbread. "When Lady Dewar asked for her writing desk, the companion claimed it had been mislaid. Her ladyship wanted to get a note to Captain MacNamara, and she would have written in the Gaelic, but Lady Standish foiled that plot. The woman is obsessed with remaining in charge of her little rural fiefdom."

"Did you convey to Lady Dewar that we're searching for Hannah?"

"We did," Hyperia said, "and we further conveyed that you have a knack for resolving difficulties such as this, and without bringing scandal down on the parties involved. Lady Dewar cares nothing for Society's opinions. She wants her granddaughter found."

As did I. "What else did she have to say?" The meat pasty was delectable. I could have eaten six, but that was the hamper's entire complement. I limited myself to a second. I also drained the flask of cool, sweet meadow tea only to note a smug gleam in Hyperia's eye when I put the empty vessel back into the hamper.

Hungry and thirsty, guilty as charged. No need to gloat.

"Hannah was reading *The Wanderer* in the shade of the wall below the foot of the garden when she was accosted by two men," Hyperia reported. "The librarian hinted again that she'd like the book returned. It's fairly recent and much in demand. The local goodwives would rather read Mrs. Burney than the library's collection of political pamphlets and sermons."

As would most rational adults. "What did the men look like?" I dove for a cherry tart and found only one remaining. "Ladies, does either of you care for the last tart?"

They sent me matching pitying looks.

"Hearing no objection…" I popped the tart into my mouth, glad in some ungentlemanly corner of my soul that Atticus was not on hand to see my lapse in manners.

"Lady Dewar said the two men wore riding attire," Hyperia went on. "They were nicely turned out. Hannah did not appear flustered by their appearance. Hats precluded specific identification."

As would the retaining wall that kept the garden above the level of the park beyond it. If Hannah had sought the shade provided by that wall, she would have been out of sight of all but the uppermost floors of the house.

"I've had enough to eat," Hyperia said. "Julian you must finish the meat pasties. In this heat, they will just go to waste if you don't."

"No more for me," Lady Ophelia said. "The weather saps my appetite."

"Does Lady Dewar know of the ransom note?" I asked, leaving the last two pasties in the hamper for the present.

"She does." Lady Ophelia yawned delicately behind a slender hand. "Her companion and lady's maid are heavy sleepers. They tipple, of course, as does Claypole, the lady's maid assigned to Hannah. Lady Dewar simply waited until they were asleep, went to the study, opened the safe, and read the note. Her eyesight is quite good. She considered writing her note to the captain by dark of night, but wasn't sure it would be delivered. Then the butler came along and escorted her back to her cell."

"Does Lady Dewar happen to know where the gold has got off to?"

"The gold is gone?" Hyperia asked. "That's bad news. Are you sure?"

Well, no, I wasn't. "Lady Standish and Strother suggested the gold was stolen at some point in the past. They claim not to know when or by whom. I have several theories. First, the gold has long since been liquidated by the viscount or his progenitors, but of course, one doesn't let that get out. Second, Strother has been selling it off to cover his debts. Third, the viscountess has frittered it away on keeping up appearances. In the alternative, the two of them in combination borrowed pieces intending to pawn and then redeem them. They cannot now admit their perfidy, so why not blame Hannah?"

"We will have to consult the goldsmiths," Lady Ophelia said. "I know them all. The ones with the pretty shops on Ludgate Hill and the ones in less prestigious establishments."

"Do you have any more theories, Jules?" Hyperia reached into the hamper and passed me one of the remaining pasties.

"I'll save that for now," I said. "My final theory is that Hannah, knowing her family to be in want of funds, and knowing herself to be, in her father's words, the brains of the operation, hid the gold. She alone knows where it is, and she cannot communicate that information to her family without revealing the location of the whole hoard to her kidnappers. If she fails to get word to her family, her life might be forfeit."

Hyperia put the food away. "From bad to worse. What we know of the lady says she won't betray her family's means of social survival even to save her own life."

"The tabbies will love this," Lady Ophelia muttered. "Lady Standish's bluestocking daughter ruined, the family fortune gone, and Strother taken up for debt. The viscount will likely drink himself to death. This is Lady Standish's worst nightmare. One almost pities her."

I might pity her more if I understood her better. "We haven't time to pity her. If we cannot locate Hannah, we must locate the gold, and we have but a handful of days to do that."

The coach made a right-hand turn, sending sunshine into the window nearest me.

Hyperia leaned across and pulled down the shade. "The captain might have some insights. He and Hannah hid letters in figurative hollow logs, didn't they?"

"We will start with the captain. I doubt the gold has gone far. It's heavy, and the pieces are conspicuous. Moving it up to Town would be a major undertaking, and according to MacNamara, Hannah made only rare trips to London to purchase books."

We fell silent as the coach rocked along, my thoughts bringing me little comfort. The kidnappers had been shrewd enough to have Hannah write her own ransom note on plain paper. They had known of the treasure and mentioned it specifically, allowing the family enough time to liquidate the gold if necessary.

Our quarry had also studied the terrain around Pleasant View and acquainted themselves with the victim's movements.

We faced intelligent, well-organized, and determined foes, and we had only a few days left to best them.

I thought of the remaining meat pasties, but my appetite had deserted me.

CHAPTER ELEVEN

"Hannah never specifically brought up the gold," MacNamara said, shoving a pillow beneath his foot where it rested on a hassock. "But the topic would arise nonetheless, like mention of a tippling auntie tumbles into the conversation and has to be tucked away again."

We occupied Caldicott Hall's library, a contrast to the Stadlers' room answering to the same name. The summer curtains here were rich blue velvet hanging in long, graceful folds, the carpet a bright, floral Axminster pattern. Evening light flooded in from the west-facing windows and winked on crystal decanters, gilt frames, and an enormous pier glass opposite the central hearth.

All was comfort, repose, and elegance, but without fussiness. I had read in this library by the hour as a younger man, and also played cards here, napped, and tended to correspondence.

I poured two brandies and brought one to MacNamara. "How did Hannah refer to the gold?"

MacNamara accepted the drink. "Like that same auntie. One cannot deny the connection, but one struggles to appreciate it. I know some of the pieces were gorgeous—she'd sketched them—and the value incalculable because the age was so venerable. Hannah claimed the cache of coins could have come from the leprechaun's fabled pot, they shone so brightly. She said no barbarians had fashioned such beauty, and I believe those pieces were ancient when the Romans arrived on our shores."

I took the second wing chair and lifted my glass. "To treasures recovered."

We sipped while off in the distance a cow lowed to her calf. Such a mournful sound.

"Where would Hannah hide a lot of gold she wanted to protect from her family?"

"Gold doesn't hide easily."

And yet, history was full of tales of hidden treasure, much of it gold. "The viscountess mentioned that Hannah was forever wandering around the estate with a lap desk or a book. Why bring a lap desk? Could Hannah have been secreting gold in the lap desk or in a book altered for the purpose?"

In Spain, many a dispatch had fallen into enemy hands. The missives were always coded, though Wellington's staff managed to crack the French codes eventually, but the messages were also hidden. Stuffed into a slit in the messenger's saddle, secreted beneath a false sole on his boot, sewn into the lining of his dusty coat. The hiding places were endless.

"She might, but some of the pieces are sizable, my lord. A circlet doesn't easily fit into a bound volume of *Fordyce's Sermons*, no matter how many pages you cut away. The lap desk was doubtless for writing to Hannah's literary friends or to me. She is a loyal correspondent, as I well know."

My mind was sluggish, my spirits low. The gold could be in a cupboard in an empty tenant cottage, behind some loose stones in the belvedere, stashed beneath the bench of an abandoned privy. All of the above. Pleasant View manor sat in the middle of hundreds of acres accessible to Hannah Stadler on foot or on horseback.

"Forget the lap desk for a moment. Maybe Miss Stadler was

transporting the smaller pieces in her book or her reticule or the crown of her bonnet. Where would she take them?"

MacNamara shifted his foot. "Where would her family never look? That is the more difficult question, because as a young lady with no independent means, Hannah was lucky to have a bedroom to herself. She had no authority to order her family away from a folly or gatehouse, for example. In London, she would have been dogged by a companion and lady's maid and probably accompanied by a footman as well."

Think, Caldicott. Think like a young lady intent on literally burying treasure. "Would the staff abet her efforts to hide the gold?"

"Are we certain she hid it?"

Valid question. "We are not. Strother, a notably dishonest fellow, claims she might have, as does the viscountess. If either of them stole the gold, they would of course claim Hannah had moved it."

MacNamara grimaced. "Right. So we *hope* Hannah hid the gold, because otherwise, there is no gold and no way to pay the ransom."

"I've sent word to Town. Waltham's solicitors have been instructed to get the funds together, but a sum that size, without the duke on hand to authorize it personally, will take some time." Meaning the funds were coming from my own figurative pockets, about which not a word need be said. "And I have nothing in the way of ancient gold."

MacNamara peered into his glass. "Decent of you, all the same."

"Her Grace seconded the motion. Said one mother could do no less for another, but the sum will be all in bearer bonds rather than partly in gold as directed." I'd dispatched the requisite pigeon within the quarter hour of consulting Her Grace. "Where do we look for the gold, MacNamara?"

"The manor house is probably out," he said, sipping his brandy. "Strother, the viscountess, or her ladyship's familiars might come across anything hidden within the dwelling itself. They have doubtless looked. Hannah would have reasoned that Stadler land was the safest option. Anybody who came across a bracelet or brooch in some cow byre on Stadler property would have been obligated to assume the piece belonged to the Stadler family."

"Anybody but a thief with common sense. He'd assume good fortune had finally smiled upon him."

"Hannah would not leap to that conclusion. She is blazingly intelligent, but also... innocent."

"Good," I said, knowing exactly what MacNamara meant. "Pure of heart. I suppose I must scour the countryside, then, or at least the land adjacent to the manor." I had found needles in haystacks before, though not often and not when time was so short. "Can you draw me a map?"

A tracking hound would find too many old trails to be of use, and an army of searchers would obliterate as many clues as they found. Nothing for it but relentless hard work.

"I'll make you a map and note places Hannah frequented. I can also put at your disposal my groom, gardener, and gamekeeper. All former military. Reliable sorts and hard workers. My butler is former military, too, but getting on."

"Do I dare trust any of the Stadlers' retainers?"

"You do not. They are too terrified of the viscountess. She's the kind to sack a maid without a character if Strother takes a fancy to the girl. Hannah wrote the characters, signed her mother's name, and contributed what severance she could."

"The more I know of the viscountess, the less I like her."

MacNamara finished his drink and commenced rubbing his knee. "Don't underestimate her. She's smart—Hannah did not get her brains from old Standish—and bitter."

Her bitterness was obvious, but also off-key. "Her ladyship, a Scot of no lofty pedigree, married an English viscount's heir. Why the bitterness?"

"I don't know. Perhaps it's as simple as she *had* to marry the English viscount rather than some braw, bonnie laddie."

"And thus her daughter must be made to marry some strutting Irish lordling? Her daughter who has no dowry to speak of? Who is no longer in the first blush of youth? Who is not, meaning the lady no respect, a diamond of the first water? Too many questions, MacNamara, and not enough answers."

He sat back. "I should get up and fetch pencil and paper from the desk, but such is the contrariness of my knee that I will ask you to procure them for me."

I rose, my drink all but untouched. "Have you consulted Hugh St. Sevier about your medical woes?"

"The Frenchman?"

"The French physician who was educated in Scotland and saw more human anatomy and medical challenges on the Peninsula than you did cannonballs. He's in London these days. I know one of the clubs he frequents."

"I can't say I liked St. Sevier. He wasn't easy company, but he was a damned fine surgeon."

"He still is, though I think he limits his practice to émigrés. He'd make an exception for you." Particularly if I wrote and asked him to.

"Find Hannah, then I will fret about an aching knee or dodgy foot. Find Hannah, Caldicott, the sooner the better."

I brought him a lap desk stocked with paper, pens, pencils, and other accoutrements of correspondence.

"Please jot me a letter of introduction to whoever held the senior rank among your staff, and I'll acquaint them with the state of the campaign. They might well have heard something or seen something of interest in your absence."

"Good thought. You'll get an early start?"

Another early start. "Crack of doom."

MacNamara considered me. "I'll do what I can to assist with the ransom. My resources are modest, but my family has some means."

From the captain, that might mean his older brother was rolling in filthy lucre, or it might mean they'd somehow endure it until harvest.

"You might deploy those family means to buy up the vowels owed by one Sylvester Downing. I have no reason to conclude that he's implicated, but I cannot rule him out. He has motive, and my instincts are twitching. You'll have to move quickly and rely on London connections."

MacNamara ran a blunt finger along the lap desk's inlaid border. "Downing's younger brother recently decamped for parts distant, didn't he?"

"Probably one foot ahead of creditors." Though the Continent served the purpose just as well as the New World did and was within easier, cheaper reach.

MacNamara opened the desk and rummaged inside. "You're looking a bit peaky, Caldicott. Not sleeping well?"

"Not sleeping enough. Summer nights are too short and too hot. In Spain, the nights were brisk, even if the days were broiling. I don't miss it, but..." *Why was I talking about bloody Spain?*

"But we left pieces of our souls in Spain," MacNamara said, laying a sheet of paper flat on the top of the lap desk. "And we might never get those pieces back."

One thing I would not be is maudlin regarding my military past. "Good night, MacNamara. I'll report back as regularly as I can."

～

"We'll find her," Jimmy Dorset said, balling his callused hands into fists. He was a rangy blond, former infantryman turned gardener, and he walked with a slight limp.

"We ain't looking fer the young miss," the groom retorted. He went by the moniker Dutch, though *I detected nothing of the Low Countries in his accent.* He was shorter and thicker than Dorset, and his hair was flaxen. "We're looking fer the gold."

"We might find the young miss," Dorset shot back. "She's lively, in her way, and hauling her to parts distant would be a challenge." *Dorset was the better-spoken, but in a fight, I'd put my money on Dutch.*

The groom, who'd been artillery until he'd lost an eye, wore a green patch over the socket, probably a nod to his former regimental colors.

"We won't find anything if you two keep bickering," the gamekeeper said. "My lord doubtless has orders for us."

The gamekeeper, Carstairs, struck me as an academic sort. In addition to worn but well-made riding attire, he wore spectacles and a low-crowned beaver hat. Curling dark hair neatly trimmed, intelligent brown eyes. A gentleman's son, perhaps. I wondered how much gamekeeping he actually did.

Former rifleman, MacNamara had said. A demon in battle and never missed a target, but wrote fairly good poetry too. Carstairs did not appear demonic. He looked like a schoolmaster resigned to educating little heathens, with whom he half sympathized. He was lanky and attractive in a lonely soul sort of way, and his smile struck me as sad.

He also outranked Dutch and Dorset, so they fell silent at his order.

"Dutch has a point," I began, at the risk of causing dissension in the ranks. "Miss Stadler might well be in the vicinity. All we know is that she's missing, and the gold is missing. The family will receive instructions regarding ransom money in the next several days, if our criminals can use a calendar, so time is short."

Dutch said something under his breath that sounded like German profanity.

"*Are* we looking for Miss Stadler?" Carstairs asked.

The three of them, probably without intending to, had arranged themselves in a ragged line in MacNamara's garden. Carstairs lounged against the upright supporting a wooden swing wide enough for two. Dutch had propped a hip against a dry birdbath, and Dorset stood loosely at attention on the other side of the birdbath.

MacNamara's garden was hardly a showplace, considering that we'd reached the late spring/early summer season when gardens often showed to their best advantage. Potted heartsease provided some color, and the lavender borders were in good trim. Roses had been trellised to provide shade on a back porch, but the rest of the space boasted few flowers.

The beds looked to be full of spices, a few tomatoes, some beans... Half kitchen garden, half spice garden with a few ornamental touches as an afterthought.

A soldier's garden, perhaps. Provisions and medicinals before all else.

"The gold could be anywhere," I went on. "Miss Stadler could be enjoying the hospitality of some obscure hostelry over in Dorking. She might be housed in an abandoned tenant cottage, of which there are two. The weather is mild enough that amenities can be safely limited."

Dutch snorted. Carstairs gave me his woebegone smile.

"Miss Hannah is a lady," Dorset said, "but she isn't any fading flower. The only amenity she needs is books. Captain says the same."

"A born reader," Carstairs added. "Nose in a book, and she's happy."

The rest went unsaid: If Miss Hannah was happy, the captain was happy, and thus his men were happy. How many of these little ragtag regiments had formed all over Britain, part veterans of the war, part refugees from a land that had no jobs and no homes for its former soldiers?

"She was reading when her captors came upon her," I said. "Think of yourselves as temporarily seconded to reconnaissance. We can't spot a brooch tucked into a stone wall, but we can look for stones that, unlike the rest of the wall's face, lack moss. We won't see Miss Hannah waving to us from some sunny back-garden, but we can note human footprints on a narrow game trail or spot an old well whose cover has been set aside."

"We are looking for anything out of place?" Carstairs asked. "Is that how you fellows did your jobs?"

"Part of it. We looked for who was riding a horse of better quality than his means would allow—there's your informer. We looked for stacks of fodder higher than needed for the livestock in view—there's the man who will sell you a few head of cattle, provided the enemy doesn't see him doing it. We kept a sharp eye, or we never made it back to camp."

"Miss Hannah will make it back to camp," Dutch said, "and the captain will marry her."

On this, the whole battalion agreed.

We consulted the maps MacNamara had drawn, and we discussed, as military people would, how to implement the orders given. I did not expect us to stumble across Hannah Stadler, but the possibility bore consideration. If nothing else, we could find clues as to who had taken her, and then we might pick up their trail.

Miss Stadler had likely hidden the gold in every hollow log and stile on the property. Golden needles—and bracelets, circlets, tiaras, and necklaces—in an endless haystack.

The butler, MacNamara's former batman, would man headquarters in our absence. He was a former gunnery sergeant answering to the name of Coombs. Spare, quiet, and watchful, he could hear out of only one ear unless a storm approached, and then both ears temporarily functioned.

A storm was approaching, figuratively, and—given the time of year—probably literally. Dutch and Dorset left the garden on foot. Carstairs took the captain's extra mount.

I climbed into Atlas's saddle and prepared for the disagreeable task of once again doing battle with Viscountess Standish.

∽

"I don't understand." The viscountess sank onto the formal parlor's tufted sofa. "If Her Grace has arranged for funds, why must these, these... menials swarm over the property? We pay the ransom, Hannah is returned, and nobody will know she was ever missing."

Strother sent me a pleading look from across the room. He lounged against the mantel, the picture of young manhood at his rural leisure. His riding attire indicated that he'd been hacking his familiar route. The dust and spurs on his boots suggested he was too rattled by his sister's situation to have attended to basic courtesies upon returning to the house.

"My lady," I said, resisting the urge to pace before her, "kidnappers are felons. Felons are seldom honorable. They have taken your daughter, and she might well have fared very badly at their hands."

The viscountess turned an outraged eye on me. "You mean, MacNamara won't marry her now? The impudence of that man. He all but jeopardizes her good name, strolls all over creation at her side, allows her to gambol unescorted about his property, makes a nuisance of himself here at—"

My patience deserted me. "My lady, the captain has personally dispatched me and his staff to search for your daughter. My comments implied that Miss Hannah might have been murdered by her captors."

I despised the word—*captors*. *Captivity* was worse, *prisoner* worst of all.

"Murdered? That is preposterous. Who would murder…?" The viscountess fell silent, and for the first time, she seemed to grasp that the present situation was not intended as a mean joke to vex her tireless campaign on behalf of propriety and standards.

She put a hand to her throat. "Strother, please ask his lordship to leave. He's spouting nonsense."

"Mama, he is not. I will ask him to leave, though, so that he might search for Hannah. My lord, I'll see you out."

I went with him gladly. "Your mother has had a shock. Best send her to bed with a tisane."

"She doesn't send to bed very well, my lord. Won't be seen to tipple before the servants either." Strother escorted me down a spotless corridor, scowling ancestors glowering down from the walls. The runner beneath our boots was clean, but going thin in the middle.

"Then send for her physician," I said, "and have him order her some patent remedy for the nerves. We may have worse news yet to impart."

"What's worse than Hannah missing, our fortune disappeared, and the captain's little army of the halt and the indigent roaming the property?"

I stopped several yards short of the sunny, cavernous foyer. "Those indigents lost eyes, feet, *and their lives* so that you could sleep safe in your bed, Stadler. You impugn them in my hearing at your peril."

"Do forgive me, my lord. Meant no offense. Profuse apologies. Not myself lately."

He was himself. Sly, self-absorbed, and smart enough to retreat when necessary, exactly like his father. *Cook stinted on the mustard.* Strother stinted on sincerity.

"The men are looking for Hannah," I said. "They will also keep an eye out for anywhere your gold might be hidden. I frankly hold little hope that your fortune can be recovered unless Miss Hannah is extant to tell us where it is."

"But you will recover Han eventually, because your dear, gracious, generous mama has sent to London for the funds."

He glanced over his shoulder, as if he feared a footman overhearing that part.

"The kidnappers specified that some of the ransom was to be paid in gold. Assuming the Caldicott solicitors and bankers can assemble a fortune and get it to us by the day after tomorrow, we still won't have it in the form demanded. We also might not have it in time. His Grace is on the Continent, and cash reserves between planting and harvest are generally low."

"But he's a duke. You're his heir. Surely the bankers comprehend the order of precedence?"

"To a nicety. Even His Grace of Waltham doesn't keep that much spare cash on hand, nor do the Caldicotts have much in the way of gold to contribute." Moreover, I was not His Grace. I could ask the banks to exert every possible effort to liquidate my assets. I could not order extraordinary measures regarding the ducal resources with the same authority the duke could have.

Strother continued into the foyer. "We wouldn't expect... that is. You're doing your best. You have my thanks for that. Mama's, too, or you would if she was herself."

"Meaning?"

"She's a high stickler, but most high sticklers are simply uppish. Mama believes in maintaining standards, but also in noblesse oblige. We simply lack the coin to uphold our end of the obligations. The church should have a curate, preferably a handsome, friendly bachelor who isn't too keen on brimstone. The assembly rooms need refurbishing. Pleasant View should host the occasional fete. Mama would make a fine lady of the manor, but the manor isn't doing so well in recent years. This leaves her..."

Rude? Overbearing?

"At a loss," Strother finished. "A little desperate and trying not to show it. When I view her like that, I have some sympathy for her."

As did I—grudging sympathy. "Well, prepare to have a little more sympathy for her, Stadler. MacNamara's men will tromp and ride themselves to exhaustion looking for any sign of Hannah or her captors. I doubt we'll find her, but we must try."

"What can I do to help?"

That he'd got around to asking that question at all surprised me. "Manage your mother. Look through Hannah's effects without the servants catching you at it. Poke around the house as casually as you can. Hannah would have hidden the gold where the family was unlikely to come across it, but you—being family—know the parts of the house you and your parents never frequent."

"You mean the laundry and larders and such?"

"If Hannah could slip into and out of such locations unremarked, then yes. If she could use the key to the wine cellar without attracting notice, then look there too. Where was she permitted to putter and pry without the rest of the family's interference?"

Strother's expression suggested he'd never in all his born days viewed himself as an interference. "I'll have a look around."

"Do that. Assume if you hear nothing from me that our efforts have thus far been fruitless."

He saw me out, and I was relieved to go. MacNamara's *indigents* would be free to reconnoiter the property, as would I. We *were* searching for Hannah, of course, and also for the gold.

But we were all former soldiers, albeit somewhat the worse for our military experience. Every one of us well knew the look of a fresh grave, and we'd take particular notice should we happen to spy one of those.

∼

I explained to the men how to search on a grid pattern. Whether they were scanning the landscape, rummaging around in a deserted summer kitchen, or evaluating a newly repaired stone wall, I taught them to let their gaze wander over the field of view slowly and thoroughly in the kind of half focus that notes both details and patterns.

Such a gaze required seeing with both the mind and the instincts, and the skill had taken me endless hours to acquire.

"What do you make of that stream bank?" I asked Dutch as we headed toward MacNamara's abode after a long, frustrating day of tramping.

"It's a stream bank."

His enthusiasm for finding Miss Hannah outstripped his reconnaissance skills. "Is the water higher or lower than usual?"

"Lower."

"How do you know?"

He stopped on the path and considered the opposite bank. "The plants don't grow all the way down to the water. The dirt is a different color below the plants."

"Right. How long since it rained?"

He gave me a cross look, then looked again at the bank. "I don't know."

"Look at the tracks, Dutch. Animals will come down to the water to drink at least daily, often twice a day. Do the tracks near the water look dried out or soft and fresh? Has dust accumulated in the crevices of the tracks, or are the contours sharp?"

He shook his head. "The tracks look like tracks, and if I don't get somethin' to eat soon, I'll pitch your lordship into the river, I vow I will."

"Go on in, then. I'll nose about awhile longer." We had two hours of light left, and the soft, slanting beams of a setting sun often revealed signs not as visible during bright daylight. "I'll probably follow by nightfall."

"See that you do. I'll be drummed out of the regiment if you come to harm. Captain thinks highly o' you."

The captain, who must be half out of his mind with worry. "Away with you. Save me some rations, and don't fret if I'm out all night."

"One question, sir."

"Ask." Dragonflies danced over the sluggish water near the riverbank, and dust drifted on the slanting sunshine. A beautiful time of day, though my day had been anything but beautiful.

"Dorset says," Dutch began, nodding in the direction of the manor house, "that these people aren't paying the help timely. Carstairs says their riding horses are nigh feeble, and their butler shoulda been pensioned before Farmer George went mad the first time. They got no coin, but they got that gold. Why not sell the gold, pay the help, and onward we march?"

A pragmatic question. "Much of the gold is distinctive, made into one-of-a-kind pieces that predate the Romans. Some of it is in ancient coin. It can be melted down, but that would mean finding a goldsmith willing to destroy a priceless antique *and* keep his mouth shut about it. The gold is worth more as jewelry, come to that, but finding a buyer who won't flaunt the acquisition would be nearly impossible."

"And that's the problem? Somebody knowin' that the gold was finally put to some use?"

"More or less. To turn the gold into coin would all but shout that the Stadlers were bobbing about in the River Tick. Young Strother would find himself in the sponging house, Lady Standish would become a laughingstock, and Lord Standish might well be blackballed from his clubs." Debtors' prison could be tantamount to a death sentence for a cobbler down on his luck, but Strother's fate would be ameliorated by his family's ability to keep him in amenities.

"But if they sold the gold, they could eat," Dutch retorted. "They'd have boots that fit. They'd have all this..." He gestured to the surrounding bucolic splendor.

A doe and a pair of fawns just emerging from the home wood stopped and lifted their heads at his gesture.

"They would have all of this," I said, "and more scandal than any family could live down in three generations."

"But instead, they have their gold. Except they don't even have that, an' neither do they have Miss Hannah."

He shook his head and moved off down the trail, muttering about the Quality and daft officers and how was a body to march without tucker?

For my part, I wondered how Miss Hannah was faring. Was anybody feeding her? We'd found no fresh graves, but then, if I were a kidnapper turned murderer, I'd hide the body someplace other than the victim's figurative backyard.

Where, though?

For the sake of reconnoitering, I sought the closest thing to a church steeple I could find, that being the belvedere. I made my way to the top and took out a spyglass. In all directions, the land was green and growing, whether I viewed the park, the pastures, or the home wood. In the distance, a bank of gray clouds was scudding in from the south, leaving only a band of gold between the horizon and the overcast sky.

The land was verdant, the crops and livestock abundant, and yet, the Stadlers were in straitened circumstances. I nearly fell asleep pondering that conundrum, my hip braced on the balustrade, my spyglass slipped back into my boot.

The men and I had made a grid out of the manor's immediate

grounds and spent the day traversing several hundred acres. Our emphasis had been on fixtures—an unfinished hermit's grotto, the old summer kitchen, a woodshed at the edge of the home wood. We found no sign of Miss Hannah and no sign of any gold.

Thunder rumbled, and a streak of lightning danced down from the distant clouds.

"It needs only this." Signs obliterated by a downpour, trails turned to mud, visibility reduced from even the best vantage points.

I made my way down through the dark spiraling stairs of the belvedere, prepared to get a thorough soaking on my way back to headquarters. I stopped at the bottom of the steps and glanced back up into the shadowed tunnel I'd just descended.

Spotting the hiding place was simple, especially in the limited light. The stone structure was well made and old enough to have thoroughly settled. One patch of wall, though, had suffered a loss of mortar, as would happen in old, exposed masonry. I pushed here and there, found the loose stone, and removed it.

Nothing. The space behind the stone was merely a whitewashed recess at about chest height. No brooch gleamed at me from the depths of the gap. No circlet caught the rays of the fading sun.

No letter greeted me either.

Thunder rumbled again, closer. I slapped the rock loosely back into the gap in the wall and forced myself to make double time in the direction of MacNamara's home.

A wasted day on every hand. No sign of Hannah Stadler, no sign of the gold, no sign of who might have kidnapped her. Rather than make the journey back to the Hall, I'd sent word that I'd be putting up at MacNamara's abode, the better to save time.

That I was also avoiding Hyperia had to be admitted. I loved her. I missed her when we were parted and missed her even as I felt the first cold raindrop slap the back of my neck. My feelings for her were deep and devoted, that hadn't changed.

But my circumstances were changing. I was regaining health in a manner that bore materially on my expectations of matrimony. What did that mean for my future with Hyperia?

Round and round, I pondered as I tramped the mile and a half back to the captain's dwelling. I arrived in his foyer in a state between bedraggled and sopping and was thus unprepared for the butler, Coombs, to inform me that I had a visitor awaiting me in the guest parlor.

Coombs had taken the liberty of offering Miss West a tea tray, and she had done him the courtesy of informing him that she would not be staying to supper with milord.

CHAPTER TWELVE

"The goldsmiths report no sightings of any ancient Irish gold artifacts," Hyperia said, pouring me a cup of steaming tea. She added a dash of honey and passed it over. "The fancy shops, the less savory dealers, the pawnbrokers who regularly trade on the Continent... According to Lady Ophelia, not a speck of suspicious gold in the past year or so."

The tea was ambrosial. I had tarried only long enough to change into dry attire, which hadn't chased the chill from my bones. Coombs had laid a wood fire on the hearth, the scent reminding me of myriad campfires and winter bonfires on campaign.

Hyperia fixed her own cup of tea. "If the treasure is intact, the kidnappers have no excuse for harming their victim. That has to be good news."

"I hope it's good news. Quite possibly, Lord Standish liquidated the family gold twenty years ago, and the theory that Hannah hid the gold is more posturing."

I watched Hyperia gracefully presiding over the tea tray, offering me warmth, companionship, and a friendly ear at the end of a long, hard day. She was every good, domestic, delightful thing my heart desired.

I love you. To offer her the words usually cheered me, but in my present mood, weary in body and spirit, the dismals hard on my heels, the joy that was my love for Hyperia was tinged with misgiving. The heart's desire and the body's desire were both deserving of acknowledgment and, within the bounds of matrimony, designed to amplify each other.

"Is the inn acceptable?" I asked.

"Surprisingly so." She held out a plate of shortbread. "Lady Ophelia was impressed."

Despite not having eaten for hours, and having walked mile after mile, I now wasn't hungry, but that, too, was a symptom of inchoate melancholy. One compounded the issue by ignoring food, blending ennui and physical sluggishness into a pervasive torpor.

I took two pieces and popped one into my mouth. "I am surprised the captain didn't escort you."

"He's in pain, Jules. The compresses help, but he refuses the poppy. Says he cannot afford a dull mind. He stares at Hannah's miniature and broods."

I'd had no miniature of Hyperia when I'd been in Spain. Too incriminating, for a tinker's assistant, drover, or shepherd, to be larking about the mountains with a likeness of a pretty English miss in his pocket.

"We found nothing today," I said, "and that puzzles me. We found no sign of gold, or of a prisoner being kept in one location then moved to another. We found no sign that Hannah frequented any favorite place with her books and lap desk either."

"How could you tell if a young lady preferred to read on a bench by the stream or in a half-finished hermit's grotto?"

"Scuffed ground beneath the bench, heel prints in soft earth, pencil shavings, an absence of dust wherever she routinely sat for any length of time. Game trails widened by repeated human use. Broken vegetation along the narrower trails, suggesting skirts or a cloak had swept past..." The usual signals that a closer look was in order, and we'd found none of them.

A tattoo of rain spattered the panes of the captain's cozy parlor, causing me to startle sufficiently to slosh tea into the saucer.

"You will find her," Hyperia said, kindly ignoring the mess I'd made. "You will find her, and she will be well, and she and the captain will marry."

Will we marry? Will we marry happily? "They deserve some joy."

Hyperia finished her tea. I was well aware that she and Lady Ophelia had gone to considerable trouble to see that I had all the intelligence from Town. A note would have done, but the ladies were putting on a show of support.

I appreciated their efforts, even as I resented them, and resented the whole tangle I'd taken on at MacNamara's request.

"This arrived for you at the Hall," Hyperia said, withdrawing another missive. The letter was small, the wax seal a mere white drop.

I slit the seal.

No word of the lad or anybody who knew of him, but half the town is off to the coast. I shall remain vigilant.

H. MacInnes

PS The blue specs work a treat.

"MacInnes sent a null report from Chelsea." I refolded the missive and felt a mixture of relief—I hadn't time to dash back up to Town at the moment—and despair. The trail leading to Atticus's sibling was cold and obscured by time. A better tracker than I would have difficulty following it.

"No news is good news," Hyperia said, "though when people fling platitudes at me, I usually find them anything but consoling. If Tom can be found, you'll locate him, Jules."

"The operative word being 'if.' I'll accompany you back to the inn," I said, finishing my second piece of shortbread. "Will you return to the Hall in the morning?"

"Lady Ophelia is restless." Hyperia rose as another gust of wind roused the fire in the hearth. "She's talking about returning to London to learn what she can about Sylvester Downing. Her network doesn't include many of Dublin's notables, so she's keen to check her traps before the Season ends and what few Irish connections she has go home for the summer."

I pushed to my feet as well, hips and ankles protesting the effort. "Does her ladyship seem to be declining to you?"

"'Aging' might be the more accurate word. Mentally, she's as sharp as ever, but physically, time or the social Season is taking a toll. She says Hannah Stadler reminds her of somebody, especially about the chin."

"Hannah has her mother's nose," I said, extracting a likeness from my jacket pocket. "What do you think?"

Hyperia took the paper from me. "Hannah is taller and more robust than her mother. Her father has some height, but not Hannah's... sturdiness."

We peered at the likeness for a quiet moment.

"She doesn't resemble her father at all," I said, and now I had the sense Lady Ophelia was right. Hannah Stadler's features were vaguely familiar.

"Jehovah's nightgown, Jules. Hannah has Harry's chin. His jaw, his eyebrows. She looks more like Harry than she does her own brother."

An odd tingling skipped over my nape and down my arms. "I cannot ignore the similarity. I want to blink and have it disappear, but Harry's eyebrows in particular... swooping, symmetric, and positively intimidating when arched... And you're right about the chin, too. That has to be a coincidence."

Hyperia set the sketch aside and slipped her arms around me. "No, it does not. Your papa was no saint. Your Uncle Thomas had a wicked streak and an eye for wives susceptible to temptation. This would explain why a pair of titled families two hours' ride apart barely nod to one another."

"The Stadlers' relative penury might explain that as well."

Hyperia gave me a squeeze and stepped back. "If a young and unhappy Lady Standish frolicked with a ducal Caldicott, she might well be ashamed of her past."

Uncomfortable insight. "She might have become a high stickler as a result. I concede the theory has merit." The theory had intuitive appeal as well. "I've been puzzled as to why Lady Standish is such a Tartar, so uniformly vexed with life. Perhaps she fell in love with her straying Caldicott, and he cut off relations."

Hyperia's gaze went to the sketch. "Perhaps the straying Caldicott did not secure Lady Standish's consent. Perhaps a flirtation meant to arouse her husband's jealousy turned into something sordid, very much against her ladyship's will. She could hardly hold a Caldicott male accountable for such a lapse, could she?"

My intended put forth her hypothesis with a studied detachment very much unlike her. The topic was distasteful, true, but that did not account for the bleakness of Hyperia's expression.

"Only Lady Standish knows," I said, "and we might be speculating about a coincidence of appearances common to an inbred aristocracy."

"True." Hyperia beat me to the door. "Jules, would you like me to return to London with her ladyship?"

Yes. No. Of course not. "You must do as you wish. I know I'm neglecting you terribly, but MacNamara appreciates your company, and I was under the impression Healy might soon show up at the Hall."

"You're right. I don't want to be a burden, though."

I caught her hand as we approached the foyer. "Never, never, ever could you be a burden." But what exactly would I call a wife who wanted no intimacies with a husband who desired her madly?

"The investigation isn't going well, is it?"

I draped her cloak around her shoulders and put on my own less-than-dry shooting jacket. "We still have some time, and Lady Ophelia's news from Town is more heartening than otherwise. I suspect Sylvester Downing has much to answer for."

"The scorned suitor?"

"The scorned suitor of limited means probably thought he could charm himself into a pot of gold. If he's half the strutting cockerel I think he is, that arrogance would not have sat well with Miss Hannah."

We made the short coach journey to the posting inn, and I kissed Hyperia good night. Before decamping on foot in the rain for headquarters, I nosed about for Jem Bussard, but that worthy was off duty.

I thus made my way in the rain back to MacNamara's abode, where I fell into a fitful slumber and dreamed of Harry's chin on Atlas's horsey face.

∼

"If this is what reconnaissance entailed," Carstairs said, gathering up his reins, "it's no wonder you fellows were such a peculiar lot. You stare at dog shit as if it's a fortune-teller's pile of tea leaves. You sniff the ground, you shuffle through bracken… Are you even listening to me?"

I led Atlas along the edge of the Pleasant View home wood, Carstairs and his borrowed mount trailing behind me.

"You're a gamekeeper," I replied. "Do you have hounds to track game or fetch the birds you drop?"

"A brace of hounds would be an extravagance for a household of half a dozen men. Canines require meat, and what's the point of shooting birds to feed the hounds when… Oh. I see. We're on the vast Stadler property, and the family does not keep hounds, though Lord Standish would call himself a hounds and horse man, if you asked him. Strother has aspirations in that direction too."

"Right. No hounds kept by the Stadlers, and that scat was the sign of a large dog. The tracks I found a few yards away confirm the conclusion." The beast in question was quite sizable, in fact. "If you were poaching, perhaps with the landowner's tacit consent, would you bring a big canine along with you?"

"Proper poaching is supposed to be done under cover of darkness, so I don't see what..." Carstairs stopped, his horse shuffling to a halt behind him. "You mean to imply that a poacher would not want his notably large canine companion leaving tracks all over creation to announce their passing. As a gamekeeper, even I'd notice such evidence and mention it to the captain."

We reached the bridle path Strother and I had traversed only days ago. "Are you a gamekeeper, Carstairs? I confess you look more like a younger son down on his luck."

He was pleasant company, alternately jocular and quiet. To make the leap from pawprints to penury to trespassing required a nimbleness of the imagination that Dutch, at least, lacked.

"As it happens, I am a younger son, but as for luck, I am awash in luck."

You don't sound like it. I mounted up rather than contradict him. He climbed into the saddle too.

"You maintain a diplomatic silence," he said. "Ever the gentleman. You are correct. I am the second son born to Lord Dunsford, Baron Dunsford, and as such, I was given a choice of the Church or the military. My oldest cousin chose the Church and discouraged me from that path. Until Papa can finagle Cousin Peter into the living at Dunsford's local pulpit, poor Petey is doomed to meager wages, ailing beldames, and weak tea."

"Papa scrounged up a commission for you?"

"Captain in a cavalry regiment. Worst mistake of my life. Wellington hated us, and we deserved his ire. There is a difference between being able to stick in the saddle and having the skill to actually ride."

A vast difference. "But you were among officers, your regiment fairly well provisioned, and you survived."

I watched the ground beneath as the horses ambled along. The path was pretty, passing under the arching oaks, meandering along the stream, but not that well traveled. Perhaps that's why Strother chose it, rather than to ensure he could be easily encountered by tenants.

"We come to the lucky portion of my existence," Carstairs said. "I survived. I transferred into a rifle battalion. I survived yet longer. All across Spain, the push up into France, and even Waterloo. On my worst days, Caldicott, I must still be grateful for the very fact of survival."

His cousin might be the parson, but Carstairs was capable of a gentle sermon. "As must we all."

"My younger brother was not so fortunate. I walked away from battle after battle. Bullets missed me by inches, sabers were swung at my very head, my horses went down, and more bullets missed me by inches precisely because the beast fell when he did... and here I am, upright and hale."

A not-so-gentle sermon, rather. "How did he die?"

"Damned lung fever at university. He wasn't sickly by nature, so he didn't take illness seriously. From his perspective, a head cold was nothing to worry about, not compared to the whole French Army. The head cold progressed into influenza and lung fever, and my baby brother was three weeks dead before my older brother could bring himself to write to me with the news."

Rain had obliterated much of the tracks previously laid on the bridle path, but we reached a place where the path passed under a bridge, an ancient arched construction no doubt of Roman provenance. Some considerate engineer had left enough room on the riverbank that a towpath might have been fashioned where the bridle path lay.

I brought Atlas to a halt in the blessed gloom beneath the bridge.

"Is this why you became a demon in battle?" I took out my flask and drank sparingly. "You were trying to get yourself killed?"

"I was not purposely risking my life, but I was unleashing my fury on the French. I should have stayed home. I should have made sure the tutors were more conscientious. I should have never complained in my letters that soldiering was mostly gratuitous hardship."

"Instead, you tramp the captain's woods, keep an eye on his infantry, and brood." A change of subject was in order, though condolences were too. "Your sainted brother *of all people* would tell you to lay the grief aside at the first opportunity. Do you notice anything odd about the tracks here under the bridge?"

"They're dry."

"Look along the edge of the path, Carstairs. Pawprints."

"Large pawprints, and that's either a large riding horse or a small draft animal. Strother's gelding is a bit pigeon-toed, and this beast travels straight. I'd say whatever equine left these tracks is of Atlas's generous dimensions or perhaps larger."

"You've been paying attention."

"Trying to. You are right that I brood too. I grant myself one hour a day to wallow and pine and be bitter, but then I go about my appointed rounds as best I can. Jasper would never countenance grief turned into a ridiculous fixation, you are right about that too. I will always miss him, but I must also be grateful that he was around as long as he was. What do you make of this horse-dog duo?"

"I'm not sure. Let's meet up with the other fellows and see what their morning has revealed."

By agreement, we gathered back at the captain's house for lunch. I considered dropping by the inn to look in on the ladies, assuming they had lingered in the area, but Hyperia had not asked that of me. More to the point, the fortnight's grace intended to facilitate amassing of the ransom money would be up in a day, and we'd found no sign of Hannah or the hoard.

When we reached the portion of the path that swung away from the river, I halted Atlas again. "I'd like to stop by the belvedere if you don't mind."

"Take a gander at the landscape?" Carstairs asked. "Look for smoke rising from deserted chimneys?"

"Yes, and for places we might have neglected in our searching thus far. Tell Dutch and Dorset that they eat all the victuals at their peril. I'll be along shortly."

He gave me a keen appraisal, reminding me that a baron's younger son, of necessity, was a shrewd fellow.

"She's very pretty, your Miss West. Coombs put out the company tea service."

And the fresh shortbread. "She's very sweet, too, and we are engaged to be married, so no more need be said on the matter."

Carstairs's smile went from sad to smug. "Dorset just lost a bet. Good day, my lord."

He kneed his horse onto the diverging track and left me alone with my thoughts, where I preferred to be. I'd had much of his life story out of him in the course of a short hack, and that was a symptom of our shared military experience.

Barriers eroded on campaign. Among officers thrown ceaselessly into one another's company, confidences were inevitably shared along with regrets, dreams, and hopes. I preferred to work alone in the field in part for that reason.

A man who allowed his inmost thoughts to escape into the keeping of any other fellow lounging around the campfire was a man with vulnerabilities. He might have friends, too, but he most certainly opened himself up to betrayal.

I returned to the belvedere and again ascended to the lookout. All was yet sunny and green, and no helpful plumes of chimney smoke rose up from suspicious locations. None rose from the manor house either, though the summer kitchen was apparently in use, as was the laundry.

I descended along the gloomy twisting staircase and considered what Carstairs and I had found. A large canine loose on the property, or in company with somebody riding a good-sized horse. Town dandies often kept sizable dogs as companion animals, mastiffs being currently in fashion. Strother struck me as exactly the sort to keep such a pet as an ornament.

At the bottom of the steps, I paused to put my blue specs back on, and the little recess where the captain had left his *billets-doux* caught my eye.

I'd wedged the stone loosely into place when I'd visited the previous day. Its position was minutely different now.

Interesting. I followed up that discovery with a more careful examination of the stone steps, finding faint hints that somebody had made the ascent with boots wet enough to leave an outline in the coating of dust ever present in outdoor structures.

I was still pondering my findings half an hour later when Coombs set a tower of sandwiches before me in the captain's breakfast parlor.

"Cider or ale, my lord?"

"Ale, please, or meadow tea if you have it."

"Spearmint or peppermint?" His old eyes gleamed with satisfaction to be able to offer a choice.

"A blend of both, with a dash of honey."

"Very good, sir. Most refreshing."

"Ale's not good enough for you?" Dorset asked, grinning over his half-empty plate. "More for me and Dutch."

"Ale goes right through you," Dutch said. "Learned that on my first march."

"My lord," Carstairs said, setting down a tankard of cider. "You have learned something. Best spit it out. The news is doubtless bad."

"Not bad, puzzling." I waited until Coombs had rejoined us, because he was assigned to the same mission we all were. "We're looking for Miss Stadler and for the gold. Somebody else is looking, too, though I can't say whether they hope to find the lady or the treasure."

CHAPTER THIRTEEN

"What do the solicitors have to say?" Lady Ophelia asked as I folded yet another missive from Town and stashed it in my pocket.

Hyperia kept silent. I sat beside her on a small sofa in the sitting room attached to Godmama's overnight quarters, and I could feel my intended's curiosity about the solicitors' epistle. Hyperia had the gift of silence, of composure in the face of chaos, and how I envied her that quality.

"The bankers are most apologetic," I said, "but given that the Season has emptied many a pocket, raising the sum requested in the time allowed hasn't been possible. I had only stocks to liquidate in the immediate term, and apparently my investment choices aren't that attractive to polite society."

"*You* intended to pay the ransom?" Lady Ophelia traced a slender finger around the rim of her glass. The ladies were drinking hock, a libation I preferred to avoid.

"If necessary."

This little parlor enjoyed a view of the pastures stretching out behind the inn. To the west, a haying crew was making slow progress scything in two ranks across a field of tall grass. The first rank sang the verses to an old haying song. The second rank, coming between and behind them, joined in on the choruses.

I knew the words, I knew the feel of a scythe in my hands, I knew the exquisite variety of pain across the shoulders, hips, and back that resulted from the first long day's work, and how it was possible to get blisters even when wearing gloves.

Something about the sharp blade cutting down rank after rank of verdant grass made me want to bellow at the lot of them to stop, to leave the grass to its season of flowering in the sun.

"Julian?" Lady Ophelia said, clearly not for the first time. "Might I lend you some coin?"

"Generous of you," I replied, "but our deadline approaches, and by the time your bankers did your bidding, it might be too late."

I was furious with my bankers and solicitors, certain that if Arthur had done the asking, the coin—come fire, flood, or flaming thunderbolts—would already be in Caldicott Hall's safe.

But then, it truly was the end of the Season, when even the best families had beggared themselves shopping, entertaining, and being outfitted to be entertained.

"What do we know of Sylvester Downing?" I asked.

"Not enough," Lady Ophelia replied. "I'd thought to return to Town and see what I might learn, but I would have nothing of value to share for another few days. He's not awful, but also not seen as a catch."

"Why didn't Hannah Stadler give him a second look?" This bothered me. "She is supposed to be practical, and a viscount's heir would have been a suitable match."

"Not if he was stupid." Hyperia spoke up for the first time, and with surprising vehemence. "Not if he was arrogant. Hannah clearly has standards—in that sense, she is like her mother, though Hannah's standards are not limited to etiquette and deportment. The captain meets her standards. Mr. Downing did not. If she was to marry a man of limited means, why not at least marry the one who charms her and values her gifts?"

What wasn't my beloved saying? I valued her gifts, but as for charming her... a work in progress, at best.

"Hannah had gold," I replied. "That likely explains Downing's interest in her, and if he was obviously mercenary in his wooing, she might have objected to that. Could I borrow the coach for the afternoon?"

"We are at your disposal," Lady Ophelia said, setting aside her wineglass. "I will expire of boredom if you don't give us an assignment, Julian."

Couldn't have that, though much of military life had been a battle with boredom. "The errand is beneath you, my lady. I have reason to believe that somebody with a sizable canine has been wandering at large over Pleasant View holdings. The dog's owner appears to be mounted on a substantial horse. I cannot rule out poachers." Though poachers would tend to hounds and spaniels rather than larger canines.

Interesting thought.

"Poachers typically leave their horses at the edge of the woods," Hyperia observed, "and check traps and whatnot on foot. Have you found traps and snares and the like?"

Right to the point. "We have not. The wildlife is abundant in Pleasant View's woods, and if the family is short of coin, that makes sense. They would need that game to fill the lockers and larders."

Her ladyship rose. "Then what is our errand?"

Manners had me rising as well. "I had thought to dispatch one of the captain's men to chat up the local butchers. Who has been pestered to part with his last juicy hambone daily for the past two weeks? Who has a new customer coming around for an order of tripe? It's an unlikely gambit, but as Carstairs pointed out, dogs eat meat, and large dogs eat large quantities of meat."

"Especially," Hyperia said, standing too quickly for me to assist her, "if that dog is gallivanting all over the countryside. We'll ask the innkeeper for a list of village butcher shops in, say, a ten-mile radius."

"Avoid the smallest villages. If we are looking for a well-dressed Irishman on a fine horse,

he'll be drawn to the market towns, where he has a better chance of blending in."

"Also," Lady Ophelia said, "avoid the establishments in the immediate surrounds, because if our man is Sylvester Downing, he might be recognized from his earlier attempts to court Miss Stadler. The list should be short."

"We will chase hambones," Hyperia said, "while you do what?"

"I will consult with my eyes and ears here at the inn, assuming I can find him, and pay a call at Pleasant View. To provide ransom instructions, the kidnappers must somehow contact the manor. The how and when that feat is accomplished might provide some insight into from where and from whom the instructions are coming."

I was grasping at straws, in other words. Days of fruitless searching, a resounding failure at the bank, the Stadler family resenting my every question, and all I had to show for my efforts was ongoing suspicion directed at Sylvester Downing.

Wherever he might be.

"Don't give up." Lady Ophelia patted my cheek. "'It is always darkest just before the day dawneth,' and so forth."

I had no idea which pontificating cleric had coined that phrase, nor did I care.

"We live in hope." And my hope was somewhat justified. If Downing was our man, he apparently hadn't found the gold either—the signs I'd seen of his passing were fresh—and he thus had every reason to keep Hannah alive and well.

"I still don't understand the why of all this," Hyperia said, studying the field where the haying crew slowly advanced. "If Downing lacks funds, then he should have spent the past month assiduously courting some heiress in Town."

"So should Strother," I countered, "but he wore out his welcome with the shops. He probably came home to cozen more funds from Hannah, but she's not on hand to bail him out this time."

"Money, money, money," Lady Ophelia muttered. "So tiresome. Hyperia, will you consult the innkeeper regarding the various abattoirs?"

"I shall."

She decamped with me, and when I should have offered some flowery bit of verse alluding to loverly longing, I instead paused with her outside Godmama's door and simply held her.

"You're worried," she said.

"Nigh panicked. I have no earthly idea where Miss Stadler might be, no inkling why Downing thought he could get away with kidnapping her—if Downing is even involved."

Hyperia stepped back. "He is, Jules. What other well-dressed young man could accost Hannah in her own park and talk her into strolling away with him? Granted, she was within view of the house—the proprieties were observed up to a point—but then, she wasn't within view of the house, and still she wasn't unduly alarmed."

That we knew of. "I feel as if I ought to be back at the Hall, explaining my lack of progress to MacNamara, and at Pleasant View, shaking some overlooked detail from the viscountess or her clodpated son. Then I recall that Hannah's own papa went haring off to Town like the proverbial thief in the night at the first sign of trouble. And speaking of London, why hasn't our lookout in Chelsea seen anything of interest?"

The boy Tom haunted me, not as relentlessly as Harry did, but the child lurked in the back of my mind, a shade composed equally of guilt and ignorance.

"If Tom is alive," Hyperia said, "he has likely spent the past two weeks in relative safety and comfort. This is the most pleasant time of year, the gardens are yielding their bounty, the soft fruits are ripe, the pastures lush. You will find that boy if he's extant to be found."

I wanted to find him that instant. I wanted to find Hannah Stadler in the same instant, and, for good measure, I wanted to summon Arthur home.

I kissed Hyperia's cheek, taking in a whiff of roses. "Thank you.

You steady me. Off you go on the trail of hambones. I will locate Jem Bussard."

She made for the common and would not hesitate to intrude on the kitchen beyond if necessary to locate the innkeeper.

My objective was less clear, but to my surprise, I found Jem lounging in the shade of a large oak that spread over half the innyard.

"Milord." He scrambled to his feet, hastily setting aside a bound volume as he jammed a pamphlet between the pages to serve as a bookmark. "Fine day, isn't it?"

I had the impression he was struggling not to salute me. "Beautiful weather after last night's rain. Nothing to report, Jem?" I did not eye the book that had so absorbed him. Even a stable boy well knew that reconnaissance meant keeping eyes open, not trained on some Gothic novel.

And he hadn't been pretending to read. He'd been utterly absorbed in whatever tale the book told.

"I've seen nothing, sir. The usual coaches at the usual hours, the usual nonsense on darts night. My cousin says Viscount Standish has took off for London, but his lordship does that on the regular. Haying has begun, but that's not news."

"If you were a hungry coach horse, the hay crop coming in would be wonderful news. What are you reading?"

"A novel." He seemed torn between pride to be reading a sizeable tome and self-consciousness that his interest was piqued by fiction rather than *literature*. "It's long and seriouslike. Miss Ellington don't have no patience for slow readers, so I'm keeping at it."

"I'll let you get back to your reading, then." I did not tell the boy I was intent on physically beating the bushes in hopes of locating his personal heroine, but to leave him whiling away the afternoon while I...

Bother. I was abruptly exasperated with myself and my investigation. I had a young lady to locate and a fortune to find. Either objective could thwart the villains behind Miss Stadler's present difficulties. I'd stop by Pleasant View, make my report, and then get back to the job at hand.

Napoleon hadn't been vanquished in a day, after all.

∼

Strother occupied his usual location at the edge of the battlefield. He took a three-quarter profile stance by the windows, out of which he doubtless longed to leap. The viscountess's fussy, desiccated formal parlor seemed more forlorn than usual compared to the glorious summer weather that had followed on last night's storm.

"The bankers refuse to aid us?" Lady Standish muttered. "I'm not at all surprised. That lot trades in scandal and misery, for all their polite airs. They profit from a family's ruin and—"

"Mama, please recall that Lord Julian tried his best for us and that time is very short."

The viscountess rounded on her son. "A gentleman never interrupts a lady."

"A lady," I said, "does not react in anger when others are trying to aid her cause. I can donate three thousand pounds in banknotes to the total ransom, and Lady Ophelia has sent for some of her own gold jewelry." Her ladyship had lit upon this measure as a ploy to fool the kidnappers long enough that Miss Stadler might be freed.

I hadn't offered a word of protest. Desperate times were upon us.

The viscountess indulged in a great sniff of affronted dignity. "His lordship," she said, addressing her son, "has been as useless as a heroine in a Gothic novel who hardly deserves the label because all she does is lament her vicissitudes and pine for her horse or her dog or her loyal footman, who is, of course, a long-lost prince in disguise. Life is not an adventure story, and nobody is ever rescued. We are ruined, I tell you. Of course the bankers are unavailing. Of course Lord Julian has found nothing. Perhaps it's for the best that our downfall is not simply financial. You two will expect me to thank Hannah for that."

"If the heroine had a dog," Strother retorted, "her loyal hound might have defended her from those perils in the first place." He turned his face to the window rather than huff and puff.

I wanted to bang their stubborn heads together. "Madam, I have been dressed down by Wellington himself on at least three occasions, only one of which I halfway deserved. I will take your remarks as proof that you are distraught over your daughter's unfortunate situation. Strother, if you would give me some privacy with the viscountess, I would appreciate it."

Strother bowed shortly and left before his mama could fashion a counterorder.

I closed the door to the parlor, and her ladyship watched me as a house cat watched a pensioned hound new to the privileges of the hearth.

"Anything you have to say to me can be said before my son," her ladyship said, now that that worthy was well out of sight.

"No, it cannot. Is Hannah's progenitor the late duke or my late uncle Thomas?"

Lady Standish fisted her hands against her skirts. "How *dare* you? How *dare* you even intimate, suggest, or imply such a thing!"

"Reluctantly, that's how, but Hannah is in significant danger, and your reaction as a mother has been ambivalent. You blame her for this great misfortune even as you worry about the scandal of it all. She could be dead as we speak, and yet, you fret over the family's reputation rather than the family's loss."

The viscountess stalked to the wing chair nearest the cold hearth and sat with less-than-perfect grace. "I love my daughter. You are unnatural and mean-spirited to imply otherwise."

"You also resent your daughter. If she was the inconvenient result of a regretted liaison, that might make some sense. She is headstrong and intelligent—two more strikes against her from your perspective—but no young lady deserves to be hauled away from her home and held for ransom."

The viscountess fussed her skirts, the first real sign of nerves I'd seen from her.

"Every young lady of good family is hauled away and held for ransom, my lord. We refer to the practice as holy matrimony. Hannah should have accepted Sylvester Downing when he was of a mind to offer for her. I will never understand her refusal, much less why she'd prefer that limping Scotsman."

One could only pity a person who had no comprehension of love.

I took the second wing chair and to blazes with the etiquette manuals. "My question stands. Was it His Grace or Lord Thomas who tempted you to stray?"

To give the lady credit, she put up a rear-guard action. "What possible relevance does ancient history have on the present looming disaster?"

"If it's any consolation, I am one of very few who know that Lord Thomas tempted even the duchess herself." More specific than that, I need not be. For all her vitriol, Lady Standish was no fool.

"The duchess? *Her Grace of Waltham*? Tempted?"

I kept my peace while Lady Standish doubtless inventoried memories. Odd moments, chance sightings, peculiar notions dismissed as pointless imaginings. What I suggested—temptation resulting in tangible regrets—was only too possible.

"My lady, you were right to dissuade Hannah from riding to hounds. Harry loved the hunt meets, the informality and good cheer of the institution. He and Hannah bear a close resemblance, and though Harry is gone now, his memory—and the memory of his appearance—will linger."

Her ladyship regarded me for the first time without visible animosity. "*Even the duchess*. I never... His Grace and Lord Thomas had a fraternal resemblance, though Lord Thomas had more dash. Mama once said... Well, no matter. I was an idiot, and furious, and Standish didn't care provided a spare showed up before such a thing was no longer possible. He regrets that now. Were he alive, Lord Thomas might have a few regrets too."

Said with more rue than relish. "This is why you wanted to see Hannah safely married to Downing and bundled off to Ireland, isn't it?"

"Oh, of course. She's too headstrong, too outspoken, too bold. Thank heavens she hasn't much use for Town, or some old tabby would sooner or later remark that my Hannah bears a resemblance to the late Lord Harry or late Lord Thomas. People would suspect Waltham of philandering too. He was a challenge as a husband, anybody could see that."

Had my mother felt kidnapped into the institution of marriage? Probably not at first. "Did you collude with Sylvester Downing to have Hannah kidnapped, my lady?"

She stared at the carpet, her profile revealing a beauty that had likely been stunning before time and bitterness had taken their tolls.

"That would make sense, wouldn't it, given what you know of me. I am pleased to say that you are wrong, my lord. I truly do care for my daughter and want only her happiness. She would be a fool to settle for the captain, even now, if a viscount's son is willing to have her. You must understand that much. But Hannah has a third choice —she needn't marry anybody. She will always have a home here. Lady Dewar will leave Hannah a competence—and a competence for me as well, thank the heavenly intercessors.

"This drama is not of my making," she went on, rising. "To court scandal like this is the last thing I'd do. The very last thing."

Valid point, but I didn't entirely believe her. She had raised the creation of drama to a high art. Pleasant View and surrounds were her stage, and her performance as the Royal Arbiter of Standards and Dignity would cast Mrs. Siddons into the shade.

I pushed to my feet, happy to conclude the interview. "Nonetheless, my lady, Hannah is yet at risk, and I still have many hours of daylight left to search for her. Where should I be looking?"

"You've given up hunting for the gold?"

Just when I was tempted to dismiss the possibility that Lady

Standish was the mastermind behind the whole affair, she asked a question like that—and with a particular intensity to her query.

"Hannah is the greater treasure, is she not? Find her, and you have no need to surrender the gold."

"We need that gold, my lord. We desperately need that gold."

Wrong answer, and because I was disappointed in the viscountess, I gave the Stadler family bushes one more whack.

"My lady, has it occurred to you that Strother might be reluctant to marry because he's hesitant to ask a bride to share a home with you?"

She smiled a genuinely warm and humorous smile. "Oh, of course. I am difficult and domineering. My husband calls me formidable as he's leaping into his coach to run once more for the safety of his club. I am the scourge of the ladies' charitable committee, and I would terrorize Strother's wife without mercy. I have forbidden him to have a dog. He retaliates by refusing to wed. My son is such a paragon."

She strode for the door, skirts swishing. "Do you know what I want, my lord? What I really, truly want?"

World domination came to mind. "Your daughter returned to you hale and happy?"

"Oh, that, too, despite what you think. I want grandbabies. Not an heir and spare, but grandbabies who squall and drool and grin. My daughters have four children between them, children who are never brought here to Pleasant View, children in whose upbringing, I have no role.

"I want grandbabies who grow up right here at Pleasant View, little cherubs who toddle around the garden and sit on granny's lap while she reads them stories. That's what I want. If Strother and his bride can manage to have a few babies here at the family seat, the ladies' charitable committee will never hear from me again."

She put her hand on the door latch and spoke with her back to me. "But Strother truly isn't inclined to marry. He's too much like his father, too featherbrained and foolish. He relies on Hannah to do his thinking for him, and she willingly obliges. He has asked repeatedly to have a wretched, stinking dog, though about taking a bride, he is curiously silent."

She left me in the sterile parlor.

Left me with much to think about.

Her ladyship had doubtless been different as a younger woman and younger wife, but not that different. She was no wanton, and she truly resented her youngest daughter. She might have flirted with Lord Thomas to spite her husband, as Hyperia had suggested, though a liaison before a spare was on hand…?

She was dutiful. Perhaps grudgingly so, but duty meant much to her.

As I saw myself out into the summer sunshine—spectacles donned before I left the house—I pondered the possibility that Lord Thomas had indeed pressed his attentions on a reluctant party.

She could not have cried foul—not against a ducal scion whose advances she'd encouraged, despite her marriage—so she'd explained the situation to her husband, who'd understood the dilemma she faced and borne her no malice.

The pieces fit, right down to the sort of backward fondness Lord and Lady Standish seemed to feel for each other. Right down to the social distance between two titled families in neighboring surrounds. Right down to Hannah being a constant reminder of folly paid for in very dear coin and of all that could go wrong for a viscountcy teetering on the brink of ruin.

And yet, her ladyship still hoped I would find the treasure.

Families were the greatest puzzle of all. On that eternal verity, I left Pleasant View and sought out the searching party whose efforts thus far had been in vain.

CHAPTER FOURTEEN

Because Atlas was enjoying a needed day off, my first order of business was to return the hack I'd rented to the coaching inn. I was surprised to find none other than Captain James MacNamara making a careful ascent of the inn's front steps as I approached.

"My lord." He nodded, probably as close to a bow as he could accomplish when leaning heavily on a walking stick.

"Captain." I swung out of the saddle and passed the reins to a stable boy. "Shall we appropriate the snug?" MacNamara's pale and drawn appearance suggested he hadn't been sleeping much or well. We'd need a private setting if he intended to let fly with his temper.

"The private parlor would suit me better. I grew impatient with your dispatches. 'No new developments. Search continues.' What sort of report is that?"

"One that tells the enemy nothing, should it fall into his hands."

"Ah. Of course. But who is that enemy?"

"Sylvester Downing, would be my guess. Hell hath no fury like a fortune hunter scorned." I spotted Jem on his shaded bench, nose still in a book. "My sentry is all but asleep on duty, thanks to some scribbling novelist. That boy will go for a schoolmaster, given the chance."

The captain made a laborious climb up the steps, one hand on the railing, one on his walking stick. "Jem? He would like that. Hannah would encourage him too."

I waited until we had secured the private dining parlor before making my report. "Of Hannah, we have seen no sign, which is odd."

"'Odd' is putting it politely." MacNamara lowered himself carefully to the seat at the head of the table. "Grown women don't just disappear from their own backyards, Caldicott. Order us some tucker. I was up before daylight. Couldn't sleep, figured I'd be of more use here. The Hall is lovely, but without the ladies to keep me company, I grew restless."

I gave our order to one of the serving maids, returned to the parlor, and closed the door.

"When I say we've come across no sign of Hannah, I mean... none. Nothing." Our utter failure had bothered me increasingly. Hannah had lived her whole life at Pleasant View, but for all the evidence of her passing, she might as well have been a ghost.

Where was she lurking on those frequent outings on foot? "We found a pair of Strother's gloves in the unfinished grotto," I went on. "The stable lads have been using the empty tenant cottage as a place to tryst and dice. The bridle paths and trails show that even the viscountess has been out and about on the property—her tread is heavy, even out of doors—but Hannah might as well never have set foot on the place."

MacNamara took off his hat and laid it on an empty chair. "She was frequently out of doors nonetheless. She left me regular notes in the fishing cottage, which I disdained to lock as a result. She was forever conferring with Mrs. Ellington at the lending library, and she kept a friendly eye on the tenants and neighbors."

As a true lady of the manor would. "She also retrieved your notes from the belvedere, but we found no discarded handkerchief, no forgotten fan, no riding crop laid aside in a distracted moment. She left no sign of even regular passing."

"Hannah is a tidy person. In her thoughts, in her habits. She is in Paris by now, for all we know."

She might be dead. Neither one of us needed to say that.

The food arrived, an early lunch for me, and I was hungry enough to partake. "She's not in Paris," I said between bites of a ham-and-cheddar sandwich. "That would require travel expenses as well as documents and run the risk of meeting other travelers fresh from Town who know her. Difficult for her to pull off on her own, even harder for her kidnappers."

"Documents can be forged, but I agree. No point in dragging her off to France. The easiest way to hold a captive is to secure them behind stout walls under trustworthy guard."

I put aside the uneaten half of my sandwich, assailed by images of a stone fortress on a bleak French mountainside. Dread pressed in on me, and I had to force myself to take an even breath.

Stone walls formed one sort of prison, despite what the poet claimed. Memories could form another.

MacNamara took up another sandwich, his appetite apparently in good repair, despite the situation. I tried for a sip of my ale, managed that much, and set down my tankard.

Where had I been before my mind had snatched me back to hell? "We know Hannah did not struggle when her captors approached her. She went with them willingly. Two men in gentleman's riding attire." As I had gone willingly with my captors.

Cease and desist. I aimed the order at my own ghosts, Harry among them, of course.

"You think her captors were neighbors?" MacNamara paused in his demolition of the food. "Somebody who has had enough of the viscountess's snobbery? I could see the ladies taking up against the viscountess, but not by snatching Hannah from the garden. I hate not knowing who my enemy is."

I tried another sip of ale. "Like Spain. Whose side is the tavernkeeper on? The cobbler? The latest batch of double deserters? Can the laundresses be trusted? Too many puzzle pieces to consider at once, and the formerly loyal cobbler might have switched allegiance because the bandits threatened to slaughter his mule."

"I don't miss it." MacNamara selected one of the two remaining sandwiches. "Especially at this time of year, with the heat coming on, the forced marches that never ended, the damned sieges... I don't miss it. I miss Hannah terribly."

"She hasn't gone far. Of that, I am increasingly certain." I apprised the captain of the situation with the gold and jewels, and he allowed as how he'd put together a few thousand pounds himself.

I thought of his modest cottage, his unprepossessing employees, his treatment at the hands of Lady Standish.

"Why hide your wealth, MacNamara?"

"I am not wealthy, not personally, but my family builds ships. We've coin enough when we need it. The day will come when the ships will be too big to navigate the River Clyde—steam is changing everything—but for now, we're managing. I also located a number of Sylvester Downing's debts—thank you for the suggestion—which I've secured. For good measure, I tried to locate the younger brother's vowels, too, but couldn't turn up even the smallest unpaid sum from any quarter."

"You were following a cold trail in dense undergrowth. Well done regarding the honorable Sylvester, but you are attempting to change the subject. You have been discreet about your means because you did not want to put Hannah off with your wealth." What other secrets was MacNamara keeping, and from whom?

"I haven't misrepresented myself, Caldicott. She knows my family's situation, more or less, but I was born a younger son, and I learned to be comfortable in that role. Besides, the MacNamaras, despite the title, build ships, and that qualifies as trade. Lady Standish barely lets me in the door as it is. And her a Scot."

That last was said with a sort of disgusted humor.

"Her ladyship is quite keen that we find the gold while we're trying to locate Hannah."

He muttered something in Gaelic. "Truly, I must be smitten with my Hannah, or I would never contemplate taking on that besom as my mama-in-law." He finished his ale and thumped the empty mug on the table. "Find my bride, Caldicott. For the love of leaping salmon, find her, please."

"I'll be about my appointed rounds, then, and you can pay the shot."

He nodded and went for the last sandwich.

I donned my specs and prepared to make what use I could of the last half day available before ransom instructions were due. Jem was still under his shady tree, absorbed with his novel. Truly, the Regent could have paraded before him resplendent in royal regalia, and Jem would not have noticed.

"Jem, greetings."

He slipped his pamphlet bookmark between the pages and rose. "My lord. A fine day, isn't it?"

A fine day to idle away with a book. Not such a fine day to search for a kidnapping victim. "I take it you've still seen nothing suspicious?"

He slid a glance at his tome. "I've been keeping an eye out. Captain MacNamara's back, and Lady Ophelia and the young miss went off on some errand. Took the coach, but said they'd return for supper."

He wasn't entirely oblivious to the world. "Where does Miss Stadler like to go if she's just hacking out for pleasure?"

He considered his book, the volume bound in red Morocco leather, Mrs. Burney's name embossed along the spine.

"Miss Stadler doesn't hack out for pleasure, sir. She takes the mare if she wants to go to the library or sometimes to call on the neighbors, but the mare is old. Miss Hannah spares the horse if she can."

Because that horse had to last. "Then where did the lady prefer to walk if she was simply going for a stroll?"

The book received a more studied perusal. *The Wanderer*, which had taken the author years to complete, many of which she'd spent exiled in France with her French husband.

"Miss Han isn't the strolling type either, sir. She goes afoot between the manor and the village and will often walk home from services, but she's not one for idle rambles."

And yet, her family said she was forever off the premises. Taking a book or her lap desk...

While Jem shifted from foot to foot, an obscure fact marched forth from the recesses of my memory. "Jem, let me see that book."

He passed it over. "Mrs. Ellington said I can have it until Monday noon. I'm reading as fast as I can. It's not like Mrs. Burney's earlier novels. No real villain, so far."

The villain was Society itself. I examined the book closely. "This is from the lending library?"

"The only copy they have. Look in the back for the stamp."

The binding was whole. No slits in the edges, nothing slipped down between the leather and the spine. I opened the book spine up and shook gently. Nothing fell out save Jem's pamphlet bookmark.

"Sir, you oughtn't to treat a book thus. Mrs. Ellington won't have it."

I picked up the pamphlet. "Where did you get this?"

"Was between the pages. People forget where they stash things. I found a pressed daisy in a library book once. Mrs. Ellington would have rung a peal over somebody's head for that."

I kept the pamphlet, more screed from Eve's Advocate, this time aimed at the perfidy of the Corn Laws. "Where might I find Mrs. Ellington?"

"She's usually home on Saturdays. It's not a library day. Take the lane past the church, go a quarter mile. Her door is green, and the house is fieldstone with white shutters."

I departed at quick-march time and reached Mrs. Ellington's doorstep half out of breath—but only half. I pounded her knocker as if the hounds of perdition were in pursuit of me. After an eternity and a half, a housekeeper finally deigned to admit me.

"My lord, do come in. That you would call upon my humble cottage is an astonishing pleasure." Mrs. Ellington gestured me into a parlor awash in chintz. Cabbage roses abounded on the upholstery, violets and forget-me-nots were sprinkled over the wallpaper. The pillows on the sofa were embroidered with more flowers, and every table in the room was covered in more matching chintz cabbage roses.

Atop the spinet, a glass bowl held cut pink specimens of what must have been Mrs. Ellington's favorite flower.

"You might better characterize my imposition as an astonishing presumption, Mrs. Ellington. I regret that we have not been introduced."

She was built on substantial, matronly lines, with golden hair going flaxen, blue eyes, and a lady's smooth complexion. Her dress was a modest, pale blue walking ensemble, devoid of flounces and fussiness. The gleam in her eye suggested a courtesy lord in her parlor would give her *much* to discuss when next she held court in the churchyard.

"Nonsense," she said, gesturing me into a wing chair. "We find ourselves quite in the shires and need not stand on ceremony. I have met your dear friend Lady Ophelia, and I suspect that the charming Miss West has caught your eye. The Misses Fortnam have intimated as much, and they are shrewd observers."

A sturdy maid rolled in a tea trolley heaped with enough comestibles to feed Wellington's infantry.

Mrs. Ellington beamed at the offerings. "Thank you, Peters. You are excused."

Peters gave me a curious glance that might have seen her sacked in Lady Standish's household, then bustled out.

I rose and closed the door. "Forgive my presumption, and no tea for me, thank you, but can you explain to me how the library's copy of *The Wanderer* came to be returned?"

She poured two cups. "You look like a sugar-and-cream man to me. The tea is my personal blend, and I'm sure you'll enjoy it."

I resumed my seat reluctantly, feeling as if I were being offered pomegranate seeds as I struggled to escape the underworld. I preferred honey to sugar and cream only occasionally.

"Truly, ma'am, I come on an urgent errand. I am sorry to put you to the trouble of a tea tray, but I do need to know how *The Wanderer* was returned to your collection."

"Not my collection." She piled ginger biscuits and shortbread on a plate and passed it over. "Miss Hannah's collection. The shortbread was made fresh today, almost as if Cook had a premonition that august company might come calling. Before we discuss books, do please assure that you will remember me to your *dear* mother. Our paths do not cross frequently, but Her Grace always makes a most gracious impression."

As far as I knew, my mother hadn't had the pleasure, ever.

"I will convey your greeting to Her Grace when next I see her, I promise. About *The Wanderer*, Mrs. Ellington. Miss Stadler borrowed it, and you were concerned that she'd not returned it before going on her travels. Do I have the right?"

My hostess sipped her tea, not a care in the world. "You must try the shortbread. You will hurt Cook's feelings otherwise, and when Cook is in the boughs, we have burned toast and runny eggs. A penance, you will agree."

I took a piece of shortbread, bit off a corner, and set the remaining portion on my saucer, feeling all the while as if I'd just made a very great mistake. Mrs. Ellington would next have me escorting her on a tour of the library, volume by volume, and all the while, Hannah Stadler was awaiting rescue probably not five miles away.

"And the tea," she said. "My own blend. I order from Twinings and measure the proportions myself."

I sipped. "At the risk of giving offense, I must know how *The Wanderer* was returned to the library."

"Why is a mundane little tale of such great interest, my lord? The critics have not been kind to Mrs. Burney's latest effort."

If I stood and began shouting, the tale of my behavior would live in infamy for all the rest of my days. Mrs. Ellington would see to it that posterity was given a picture of me, barking mad, walking proof that the Quality were dangerously inbred.

"Miss Hannah Stadler checked the volume out," I said, "then decamped to take the waters. The volume was returned to you some two weeks later, and the family is concerned that somebody might have borrowed the book from Hannah, perhaps without Hannah's permission."

Mrs. Ellington's blue eyes narrowed. "Lady Standish is at it again, is she? Looking for an excuse to sack an undermaid or turn off the newest footman? That woman could pinch a penny until it confessed to murder most foul. Miss Hannah despairs of her dear mama, and that is putting it kindly."

"Peters was a casualty of the viscountess's economies?"

"Precisely. She was the under-housekeeper at Pleasant View for eight years. Her ladyship took a notion to economize, wrote the most grudging character, handed the poor woman a few coins, and offered to pay outside coach fare to Town. *Outside* fare, for a woman of mature years who had given loyal service and knew not a soul in London."

None of this was earning me any relevant information. "About the book, Mrs. Ellington?"

"Her ladyship will be very disappointed to learn that Miss Hannah kindly dropped the book off at our sister establishment in Hamden Parva. I assume Miss Hannah sought to finish reading the story as her journey began and took the expedient measure of returning the book indirectly. People do sometimes, but we librarians sort it all out at our monthly meetings."

"The book was returned to the library in Hamden Parva. You're certain?"

She took another dilatory sip of her tea. "I know my sister

branches, my lord. Lady Standish will not claim that a servant pinched that book if I have anything to say to it. Her staff must toil and moil the livelong day for precious little coin, and they honestly would not have time to read for pleasure. Young Jemmie Bussard has the honor of reading *The Wanderer* now, and he will return it promptly by noon Monday."

Hamden Parva. A direction, a hint of a possibility. The faintest of hopes, but more than I'd had ten minutes past. I finished my shortbread and gulped my tea.

"Thank you. The tea is lovely, quite unique, and the shortbread delicious. My compliments to the kitchen, and now I must fly. You have been incredibly helpful, and I will be very sure to remember you to Her Grace."

I made for the door, Mrs. Ellington on my heels. "But you cannot leave so soon, my lord! I won't hear of it. You must tell me your favorite authors and what books you are reading now and tell me of your last visit to Hatchards. We have ever so much more..."

I collected my hat from the peg the housekeeper had hung it on. "Mrs. Ellington, you have been graciousness itself, and your forthright support of truth is to be vociferously commended, but my time is not my own." I bowed over her hand, a presumption that I hoped promoted her to queen of the monthly librarians' meeting for the next five years. "Good day."

I slapped my spectacles on and left her standing on her front porch, her hand to her throat, her smile perplexed.

When I was far enough down the lane to be out of her sight, I withdrew a peashooter from the tail pocket of my riding jacket and fired two shots into the air.

All hands report to headquarters. We had the siege of Hamden Parva to plan.

~

"I know the terrain in the vicinity of Hamden Parva only in passing," MacNamara said, easing his foot onto a hassock. "Hamden Parva is to the west, and my travels usually take me north to London or south to the coast."

"But," Strother said, "if the kidnappers wanted to create the fiction that Hannah was traveling to Bath to take the waters, they would lay a trail to the east." He'd enthroned himself in the second wing chair, leaving the rest of us to lounge about the captain's study. I propped a hip on the desk. Dutch remained near the door.

Carstairs was our lookout by the windows, and Dorset roamed along the bookshelves.

I had summoned Strother to the captain's home rather than affront the viscountess by suggesting that MacNamara and his minions meet with the Standish heir under Pleasant View's roof. Then too, I was simply tired of dealing with the woman.

"Hamden Parva's right along the bridle path," Dutch observed. "Less than three miles, most of it through woods and along the river."

Strother tapped a manicured nail on the arm of his chair. "What is the significance of that?"

The others looked to Carstairs to explain the obvious. "The greenery provides cover. If your villains are also looking for the gold, as Lord Julian has suggested, that bridle path lets them travel unseen between Hamden Parva and Pleasant View."

"I travel that way frequently," Strother retorted. "I've never met anybody on that path, save for Lord Julian." He turned a curious gaze upon me.

Tiresome and predictable. "By your own admission," I said, "you travel the same route at the same time of day in a well-known rotation. Either meeting you or avoiding you is thus a very simple matter. I chose the former. The kidnappers have apparently chosen the latter."

"Nevertheless," Strother began, only to fall silent when the captain held up a hand.

"Don't be ridiculous. Lord Julian has no lack of coin and no untoward interest in your sister. More to the point, he is the only party who has done anything to find Hannah."

"I searched the entire house, and without alerting Mama to my efforts."

Carstairs sent him a pitying look. "You were looking for the gold. You've doubtless been searching for that treasure since you were twelve years old."

"I don't think Han had hid it by then. Though she might have. She's always been headstrong. Gets that from Mama, ironically."

"Hamden Parva," I said a bit too forcefully. "What do we know of it? Where in that vicinity might kidnappers keep a young lady without being detected by the neighbors?"

Carstairs propped his hips against the windowsill. "For obscurity, it's a good choice. The village used to lie in a royal forest, and thus the surrounds weren't put under cultivation until fairly recently, by local standards. The land doesn't lend itself to farming as well as other parts of the shire, and the tenancies and homesteads are spaced well apart."

Another little world, and only three miles distant.

"Hamden Magna doesn't exist," Strother observed, though nobody had raised the question. "Nobody knows quite where it might have been, assuming it ever existed."

"We have hours of light left," Dutch said as if Strother hadn't spoken. "Shall we have a stroll down the bridle path, my lord?"

"Is there any sort of butcher's shop or abattoir in Hamden Parva?" I asked.

Every pair of eyes in the room turned in my direction.

"There is," Carstairs said. "A royal forest was preserved for hunting, in the usual course, and hunting meant game to be dressed and butchered. The Dolans have been butchers from time out of mind. They still trade in game, for those with a license to hunt, and all the farmers rely on them to assist with local livestock."

"We send them our deer," Strother said, another irrelevancy. "They accept payment in kind rather than coin."

Meaning they took the best cuts, the valuable hide, the bones, and any antlers, and sent the rest back to Pleasant View for consumption.

"Hannah knows the Dolans," Strother went on. "Everybody does in these surrounds, at least in passing. They would not be a party to her kidnapping."

Hardly the point, but I did not feel the need to explain myself. "We're off to Hamden Parva. Carstairs and I will ride by the lanes. Captain, you will inform the ladies of recent developments when they return to the inn. Dutch and Dorset, you go by the bridle path. Dutch, you know which tracks to look for, though the recent rain won't make the job easy."

We gathered up flasks and buttered bread, and Carstairs and I retreated to the stable yard.

"We're still looking for a needle in a haystack," Carstairs said as he tightened the girth on his saddle. "Some parts of Merry Olde are less domesticated than others, and Hamden Parva is one of them. The land isn't good enough to support much agriculture, and as far as I know, a great deal of it is still held in common."

"All of which suggests an ideal situation for kidnappers looking to lie low." I swung into the saddle of the captain's personal mount, knowing Atlas needed his day of rest. Smooth gaits were among his many fine qualities, and his saddle was exquisitely contoured, by design and long usage, to keep both me and my steed comfortable.

"Strother is a precious idiot," Carstairs observed when we'd mounted up and gained the lane. "Or he appears to be."

"He's shrewd enough to dodge his creditors, but foolish enough to live beyond his means. How does that make him different from every other heir to an impoverished title?"

"You've been over every inch of Pleasant View," Carstairs said. "What did you think of it?"

"Not every inch." But I'd certainly inspected the grounds of the manor itself. "The property presents well. The deer are fat, the buildings in good repair, the home wood thriving, the kitchen gardens well maintained. Fences, fixtures, and home farm all appear to be regularly seen to as well."

I could have gone on. The bridges were sound—always important to a marching army—and none of the ground qualified as bog, which meant mosquitoes would not torment the troops and somebody had kept on top of drainage considerations. Lanes and bridle paths were free of potholes and clear of obstructions, which mattered very much to the artillery.

Which left...? "Strother says the tenant cottages are in want of repairs." Though I'd seen some of those cottages, and none was in shameful condition. "You're saying Strother is a decent manager, for all he comes across as a fribble?"

"He patrols the perimeter conscientiously. The locals get on with him. He might not behave with great sense when in Town, but he's holding Pleasant View together. That takes a certain dedication and savvy."

And yet, I'd caught him easily in a lie. Several lies. "What regiment had the pleasure of your loyalty?"

"95th Rifles, for my sins." He nudged his horse in some unseen fashion, and the beast took off in a businesslike canter.

If there was one group of soldiers who saw more keenly than Wellington's reconnaissance officers, it was the sharpshooters in the Rifles. I could not put my finger on what troubled me about Carstairs's observations, but he'd given me food for thought.

CHAPTER FIFTEEN

Hamden Parva was indeed another little world, much as the Dales and the Lake District, side by side, were very different terrains. The surrounds of Hamden Parva had a wildness to them, a primitive quality. The land tended to neither the majestic hardwoods of a mature home wood, nor the open expanse of moorland.

Game would thrive handily in such an environment. Scrubby trees, overgrown meadows, bramble thickets, and freshets all blended into a wilderness that had apparently been undisturbed for centuries. An occasional oak or maple had gained height over its neighbors, while yews of ancient vintage occupied higher slopes.

"The whole place feels neglected," I said as we rode into what passed for the village green after some three hours of scouting the vicinity. "Too quiet."

"No cattle bawling or horses whinnying," Carstairs replied. "Nobody practicing the organ or remonstrating with a wayward youth for all the neighbors to hear."

No ring of a blacksmith's hammer. No hound making his rounds along the single lane passing between the few houses that comprised the hamlet.

"If I were fanciful," I said, swinging down from my horse, "I'd say the place feels as if it were under an enchantment."

The buildings around us were in good repair—the thatched roofs tidy, the chimneys straight. Gates hung straight as well, as did shutters. And yet, an oak blackened by lightning poked up through the wilderness to the west of the green. Why hadn't that eyesore been taken down decades ago? No living thing stirred anywhere, not so much as a sparrow. We'd reached the time of year when birds were nesting, and yet, no winged creatures searched for food or patrolled the skies.

"No flowers," Carstairs said, dismounting by swinging his leg over the horse's crest. "It's the highest of high seasons for flowers. Not a rosebush or hydrangea to be seen."

"This village," I said, "puts me in mind of Spain, and not in a good way." How many times had I ridden into the same sort of emptiness where signs of habitation ought to be? No chickens scratching in the street. No equines dozing at hitching racks. Nothing in plain view that could be killed or plundered.

"Times are hard. How long do we wait for Dorset and Dutch?"

The sun was low enough to be obscured by the scraggly trees. I consulted my timepiece. "We're about a quarter hour early."

"One feels an urge to turn homeward."

"We're safe enough. Even if the countryside is full of bandits and poachers, the rule is mutual avoidance in a place like this. Neutral territory is integral to the pursuit of the criminal professions." Also to the dubious profession of spying. Many a time, my French and Spanish counterparts and I had sought refuge in the same cantina. We acknowledged one another with reciprocal displays of indifference and went upon our respective ways.

Honor might not thrive among thieves, but among spies, a certain understanding could be relied upon. Ours was not a violent pursuit in the normal course, and we shared a certain exasperated impatience with the blunt instruments more usually employed to wage war.

"They're here," Carstairs said, slipping off his horse's bridle and loosening the girth.

I did likewise, and both beasts took to cropping what grass was available on the expanse that passed for the village green.

"A talking raven would be of a piece with this place." Carstairs drew off his hat, swiped his sleeve across his forehead, and ran a hand through creased locks. "Or an old woman muttering curses."

"Do you feel a poem coming on?" For a gamekeeper who spent much of his time in the forest, he was quite fanciful.

"If I could pen a good Gothic tale or two, my fortunes would definitely improve. Alas, I am not that talented."

"Have you tried?"

Rather than answer, he greeted Dutch and Dorset, a dusty and oddly subdued pair.

"No sign a'nothin'," Dutch said. "Place gives me the collywobbles in me pandenoodles. Like something's creepin' up behind me, but I turn, and nothin's there."

"Nothing left in your flask, you mean," Dorset muttered. "You saw them prints too."

"Man gets parched this time of year," Dutch said. "We did see a few more of the dog's pawprints, milord, and also the big horse. Coming this direction. Can't say when."

"You can say when. Were the prints out in the open or under some sort of overhanging bough?"

"In the open. Sun-baked."

"And fairly deep, I'd wager."

Dorset squinted at me. "How'd you know that?"

Dutch spoke for me. "A'cause of the rain, dimwit. The prints were made in soft earth, after the rain, but not terreckly after. Right?"

"Correct. That tells us whoever rides the big horse is still in the immediate surrounds." We also knew that party to be shrewd enough to avoid the open lanes and well-traveled paths closer to Hamden Parva. I'd been keeping a watch for familiar hoofprints and pawprints and seen none.

"I'm ready for supper," Dorset said, patting his flat belly. "Tramping the countryside is for young soldiers and old vagabonds. Puts an appetite on a fella."

"Take my horse," Carstairs said. "I'll stretch my legs, if Dutch can bear me company."

"Dutch can take my horse," I said. "I'm of the same mind. Too much time in the saddle." I had no idea if Dutch was capable of riding, but the captain's horse, fatigued by the day's labors, would amble in the direction of home willingly enough, particularly if his stablemate was at his side.

"Obliged," Dutch said. "Dorset, let's be off. We don't want the captain to worry."

They caught the horses and were trotting west in short order.

"You will take the bridle path?" Carstairs asked.

"I thought I would. Low light is surprisingly helpful in the search for tracks." Low light, or light at an angle.

"And you would rather travel alone, I take it." Not a question, suggesting Carstairs might be in need of solitude.

"Alone or in company, suit yourself."

He glanced around at the oddly quiet village. "I'll take the lane. See you at the captain's, and I'll make sure there's some supper for you."

"Mine is the shorter path."

"But you will study it and ponder and double back and ponder some more."

Tracking was best done at a deliberate pace, and besides, I wanted to take a look at the captain's fishing cottage, an errand best taken care of without Carstairs's company.

"I propose to meet you and the captain at the inn after supper," I said. "The ladies will have a report, and I might as well."

Wishful thinking on my part.

"Then I'll see you at the inn. If you're not accounted for within two hours, we'll add you to the list of those missing in action." He touched a finger to his hat brim and sauntered off.

I crossed the green and found the bridle path, though I doubted I'd see anything worth note along the trail. Dutch had confirmed our suspicions—the fellow on the big horse was traveling between Hamden Parva and Pleasant View, the hound accompanying him.

I wanted the time to think and thus set a leisurely pace for headquarters. Hamden Parva had put me in mind of Dabney Witherspoon. She, too, had the quality of being arrested in time, bleak, and haunted.

She did not dwell on her grief so much as it dwelled upon her. And yet, I had been attracted to her, perhaps because of that quality of desolation. She had not been attracted to me. I and my rubbishing manly humors were safe to speculate in her direction with no risk of reciprocity.

My perusal of the fishing cottage yielded no insights. The space was a tidy three-room affair on the lowest floor. A sitting room-cum-study enjoyed a pleasant view over the trout pond. At the back, a kitchen did double service as a dining room. A bedroom also looked out over the pond. Steps to a garret above revealed plain sleeping quarters, perhaps for staff.

The place felt unused. No lingering scent of the captain's pipe. No recent correspondence left to dry on the desk blotter. The desk itself was serviceable, with wax jack, pen tray, and ink all to hand and a fresh supply of paper in the tray. An abacus sat atop some sheets of foolscap on which figures were penciled in a tidy hand. A stack of pamphlets sat to one side—one advocating the crossbreeding of meat and dairy cows, another railing against a government that oppressed the poor on behalf of the rich, a third extolling direct applications of honey to heal wounds.

The captain was an eclectic reader even in absentia. The room was otherwise unremarkable. Two wing chairs by the hearth, a sideboard sporting dusty decanters, a worn floral Axminster carpet on a polished oak floor. Pleasant enough, but lacking the touches that made a space comfortable and personal.

No final letter from Hannah that the captain had overlooked. No kidnappers hiding in plain sight.

Another wasted effort.

I was on Pleasant View land and once again occupied with my own concerns when it occurred to me that if Dabney Witherspoon could have her Andrew returned to her, even without any hope of marital intimacies, she would take the bargain gladly and consider it a miracle of generosity on the part of Providence.

I was still ruminating on that insight as I reached the coaching inn. When Hyperia greeted me, I kissed her on the cheek, despite the captain, Lady Ophelia, and Carstairs looking on.

∽

The ladies confirmed that the Dolans ran a tidy, prosperous establishment and that inquiries directed to Mrs. Dolan regarding dog bones and strangers met with platitudes and shrugs.

"Not surprising, I suppose." I finished my last bite of mashed potatoes. "Silence can be purchased. If the Dolans have no idea Miss Hannah has gone missing, they have no reason to suspect that Sylvester Downing is anything but a young swell hiding from creditors."

"Which," Lady Ophelia muttered from the depths of a wing chair, "he might well be."

I had taken my belated supper on a tray in Lady Ophelia's sitting room. Carstairs and the captain had arrived halfway through my meal. Hyperia presided over a tea tray, though nobody seemed interested in the requisite polite two cups.

"An inability to manage his funds does not excuse his behavior in the least." The captain, perching awkwardly in the second wing chair, appeared unwell. The strain was telling, in features that looked more drawn than usual and in the manner in which he rubbed his knee. "Our best course is logical enough."

We had debated this logical measure at some length. "You want to post a lookout at the Dolans'," I said, "and wait for an appearance of Downing or his accomplice. When our quarry retrieves his next bone or mess of tripe, we follow him and foil the kidnappers."

"I don't advise the course," Hyperia said, not for the first time. "Downing has fought two duels that I know of, and if I know of them, he's likely fought more. He knows how to use a gun and will commit violence against his fellow man."

My darling was protective of me, for which I adored her, and she was sensible, which equally inspired my admiration.

I wanted to blow Hyperia a kiss, but settled for echoing her objections. "We are not in a position to lay siege to whatever farmhouse or cottage Downing has appropriated, and that assumes that Downing or his accomplice gathers up the dog's rations and repairs straight to the place where Hannah is held. Moreover, we might wait in vain for days—the ransom instructions are due tomorrow, and Downing might have already broken camp."

"I agree with Lord Julian." Carstairs offered his support from a high stool near the hearth. "Downing—if Downing is our man—has succeeded with his scheme thus far. The ransom is due to be collected tomorrow, and he might well have already taken his victim elsewhere. Then too, Mrs. Dolan might be telling the truth, and Downing is ten miles north of where we think he is."

"When we pay the ransom,"—Lady Ophelia took up the narrative—"we will be directed to retrieve the lady from some gatehouse five miles to the south, while the kidnappers hare off with their ill-gotten treasure in the opposite direction. When we reach the gate house, we'll be informed of the lady's actual location. This would be amusing were it not so serious."

The conversation went around for another half hour, putting me in mind of countless strategy sessions in Spain. Would the French break camp because their pasture was running low? Remain where they were because water was in good supply? Would they divide their forces, or remain in place, awaiting reinforcements from distant provinces?

Did we attack? Fall back? Neither? And for every sound argument put forth, an equally convincing advocate spoke for the opposite strategy. The only certainty we'd had in Spain had been the judgment of Parliament upon us, because every option would have negative consequences, and the legislators sleeping safe in their beds at home focused nigh exclusively on those consequences.

"We're too tired to think clearly," I said when the same ground had been plowed yet again. "And we're keeping the ladies from their slumbers. The next move is Downing's. He will send word regarding the ransom. We have a reasonable facsimile thereof ready to hand over, and if that results in Miss Hannah being surrendered safely to us, we will call that victory."

MacNamara wanted to argue, of course, but he rose awkwardly and bowed his good-nights to Hyperia and Lady Ophelia. Carstairs did likewise—they had come in the captain's carriage—while I lingered behind.

"You young people will excuse me," Lady Ophelia said. "I trust if you are too tired to think, you are too tired to commit rank foolishness on the eve of battle. Julian, you will seek your bed posthaste. You are not to skulk through the underbrush in search of villains by dark of night. Your word on that, sir."

I could not give it. "I concede the wisdom of a good night's sleep before a taxing day. Any soldier would, and I do not skulk, ever."

"Hyperia, make him see reason. I am away to the arms of Morpheus."

Her ladyship retired to her bedroom, closing the door softly. Hyperia stepped into my arms in the next instant.

"I want this investigation to be over, Jules. It has gone far less than well."

"I want Miss Stadler safe and secure. By this time tomorrow, that might be the case."

Hyperia eased away and studied me. "You would truly be content with that outcome? The money and trinkets turned over to a conscienceless villain, Hannah's reputation always at risk because that same villain can start rumors against her at any time?"

I led my intended to the sofa that faced the hearth. The fire was burning low, but the night was cool enough that a bit of heat was a comfort. So was Hyperia's simple, dear presence beside me on that worn sofa.

"I survived the worst treatment the French could mete out, Perry. I cling to that fact—survival against the odds—when I want to collapse in a heap of despair because I was taken captive. Worse, I *let* myself be taken captive without a struggle. I had a responsibility to resist, to go down fighting, and I failed in that duty."

"This still bothers you."

Bothers was a gross understatement. "I failed my duty as an officer, and I failed my brother as well. Those realities would condemn me to endless shame, except that wallowing in my own inadequacy adds further dishonor to failure. I yet have *life*, and I yet am capable of making a contribution. Many others cannot say the same. I owe it to them, to the sacrifices they made, to carry on and to do so as gratefully as I can."

I had reasoned this much out shortly after coming home from Waterloo, while enduring the first volley of judgment at Society's hands. The reality of Harry's passing had descended anew along with a black miasma of melancholia.

I could have easily become another former officer who'd suffered an accident while cleaning his pistol. On my worst days, the temptation dogged me still. Reasoning one's way to a path forward and sticking to that path were vastly different undertakings.

"Then victory means Hannah Stadler's safe return, at almost any cost?"

"If the cost is coin that the captain and I can spare and a few jewels Lady Ophelia won't miss, then yes. That's victory."

"But not success." Hyperia took my arm and arranged it around her shoulders. Then she drew her feet up so she was cuddled quite close indeed.

A year ago, I would have been delighted to hold her thus, to revel in the comfort of simple affection. One part of me would forever be captive to my past, but another part of me had come a great distance in a little over twelve months.

"I want you to know something, Perry." I had not planned those words. "You have merely to listen. You need not reply."

She was listening. I could tell by the feel of her against my side.

"Go on, Jules."

"When you accepted my proposal of marriage, you believed me to be incapable of the activity that results in the conception of children. I believed myself incapable as well, and, in fact, I was incapable."

"I know this, but something has changed, hasn't it?"

"How can you tell?"

"Your touch is different. More careful, not as friendly. You invited me down to the Hall and then played least in sight, day after day. I know you are searching for Hannah, but still... a gentleman cannot cry off, and you are a gentleman."

Ye winged seraphim, she was brave. "Nor am I crying off. I am alerting you to a change in my circumstances. I owe you this report, Hyperia, because above all else, I want us to be honest with each other. We've come through some difficult moments, and I would never, ever want it said that you married me when I was flying a false flag. Mind you, I have not tested my hypothesis, but I suspect if you wanted children, I could do my part with significant enthusiasm."

Hyperia's first reaction was silence, during which I berated myself for bringing up this awkward, fraught topic at the worst possible time.

She tilted her head to consider me. "You aren't asking to cry off?"

Cry and *off* had abruptly become my two least favorite words in the lexicon. "Absolutely not. I love you. I want to spend the rest of my life with you. I promise you loyalty, fidelity, and all the rest of it on the original terms, Perry, but you deserve to know that I am fundamentally different now from the man you promised to marry."

I waited for her to muster some sort of speech about reevaluating our bargain and certain matters requiring careful thought. I did love her, I did want her to be happy, and marriage to me—to the man I had become—might not figure in that recipe.

I had not, though, meant to broach the topic at this late hour, when my reserves of fortitude were at low ebb, and the coming day might see all manner of tragedy.

"You have not changed, Jules," Hyperia said, "not in any way that should matter."

She remained in my embrace, eyes closed, perhaps dozing, or trying to make me think she was asleep. We hadn't cleared the air. We hadn't resolved all questions, but I was learning that my relationship with Hyperia was a work in progress. We muddled along in good faith, our trust waxing more than it waned with each difficult issue or unforeseen challenge.

"I'm falling asleep," she said a few moments later. "Investigating with Lady Ophelia is demanding work."

"Then I will take my leave of you, before we both drift off. Tomorrow promises to be difficult."

I rose, and Hyperia came to her feet as well. Without warning, she gathered me into a fierce hug.

"I love you too, Julian. Very much. With your honesty and trust, you honor me more than I can express." She rested her cheek against my chest, making a paper in my breast pocket crackle.

"Is there more you'd say, Hyperia? We have privacy, and I hadn't meant to burden you with confidences tonight, but I did anyway. My apologies for that."

"Yes, there is more..." She straightened and patted my chest. "Nothing that won't keep. "You seldom carry anything in a breast pocket. Is that a map?"

She had changed the subject. Were the hour not so advanced, I would have pressed for details. I had her declaration of love, though, and decided to allow that to be the last word on our romantic circumstances.

I extracted the folded paper from my pocket, somewhat surprised to find Jem's pamphlet bookmark. I recalled stashing it somewhere, a tail pocket perhaps.

"Somebody's diatribe on the Church of England's responsibility to support more legal independence for women, especially wives. Jem was using it for a bookmark in Mrs. Burney's novel."

"The novel Hannah borrowed?"

"The one she borrowed that was somehow returned to some under-librarian in the outer reaches of Hamden Parva...." I held the folded paper up to a branch of candles on the mantel. Had Hannah returned the book, or had her kidnappers tossed the novel aside, leaving some passerby to exercise a sense of civic duty? I studied the pamphlet more closely, some fact or connection trying to tickle my brain.

"What is it, Jules?"

"I saw this same pamphlet in the captain's fishing cottage. Several copies of it. Hannah might have picked one up for herself, and that means..." I opened the leaflet and scanned the printing. To see well, I needed strong sunlight, but had only the candles... "Perry, look at this closely for me, would you? Look for any marks, any faint lines, anything that indicates Hannah might have used this pamphlet to send us word of her location."

I was grasping at straws, but at this eleventh hour, I forgave myself the folly.

"Here," Hyperia said, holding the pamphlet perilously near the candles. "Somebody underlined a sentence or two in light pencil."

"Read them to me, please."

"'And what recourse has the dutiful wife, accustomed to sheltering beneath the oak of her husband's protection, when he is laid low by the lightning of misfortune, injury, or disease?' It goes on about she has neither the authority of the widow nor the safety of her husband's strength and abilities, but must be felled with him, powerless and suffering in her own right, despite having faculties and skills with which to earn coin... All very passionate. Also true."

Also damned clever. "Perry, I know where Hannah is. Not exactly, but close enough to reconnoiter my way to her doorstep."

"From one sentence in a bleating pamphlet?"

"Hamden Parva is home to an oak struck by lightning. The thing pokes up above the other trees some distance off the green. It's ugly and should have been taken down years ago, but I am certain that if I look carefully enough in the vicinity of that oak, I'll find the signs of our kidnapper's passing, and I can track him from there."

"Julian, you need rest. It's late and dark, and if you take a lantern, Downing will see you."

He might. Tomorrow was bound to be a fraught day for him too—him and whatever accomplices aided his scheme. Troubling thoughts might well keep him awake through the night.

"You aren't wrong."

"I am right. Go back to the captain's. Explain what we've found. Rest. In the morning, confer with Hannah's family before you take any risky measures. Lady Ophelia and I will be ready for orders at first light."

"You yourself said that Downing could be violent, my dear. I cannot—"

She put a finger to my lips. "Hannah might need the company of women, and she will definitely need somebody to keep her mother in check. You cannot be everywhere at once."

"You are pulling rank."

"And you love me for it."

I kissed her good night and got kissed rather thoroughly in return. Thus *mightily* fortified, I made it as far as the hammock on the captain's back porch, where I fell asleep the instant my eyes were closed.

CHAPTER SIXTEEN

I had the ability to wake myself at the hour of my choosing, at least when on campaign. A lone robin caroled in the predawn gloom when I rose from my hammock, made my ablutions, and again borrowed the captain's riding horse.

I had also appropriated buttered bread and some cheese from the larder, eating in the saddle as I had many, many times before. In terms of weapons, I'd brought only my peashooter, the knife perennially sheathed in my boot, and my wits. My mission was reconnaissance rather than freeing the captive.

That part would come later, assuming Downing had not fled the area with his victim in tow.

Or worse.

The bleak surrounds of Hamden Parva were rendered more sinister by mist rising from the river and drifting over the bracken and trees. The blighted oak twisted upward into the foggy air, the upper reaches disappearing altogether. No birds sang in this tenebrous world. No foxes stirred through the undergrowth, homeward bound after a night of hunting.

Too quiet.

I dismounted about twenty yards from the charred oak, secured the horse to a stout chest-high branch of maple, and let the stillness of first light seep into my bones. Hurry and worry made for sloppy reconnaissance, and sloppy reconnaissance made for tragedy.

I approached in slow circles, keeping my footfalls silent and flat. Many a useful sign had been obscured by a careless step, and I could not afford to be careless. I was on my third circuit of the dead tree when I spotted the faintest of trails leading through the undergrowth.

A partial pawprint of a size to belong to a large canine lay two yards from a hoofprint answering to the proper description. The tracks were fresh, less than a day old, in my estimation. Dry, no dust accumulated in the crevices.

I set aside the compulsion to jog down the game trail. I might move silently by human standards, but any large creature making rapid progress would alarm what game and birds were lurking in the silence. I proceeded carefully, keeping an eye out for more signs, and was periodically rewarded with same.

A burst of pink blooms against the misty air provided further encouragement. Rhododendrons were not native to England, but since the middle of the previous century, landowners had imported them because, in addition to gracing hedgerows with their beautiful flowers, the evergreen bushes provided year-round cover for game.

I was moving in the direction of human habitation.

When I caught a faint whiff of woodsmoke, I slowed my steps further until I spied what might have been a fairy cottage nestled at the foot of a hill, the river meandering along some fifteen yards to the rear. The cottage occupied a dish of earth, as if the land itself sought to shelter the small dwelling.

Got you. Against the foggy air, no smoke was visible—shrewd, that—and yet, fresh water was at hand, and the denizens of the surrounding forest would in the normal course sound an alarm should an intruder bumble too close.

Whoever had taken Hannah Stadler captive had studied the situation and made tactically sound choices.

And yet, city walls that stood for centuries would fall eventually, if attacked with the right artillery firing from the right vantage points. I studied the little citadel at the foot of the hill and thought back over sieges, ambushes, tragedies, and victories.

I retreated the way I'd come, taking care to leave not so much as a heel print on the trail nor a broken twig along it. The going was slow, and by the time I'd made my way back to the horse, another robin was gracing the morning with his song.

~

"For concealment," I said, "the location is ideal. Even the locals have probably forgotten that cottage, but somebody went to the trouble to seal it up before it was abandoned. The building itself is stout, the glass in the windows intact."

"If it's on the acreage of the old royal preserve," MacNamara replied, "nobody would dare vandalize the place. The sheer gall, though, of holding a kidnapping victim there... You were right that Sylvester Downing is nobody's fool. He doesn't lack for balls either."

But he did want for coin, which could make an heir with a very healthy papa desperate.

"I've seen that cottage." Carstairs helped himself to a cinnamon bun from the basket in the center of the kitchen worktable. "Has a fey quality. Roses trellised along the east side of the porch, was probably awash in daffodils last month. Do you propose we simply knock on the door and invite ourselves in for tea?"

Dutch, the former artillery man, looked up from his heaping plate of eggs and ham. "We could drop a little greeting down the chimbly. Wake up the whole neighborhood."

"And," Dorset muttered between bites of buttered toast, "blow Miss Hannah to flinders while we're at it."

Coombs, who'd apparently prepared the meal, kept a judicious silence at the sink.

"We will pay a call on the cottage." I finished a cup of stout black tea and helped myself to a biscuit. "We will also recruit young Strother to accompany us."

"Why?" MacNamara asked. "He's not entirely a bungler, but he's not in my good books these days either."

Carstairs went for a second biscuit. "Strother has the air of a double deserter. Where do his loyalties truly lie?"

Upon inspection, the biscuits turned out to be buttery, spicy heaven. "His loyalties, I suspect, lie with his tailor, his glovemaker, and so forth. He'd like to inherit an estate in good repair—he's not entirely lazy—but he's gambled and gavotted himself into a corner."

More than that, I would not say, but Carstairs's observation, that Pleasant View was in good trim despite the family's fortunes, had kept me company in the hammock as I'd slept. I'd risen still pondering that conundrum and had come to a few tentative conclusions that wanted airing at the appropriate time.

"So how do we proceed?" MacNamara asked, pouring himself more tea.

I outlined a plan, and we debated its merits. For the most part, the assemblage was in agreement. We had the element of surprise on our side, provided we moved quickly. We had an advantage of numbers, and we had the former soldier's instinct for working together to best a dangerous enemy.

We had Carstairs's talent with a Baker rifle. What we did not have was much time.

Carstairs was dispatched to give the latest report to the ladies. I was soon back on the captain's horse and trotting up Pleasant View's drive. The rest of the patrol would take the bridle path in the direction of Hamden Parva, the captain mounted, Dutch and Dorset on foot.

Carstairs, the captain, and I had synchronized our timepieces, though if the day's skirmish went like many others, our finely tuned schedule would become useless in the first five minutes of the engagement.

Such was war.

"Lord Julian!" Strother greeted me more heartily than on any previous occasion, rising from his place at the breakfast table and bowing with a piece of toast in his hand. "Do sit down and join me. Today's the day, isn't it? I must say I'm surprised that MacNamara has the means he claims to have. Surprised and gratified. Mama's unhappy, though."

The Standish heir resumed his seat at the head of the breakfast table, where he had no business being.

"You've had no further word from the kidnappers?" I remained on my feet. I would not be staying long.

"Nary a note. The day has barely dawned, though. I tell myself that by sunset, Hannah might well be among us again. Perhaps her ordeal will have shown her the folly of ladies haring about unescorted, or letting books and poems render them oblivious to all else. Probably not. Han is stubborn."

This catty, chatty drivel tried my temper. "Your sister was reading within sight and earshot of the family home, Stadler. That she wasn't safe on her own property is not to her family's credit. Cease stuffing your maw. We are off to rescue your sister."

He went still, his toast held halfway to his mouth. "Rescue? Hannah? Now?"

"No time like the present. If Downing intends to move his victim in anticipation of leading us on a goose chase while he makes off with the ransom, then we haven't much time to thwart him."

"Downing? You said Downing, as in, Sylvester Downing? The Irish chap?"

"On your feet, Stadler."

He rose slowly, his toast still in hand. "I see no need for my involvement. Somebody must stay here with Mama if you're to retrieve Hannah from her captors. You're sure it's Downing?"

"No, I am not sure. We know Hannah was escorted from the property by two men. Downing might be one of them, and we know not how many others might be involved. You will improve the numbers in our favor."

"I am not very handy with a firearm." He snitched a strip of bacon from the sideboard. "You probably don't need me, and I would really be of much greater use keeping her ladyship from rash measures."

I stuck my head out the door and found a footman pretending to arrange the fronds of a fern in the sunny alcove across from the breakfast parlor.

"Please send word to the stable that Mr. Stadler will need his horse out front in a quarter hour."

The footman, who might have been ten years my senior, straightened slowly.

"Best do as he says," Strother said. "Appears his lordship and I are going for a hack." He smiled unconvincingly, and the footman bowed before departing.

"Fifteen minutes," I called. "Not thirty seconds more."

"I cannot possibly make myself presentable in a mere quarter hour, Caldicott. The neighbors might be out and about, and really, if I'm off galivanting with you, who will be here to receive further instructions from the kidnappers? We don't want to lose Hannah because the mail went unanswered, do we?"

Had I not spent two weeks living and breathing the question of who had kidnapped Hannah, I might have taken pity on Strother and allowed him to hide behind his mother's figurative skirts.

He was overplaying his role as brainless fribble, though, and I *had* spent hours and hours, miles and miles, pondering Hannah's bad fortune. The who behind the whole business had never really been that obscure, but the *why* of it all had taken some pondering.

"The viscountess is equal to the task of reading another ransom note," I said. "If one even arrives. Upstairs with you, and no, I will not kick my heels on the terrace while you tie six successive cravats off-center. I shall valet you."

Strother did not like that suggestion at all, confirming my suspicion that he was tempted to imitate his papa and take French leave.

I bundled him up to his apartment, saw him clad in breeches, clean linen, and riding jacket, and had him on the front steps within fourteen minutes.

"This might not be a good idea," he said, swinging into the saddle. "The kidnappers have been patient, and if Hannah has been underfoot this whole time, their goodwill should be in tatters. I've heard that Downing considers himself a member of the Fancy."

The Fancy, meaning amateur pugilists. "Carstairs served with the Rifles. Guess whose odds I favor?"

And yet, I could not underestimate Sylvester Downing. Thus far, the battle had been on his terms, and every skirmish had gone to his side. I was reduced to the age-old strategy of a siege, and if sieges had one characteristic, even successful sieges, it was heavy casualties for the besiegers.

∼

Strother attempted every possible delay, from claiming that his horse had picked up a stone in the shoe to insisting the beast required a drink from the river—twice. The second time, the horse had turned his head to sniff at his rider's knee as if to question orders. The gelding took not so much as a drop to drink.

We nonetheless arrived at the charred oak on schedule.

"I'll just stay here with the horses, shall I?" Strother said when we'd dismounted. "Would not want my noble steed taken by passing vagabonds. He's a good fellow, if a bit long in the tooth."

I tied my borrowed mount to the maple and did the same with Strother's gelding. "I understand that you're anxious regarding anticipated events. Battle nerves are to be expected. What you need to do now is keep your gob shut unless the captain or I give you further orders, understood?"

He pursed his lips. "From the perspective of social standing, the captain really ought not—"

I lifted the top of my fist gently beneath Strother's flapping chin, snapping his teeth together. "Gob *shut*. We're dealing with a shrewd, desperate felon who has taken your sister captive and held her for the past two weeks with no one the wiser as to his location. Either choose to act the adult now, or accept that anything that goes amiss might well be blamed on your unceasing nonsense."

I caught a fleeting glimmer of mulish temper in Strother's eyes, but he nodded. "Serious business. I comprehend that much." His expression said he'd kill me if scandal resulted from the morning's activities, assuming his mama didn't kill him first.

We approached the cottage in silence. The mist had burned off, but the surrounding forest still had a quiet, lost-in-time quality. A raven swooped off some perch and made a lazy curve of black in the morning sky.

"Bad luck," Strother whispered.

I put a finger to my lips, though laying the blighter out cold was gaining appeal by the moment. I took up my assigned position and gestured for Strother to take the place beside me.

He did, then sidled back and to the left so he was half behind me.

The planned round of mirror signals passed without incident. The actors were in their places, and the time had come to raise the curtain.

The captain gave the requisite three flashes of his mirror, and on the count of three later, three guns went off, one of them unmistakably a rifle. A half-dozen birds took wing as the volley echoed over the surrounding trees.

"Great heavens, Caldicott!" Strother expostulated. "What on earth was that about?"

I mentally counted down from ten in Latin, then dragged him out from behind me. "Not another word." I let another half minute go by before following up our greeting.

"Downing, we have you surrounded. Send Miss Stadler out, and your life will be spared." I was the chosen spokesman, because Downing did not know me. To the captain, he would attribute lameness, to Strother, dull-wittedness. He might attribute lesser standing to any other member of our party, had he taken notice of them when he'd been in the area previously.

My answer was a gun blast, the bullet whizzing by several feet to my right. To my left, Strother dropped flat to the ground, a surprisingly sensible choice. Downing had fired from a slightly raised window, his weapon a musket, based on the muzzle blast.

Dutch could have told me a specific make and possibly the year of the pattern.

"By all means," I called, "use up your ammunition. We include ex-riflemen among our contingent. The range of their weapons far exceeds yours. We'll provide you a demonstration of their accuracy. Get away from the window you just fired from, and do it *now*." The east-facing window, which seemed appropriate, given the early hour.

Carstairs gave the occupants a moment to heed my warning, then blew the window to smithereens.

"Caldicott!" Strother squeaked, getting to his feet. "You cannot risk Hannah's life!"

"I didn't. Downing was given a specific warning and time to safeguard himself and his prisoner. He's facing long odds now, but he's not yet a murderer. He's a bright sort, and he won't cross that line willingly." The captain had put forth that reasoning, which had decided the matter over my objections.

Downing was, though, bright enough to use his prisoner as a shield to ensure his own safe passage from the cottage.

"Send Miss Stadler out now," I called, "or prepare for the south-facing window to be demolished." If we were following our plan, Carstairs had already shifted to the position necessary to hit the next target.

"Hannah!" Strother called from behind my shoulder. "I'm here, dear sister! We've come to rescue you! Don't do anything rash, please! Lord Julian Caldicott and—"

The stout application of my elbow to Strother's solar plexus stopped him from disclosing the meager strength of our forces.

"If you speak again without leave, Strother, I will march up to the cottage door with you before me." Actually not a bad idea, given my present theories of the crime, though Strother had unwittingly done his part in the plan simply by announcing his presence.

"Downing, get away from the south-facing window," I bellowed, "unless you seek both death and dishonor."

Carstairs again gave Downing a decent interval to duck out of the line of fire, then let loose another blast.

At this rate, every denizen of Hamden Parva would soon be on hand to watch, and that would not serve Hannah Stadler's reputation any good whatsoever.

"Send Miss Stadler forth immediately," I yelled. "You will run out of ammunition long before we will, and then you will run out of provisions. Or we can settle this civilly, provided the lady is unharmed. The choice is yours."

"I want the gold!" The voice was masculine, furious, and determined. "Bring the gold, and Miss Stadler's life will be spared."

Downing held that high card, but he'd played it too soon. Moreover, did he truly expect us all to sit about for hours while a lot of fancy jewelry was fetched? I judged Downing to be a man with considerable passion for living. He had been given a gentleman's upbringing and could anticipate a peer's honors—or could have, before embarking on present felonies.

Taking the life of an innocent woman should be beyond him, particularly when that act would seal his own doom as well. This, too, had been the captain's reading of the matter, and I trusted MacNamara's judgment.

"Send Miss Stadler to us unharmed. We know who you are, we know the extent of your indebtedness, and we know the identity of your accomplice."

I expected Strother to start squawking, but when I looked about, I found that the Standish scion had made a disorderly retreat. Perhaps for the best.

"The west-facing window is next," I informed my opponent, "and we have sufficient numbers to attack while you attempt to reload."

Barely, but we did. "Your days are numbered," I went on, more loudly. "The sun will soon go down, and you with it."

The translation was a bit faulty, and I had no idea if the captive inside was even listening to me. An interminable silence went by, moments that felt like eternities. Downing and his accomplice might be arguing, or Miss Stadler might be attempting to reason with desperate men.

I tried again. "That busy old fool, the unruly sun, will make his motions, and still we will besiege you." Awkward wording, but apparently effective.

In the next moment, a tallish woman, hands bound, levered herself over the east-facing windowsill and bolted across the clearing into the woods. Though Hannah could not know it, she'd made straight for where Captain MacNamara should have been concealed.

CHAPTER SEVENTEEN

"Damn you, woman!" Downing bellowed. "Damn you to the infernal fiend, and damn this lot you've brought down upon us."

Why was it, that even when exasperated to the point of profanity, the Irish accent was so euphonious?

"Toss your weapon out the same window," I said. "You have the word of an officer and gentleman that you'll not be harmed."

A musket was ejected from the east-facing window.

"Your pocket piece too."

A derringer followed.

"The same for your accomplice, Downing. Don't be tedious, and don't try to be clever."

"Don't push your luck, English."

Another pistol followed.

"And the fowling piece," I called. If one firearm could be carried through the English countryside without raising suspicion, it was a fine, long-barreled fowling piece. An item fitting that description joined the growing collection at the foot of the cottage steps.

"Send your brother out first." While I spoke, the captain and

Miss Hannah joined me. Dutch was covering the eastern side of the cottage, Carstairs the north, and Dorset the west.

A young gent in somewhat wrinkled country attire emerged from the cottage and came down the steps. He hadn't put his hands in the air, nor would that show of harmlessness have been convincing.

"Brian Downing, at your service." He bowed stiffly. "My older brother had little to do with this. Leave him in peace, and I'll take what's coming to me."

"Noted for the record," I said, though in truth, he'd surprised me. "Sylvester Downing, show yourself."

Miss Hannah's erstwhile suitor emerged from the cottage. His fine clothing was also overdue for a wash and ironing, and he'd apparently parted company with his razor, perhaps in an effort to disguise his appearance. Dark whiskers gave him a piratical air, but around the eyes, he resembled his younger sibling.

"You mustn't kill them," Miss Hannah said. "They deserve to live knowing they've failed."

"Not an Irishman born who doesn't know the taste of failure," Brian said. "Largely thanks to you lot. Summon the king's man if you must, but leave my older brother out of this."

Sylvester remained silent, which did not raise him in my esteem. The younger brother was defending the heir, a noble if misplaced display of loyalty.

"Do we tie your hands, or will you come peaceably?" I asked.

"We come peaceably," Sylvester said. "Provided nobody quotes us any damned poetry, or great literature, or Bible verses. That blasted female can go on in French and German and Italian too. Damnedest thing I ever heard."

Hannah and the captain beamed at each other.

"Dutch, Dorset, Carstairs! We've prisoners to escort."

The three of them materialized from the forest. Dutch collected the discarded firearms, passing a pistol to Dorset. Carstairs, cradling his rifle over his arm, considered the brothers Downing.

"We have a three-mile hike along the river before us," he said.

"Any man attempting to escape before we reach the captain's property will be shot in the foot, compliments of the 95th Rifles."

"My horse is at the livery," Sylvester said.

"And what of your dog?" I asked. Man's best friend had helped give away the Downings' game. I and the local chickens and rabbits would doubtless rather see the hound taken in hand.

Brian put his fingers to his lips and emitted a piercing whistle. "Was the dog that started it all, really. Boru is a good fellow. Kept us company, you know?"

"Whoever is righteous has regard for the life of his beast," Hannah murmured, "but the mercy of the wicked is cruel."

"Proverbs," the captain replied. "Chapter 12, verse 10."

Sylvester groaned. Brian scanned the perimeter, and the panting canine revealed himself, tail wagging, tongue lolling.

"What of Strother?" Hannah asked. "He was here, wasn't he?"

The Downing siblings exchanged an unreadable glance.

"He was here," I said. "He was concerned for your welfare, but the gunplay did not sit well with him." I would have said more, except that voices drifted to us from the direction of the charred oak.

"Reinforcements have arrived," Carstairs observed. "Gentlemen, using the term loosely, let's be off with you to the bridle path."

With Dutch and Dorset flanking the prisoners, they trundled away through the undergrowth, the dog bringing up the rear, in apparently great good charity with all.

"I hear ladies," Hannah said. "Is Mama on hand too?"

"Not if God is merciful," the captain replied. "I believe that's Miss West and Lady Ophelia. Carstairs must have overstepped his orders. He does that from time to time."

"I like Carstairs," Hannah said, taking the captain's arm. "He's very well-read, and in any man, that is an attractive quality."

She led MacNamara down the path as she continued to hold forth, acting as his human walking stick on the uneven ground. I took one last look about—I'd see the windows replaced, of a certainty—and thanked the celestial powers that Miss Hannah was safe and free.

The battle was over, but the day's work had only begun. I was calculating just how long it would take Strother to reach London when I joined the captain and Miss Hannah beneath the oak.

To my great surprise and satisfaction, Strother waited with them, accompanied by Lady Ophelia and my dear Hyperia.

"Mr. Stadler was good enough to keep us company," Lady Ophelia said. "He did try to ride off, all the while mumbling something about forgive-me-must-dash. We couldn't allow that. I ask you, what could be more pressing than a gentleman's duty to protect a pair of helpless ladies when firearms are in use in the forest primeval?"

"Nothing on earth could be more pressing to a man of honor," I replied. "How did you dissuade him from fleeing?"

Strother studied the blue sky above. Lady Ophelia looked smug.

"I loosened the girth on his saddle," Hyperia said. "He tried to mount up and gallop off. The horse took exception to the saddle slipping halfway over the side, and by the time Mr. Stadler had the beast calmed, Lady Ophelia had located her peashooter."

Reinforcements, indeed. "Well done, ladies. If Wellington could have commanded such as you, Napoleon would have been defeated in ninety days flat. Strother, we will accompany the ladies back to the captain's house in their coach."

"March, young man," Lady Ophelia said, shaking a gloved finger at him. "I suspect you have been naughty, and naughty fellows must take their punishment."

He flashed me another one of those sullen glowers, then shuffled down the trail with Lady Ophelia in his wake.

"Was he naughty?" Hyperia asked, "or merely a coward?"

"A bit of both. I'd rather not let him out of my sight, if you don't mind."

"Right." Hyperia led the way. "No telling what her ladyship might do to him in a moment of inspiration."

"Hyperia?"

She paused on the path and regarded me over her shoulder. "Jules?"

"Loosening his girth was brilliant, and I love you."

"Thank you, Jules. The sentiment is entirely reciprocated." She allowed me to steal a kiss, and then we resumed our progress to her ladyship's coach.

∼

The captain's guest parlor was crowded. MacNamara, flanked by his intended, occupied the sofa. Lady Ophelia and Hyperia had the wing chairs. Carstairs did sentry duty by the windows, and Dutch and Dorset guarded the door. The Downing brothers, trying to look at ease and failing miserably, idled by the empty hearth.

Strother had all but secreted himself in a corner at the end of the sideboard, and when his mama the viscountess joined us, he appeared to shrink in on himself yet further.

"Sit with us, Mama," Hannah said, patting the place beside her on the sofa.

"Hannah." Lady Standish regarded her daughter quizzically. "You're looking well." She took the seat Hannah offered, that cushion being the only free perch in the room. Her ladyship sat gingerly, as if she expected riot and mayhem to erupt at any moment.

Whatever reaction I'd anticipated to the reunion of mother and daughter, it hadn't been *you're looking well*. No sign of relief, frustration, joy. A platitude alone, and that was apparently all Hannah had learned to expect.

I remained before the sideboard, feeling somewhat like Headmaster before an assemblage of the school's most reluctant scholars.

"I am well, Mama," Hannah replied evenly, once her mama was settled. "I am very well, thanks to James and his friends."

The use of the captain's given name inspired the viscountess to a minor sniff. "I see Mr. Downing has returned to the area."

Sylvester offered her ladyship a bow. "My lady, greetings. May I make known to you my brother Brian, late of County Mayo."

"My lady." Brian's bow was all that was polite.

Hannah was having none of that. "Sylvester has behaved very badly, Mama. He lured me from the property with talk of having found the perfect dog for Strother, and the dog is quite nice. What followed was not nice at all."

Strother's ears had turned pink.

"You should have known better," the viscountess retorted. "I would never allow Strother to have a hairy, slobbering, shedding creature turning Pleasant View into a kennel. Strother is well aware of this."

That the viscountess had disparaged her daughter was apparently also to be expected, but her vituperation of the dog earned her censorious looks from every other occupant of the room.

"He's a good dog," Brian said softly.

"But Sylvester has not been a good brother, has he?" I put the question to the sibling whom I judged the most sensible. The younger son, who'd gone along to prevent disaster, and found himself in the midst of worse trouble than he could have imagined.

A singularly unpleasant experience.

"Sylvester is our dreamer," Brian said, though that observation served as neither explanation nor apology.

Sylvester ceased pretending to study the carpet. "Bri, hush. If Lord Julian wants to send for the king's man, let him. It will be my word against Miss Hannah's, and under English law, that ought not result in any hangings."

"Right," I said. "And you will intimate that Miss Hannah went with you willingly—which she apparently did at first, though, of course, she was trusting your lies at the time. You would further suggest she was ready to embark on a very abbreviated and unconventional sort of courtship at the romantic little cottage. She threw herself at you in desperation, given her advanced age and paltry dowry."

The viscountess looked thunderous. "Hannah absolutely can and will marry Mr. Downing. If they spent days alone together, they must marry. Mr. Downing will not dare cast aspersion on his own wife. For Hannah, a quiet life in Ireland will hardly be a penance."

"Mama, how on earth can you possibly—?"

Hannah fell silent when the captain patted her hand. "Your mother is concerned for your reputation, and we must not judge her for that. You need not consider marrying Downing. At Lord Julian's suggestion, I have taken other measures to ensure that Downing behaves as a gentleman."

Sylvester went back to studying the carpet.

"You bribed the magistrate?" Brian asked. "Of course you did."

"Save your martyrdom for the stage," I said. "The captain bought up Sylvester's debts, all of them. The vowels, the outstanding bill from Tatts, the balance due from Hoby's, the substantial rent owing to his landlord. The sums individually aren't exorbitant, but several years of fortune hunting has resulted in a staggering pile of debt."

"But how...?" The viscountess fell silent rather than discuss coin directly.

"James, you clever, clever man." Hannah Stadler was quite attractive when she beheld the object of all her affections. The room should have glowed so clearly did she honor the captain with her esteem and so clearly did he reciprocate her regard.

"Clever enough that I could puzzle out who Sylvester's accomplice was," I said. "The captain tried to locate and buy up Brian's debts as well, but Brian had left no debts behind when he supposedly left for the New World. That suggested Brian hadn't taken ship at all, and here he is, embarking on a life of crime at the instigation of his elder sibling."

Brian smiled ruefully, while Sylvester swiveled a glower at the captain.

"Then you can have me jailed for debt," Sylvester said. "Shooting would be more merciful. I started the rumor about Brian leaving Town ahead of his creditors. I did not want polite society knowing he'd become a ruddy schoolteacher."

"Headmaster," Brian said. "The work is honorable, and I was good at it."

"That's why you knew all the Proverbs," Hannah said. "Your Shakespeare is decent, too, but your poetry wants work."

Lady Ophelia's gimlet stare landed on me and then on Strother.

Right. Enough pleasantries. "Strother Stadler, you owe your sister an apology."

The viscountess sat up very straight. "Leave my son out of this. He has done his best to assist with all efforts to find Hannah and safely retrieve her. Those efforts have been successful. I will not hear a word against him."

"Yes, you will. Several words, in fact. When I looked about for who had motive to put Miss Stadler in disgrace and who had motive to get his hands on the gold, Strother fits on both counts. He is in debt, not quite as spectacularly as Sylvester Downing is, but that's only because Miss Hannah has been bailing him out to the extent she could. He resents her aid bitterly and, worse, resents her support of his efforts to manage Pleasant View."

"Now that's quite enough," Strother snapped. "I ride the property by the hour. I chat with the tenants and neighbors. I meet with the steward, and I call upon the landowners who border our property. I do Hannah the courtesy of discussing the property with her from time to time because Pleasant View is her home, but she is hardly, that is, I mean… Tell them, Han."

"She reads agricultural pamphlets by the score," I said when Hannah made no comment. "She does the calculations of income and expenses and explains them to your father. She inspects on foot the property you trot over on pleasant mornings. She calls on the neighbors with or without you, and she is the brains that has managed Pleasant View's dwindling resources."

The viscountess stared doom at me. Hannah merely looked shy.

"Han, you have to tell them. I *do* meet with the stewards, and I *do* chat with the tenants, and Pleasant View *will* one day be mine, and I *am* looking after my inheritance."

Hannah's gaze became sad. "I meet with the stewards and tenants first, Strothie. They all like you, and Pleasant View will be yours one day. You are right about that."

For her honesty, Hannah got one of those furious-boy glowers, which, now that mother and son were in the same room, revealed a resemblance between Strother and his dam.

"Do I take it," Lady Ophelia said, "that two intemperate young men schemed together to dispossess the Stadler family of its wealth and Hannah Stadler of her reputation?"

"Strother would never do such a thing." The viscountess rose and treated the room to general sniffing and glaring. "Never. My son is honorable."

"Your son," I said, "is headed for debtors' prison, and if Hannah married MacNamara, debtors' prison would become inescapable. Married women have no control over their funds, a fact of law Miss Hannah has made sure all in her ambit are well aware of. Without her to guide management of Pleasant View and keep the worst creditors at bay, Strother would soon sink."

"I'm told Boston is lovely," Brian muttered.

"Hush," Sylvester said, shoving his brother's arm.

Brian shoved him back. "Well, Lord Julian has the right of it. If you'd told Strother to take his harebrained scheme to the devil, we'd not be in this fix. But no, you thought only of the gold and of sending the only woman to put you in your place to Coventry. I despair of you, Syl, but I'm not lying for you."

"You have no proof." This, from Lady Standish. "Strother denies the allegations, as does Mr. Downing—Mr. Sylvester Downing."

I had hoped to avoid going into sordid details. "Strother has given himself away, ma'am. You claim he aided my investigations when, in fact, he thwarted them at every turn. He could not recall the name of the friend whom Hannah visited at length last spring, though he propositioned that same friend when she was new to first mourning."

Hyperia's expression became very severe at that revelation.

The viscountess was undaunted. "Young men flirt, and Strother can be forgetful."

"Strother is forgetful," I replied. "He forgot to mention the ransom note to me when I was the only party making a thorough search for his sister. He also observed that the kidnappers would have returned Hannah's library book to Hamden Parva if they wanted to lay a false trail in the direction of Bath. It must have slipped his mind that the only parties claiming Hannah decamped to Bath were you and your son."

"We turned in the ruddy book because she would not stop going on about it," Sylvester said. "I might well be hanged for this day's work, but I will never regret that my attempts to court Miss Stadler failed."

MacNamara was half onto his feet before Hannah pulled him back to the sofa. "Sylvester merely states the truth, James. We would not have suited. I'm glad we're in agreement, though all he ever sought at Pleasant View was the gold. I suspect he would have married me to get it, which is surely a symptom of some sort of brain fever."

"What has suiting to do with anything?" the viscountess asked. "Given recent events, nothing could be clearer than that Mr. Downing must pay Hannah his addresses."

Even Strother looked puzzled by the viscountess's insistence. "She'd quote him to death, Mama."

"Strother, you are a son to try any mother's patience."

"Strother is also an accessory to kidnapping," I noted. "He wanted the gold. He wanted Hannah disgraced. His motives and Sylvester's marched to a nicety. I suspect Hannah has little idea where the gold is, though."

"Little idea," she said. "Not none. Papa can be devious, and when Mama and Strothie attributed relocating the gold to me, I decided I could be a bit devious too. I know the gold is somewhere on Pleasant View property, but not the specific location."

"But why...?" Again, the viscountess did not finish her remark.

"Because you and Strother would have wasted it," Hannah said gently. "We don't need it. We're managing."

Hannah was managing, and rather splendidly. "Rather than debate that topic," I said, "might we decide what's to be done with the Downing brothers?"

"Sylvester believes the gold is rightfully his," Hannah said. "He harangued me about the plundering English and Downing lands seized by the crown and justice being in the eyes of the invaders. I cannot refute his tale—he claims the whole hoard was found on Downing land—but he also provided no supporting evidence."

Strother stepped away from the sideboard. "Downing, you never said a word about this."

"Did you really think I wanted to marry your sister?"

Strother took another step toward Sylvester. "You *promised* you would, if the need became imperative, provided you got half... Downing, *you lied*."

"And you were in complete earnest when you said I'd get half the gold?"

Now the viscountess was staring at the carpet. Never had a pretty little pattern of roses and greenery fascinated so many people so thoroughly.

"The gold is Irish in origin," I said, "but possession is nine-tenths of the law, and Lord Standish is apparently quite in possession of the goods, while Captain MacNamara holds your debts as well as your fate in his hands. Captain, what's to be done with the Downings?"

"For a pair of dunderheaded felons, they were reasonably solicitous of a lady's welfare, according to Hannah. My judgment of their deserts is not relevant, fortunately for them. Hannah shall determine their fate."

Hannah rose and approached Sylvester. "If you worked half as hard to right your ship as you've worked to sink mine, you'd be solvent and happily married. *Grow up*, Sylvester. That is my judgment upon you. Grow up, and leave Brian in peace. He's been sorting out your scrapes long enough."

She shook a finger in Sylvester's face. "Forget about a lot of pretty gold baubles that changed hands two centuries ago. Until the captain has been repaid for every penny of your debts, you'd best avoid England, but that's between you and him as debtor and creditor. I never want to lay eyes on you again."

With the dignity of a queen, she resumed her place between the captain and the viscountess.

MacNamara possessed himself of her hand. "I'll send an accounting to the Downing family seat," he said. "If Hannah is content to see you banished, then I am content. If I hear one word spoken against her that can be traced to you, Downing, you had best put your meager affairs in order, and quickly."

I could see that neither Hyperia nor Lady Ophelia was content with this lenient judgment, and I wasn't all that happy with it myself.

And yet, we had more malefactors to deal with, and Hannah was a lady who knew her mind.

"The brothers Downing may depart," I said. "Take the first ship for Dublin you can find, and don't think to leave the dog behind. Dutch and Dorset will see you on your way."

"I wouldn't abandon Boru," Brian said.

I believed him, though I doubted his days of sorting out Sylvester's scrapes were over. Loyal younger brothers with harum-scarum siblings had a thankless lot in life.

They made for the door, heads held high, Dutch and Dorset glaring daggers at the pair of them. Brian was the last to leave, and he paused before passing through the door.

"If it's any consolation," he said to Hannah, "I think Syl was smitten with you, with your brains and self-possession and great, robust talent of taking matters in hand, but he could not admit that to himself. Our grandmother was always going on about the gold. I do apologize. The whole scheme was farfetched, but Strother was convincing, and Sylvester talks himself into things, and one doesn't... I am sorry."

Hannah pointed to the door. "Apology, as belated and inadequate as it is, accepted. Now go."

He bowed and withdrew, closing the door silently.

Good riddance and all that, and yet, there was more to be dealt with. "My lady, you owe your daughter an apology as well, and one for the captain wouldn't go amiss either. Let's be about it, shall we?"

CHAPTER EIGHTEEN

The room still felt crowded, with awkward truths and the lies used to hide them rather than human presences.

"Perhaps I should be going." Carstairs abandoned his post by the window and made for the door.

"I'd rather you stayed," I said. "Your observations about the state of Pleasant View put me on to the secret driving this whole mess. I was too busy searching for the gold and for Miss Hannah to follow the money, as the saying goes. You had your eye on the more relevant target."

"His lordship speaks in riddles," Lady Standish muttered. "I know not who that fellow is, but he has no right to become a party to difficult family conversations."

"Mama, don't be ridiculous. That is Mr. Bryson Carstairs. I've introduced you often enough in the churchyard. His papa is Lord Dunsford, of the Hampshire Carstairs family. Our Mr. Carstairs served honorably with the Rifles, as you well know."

"The Rifles?" Strother said. "I had no idea, but I suppose that's why you could demolish all those windows."

A tipsy dowager with passing experience of a fowling piece could have blasted out those windows, though Carstairs had fired not birdshot, but single bullets angled to bury themselves in the cottage floor.

"I still see no reason for further discussion," the viscountess rejoined. "In fact, I have had quite enough of present company. Hannah, if you are determined to accept the addresses of this, this..."

"Hush." I spoke on behalf of every soldier ever denigrated for his injuries and on behalf of my own dwindling patience. "Your ladyship may leave when you have made your apologies, and when Miss Hannah and the captain have decided what is to be done with your son. He schemed against his own sister and against you, madam. Strother wanted that gold, and not so he could catch up on repairs to the tenant cottages. He's been the profligate man-about-Town, no credit to his patrimony, and a frankly traitorous sibling."

"I wouldn't have put Han out," Strother said. "I simply wanted my debts cleared and a few amenities restored to Pleasant View."

"Amenities," Hannah said, "like fancy hunters who need vast quantities of grain daily while the Corn Laws price that same grain beyond a poor family's means. A new phaeton when our vehicles are perfectly serviceable. Autumn in Paris. Memberships in clubs far too smart for a viscount's impecunious heir. Even Papa despaired of you, Strothie. You don't just build castles in the air, you dwell in them."

"Hannah! When Papa cocks up his toes, I shall be the viscount. You disrespect me at your peril."

I heard again Hannah's sentence on Sylvester Downing—*grow up*. For Sylvester, I held a modicum of hope that he might eventually gain his parole. Strother was proving beyond all aid.

"Strother, what made you conceive of this scheme in the first place?" I asked. "Sylvester was after the Irish gold, and I must assume that's why he befriended you, but you took matters far past a sham courtship."

Strother examined the decanters on the sideboard. "Downing wasn't entirely shamming. He initially came calling to have a look around the estate—he'd heard me bemoaning the fact that the gold had gone missing—but then he met Han, and his eyes took on a determined gleam."

"Determined on matrimony?" MacNamara asked.

"Marriage to Han, and I think she might have allowed it," Strother said, "but then you were always limping about in the churchyard, dropping some witty quote, and willing to argue with Han. She loves to argue. Mama says it's unnatural for a lady to be so contentious."

The viscountess would be shocked to meet my sisters, then. "Then you and Downing began discussing your mutual disappointments in life and came up with this scheme to steal the gold, ruin your sister, and bring scandal down on your parents. How *clever* of you."

I chose the word to wound and apparently hit my target.

Strother rounded on me, an empty crystal decanter in his hand. "You try being the family dullard, Caldicott, your sole value that you are born male. I endured Mama parading me about before the local squires' daughters as if I were some prize bull calf. All the fellows in Town expect me to stay bang up to the minute with fashion and gossip. I am begrudged even the occasional wager beyond what passes for the pittance referred to as my allowance. It's not to be tolerated. Mama agrees."

"Your mother," I said, not even glancing at the potentially lethal weapon in Strother's hand, "has chosen to foster her own bitterness rather than rejoice in her many blessings. She set you against your sister, encouraged your petulance, and must take some blame for goading you into selfish stupidities."

Strother's air of seething resentment eased. "Mama is a penance, can't argue there. I love her dearly—no offense, Mama—but she does wear on a fellow's nerves."

Strother clearly liked the idea that he'd been the victim of his mother's harping. "Your mother encouraged Sylvester Downing's interest in Hannah."

Hannah stirred on the couch. "Mama all but saw us compromised on two occasions, which is what got my back up in the first place. Years of telling me I could not expect to marry well, of ensuring I was nigh cloistered here at Pleasant View. One glib Irishman comes down from Town with Strother, and I am to be crimping my hair and wearing too much perfume and putting new trim on all my bonnets.

"I've had other suitors," she went on, "most of them good, solid fellows, but only Downing passed muster with Mama."

And Hannah herself had not yet figured out the why of it. "Explain to your daughter the real reason you wanted to see her sent across the Irish Sea and immured in the countryside for all the rest of her days."

The viscountess tried her signature glower on me, which was beyond tiresome.

"My lady, you are wasting the time of a number of people who have better things to do than humor your pouts and airs. Explain that you took exception to your daughter's literary ventures and sought any way in the world to bring them to an end."

Hannah was clearly surprised and Strother befuddled beyond his usual slouching attempts at reason. Carstairs appeared amused, while the captain was back to smiling fatuously.

Hyperia and Lady Ophelia were beaming at me, a pleasant change from Lady Standish's ungracious treatment.

The viscountess, for the first time, appeared bewildered. "Must we discuss this?"

"Oh, we must," MacNamara said. "Hannah Stadler's ability with a pen will see the crown shamed into moderating its excesses and repealing those wretched Corn Laws. She is fearless and articulate on any number of subjects."

Hannah considered her intended quizzically. "James, you knew?"

"Why else do you think I had the fishing cottage kitted out as a writer's hideaway? I'm certainly not going to hike all that way to read what I can perfectly well enjoy in the comfort of my own hammock."

"You knew I was... secreting myself in your fishing cottage by the hour?"

"I knew, and I took great encouragement from the fact that you enjoyed the little study I'd fashioned for you. You made yourself quite at home there, and I delighted in thinking of you, gazing out across the pond, fire in your eyes while you vanquished the dragons of injustice and hypocrisy."

I felt compelled to register an objection for the record. "You might have said something to me, MacNamara." Had the captain been honest about the destination of Hannah's perambulations, I might sooner have seen the pattern that drove the whole contretemps.

"Not until I was dozing on your hammock," I went on, "watching the stars turn in their inevitable paths, did it occur to me that your fishing cottage lay at the center of the maze."

"I had suspicions only, my lord. Suspicions a gentleman would not air without the lady's permission. How did you light upon the truth?"

Spare me from true love in full blush. "The cottage bears no scent of pipe smoke and has no hassock or footstool. No ash trays anywhere. Clearly, you were not spending much time there, but somebody else was. An abacus, ciphering, a goodly supply of fresh paper untouched by spring's pervasive damp... and the pamphlets."

"The wretched, wretched pamphlets," the viscountess snarled. "The pamphlets that will see my daughter arrested for sedition. The day those ravings are attributed to you, Hannah, your brother's creditors will be down upon us like vultures flocking to carrion. Polite society will titter behind their hands at Lord and Lady Standish's bad fortune, and poor Strother will never be able to marry well."

Hence the viscountess's willingness to dwell almost exclusively in the country. Cheaper, of course, also *safer*. Much, much safer to rule in obscurity than to face the eventual scorn of Mayfair.

"I gather Miss Stadler's quotes gave her away?" Lady Ophelia asked. "I do like that one about whoever oppresses a poor man insults his Maker, but he who is generous to the needy honors Him."

"You read her shameless drivel?" Lady Standish spat while the captain murmured about Proverbs, Chapter 14.

"Her shameless drivel is the delight of my better-read female acquaintances," Lady Ophelia retorted. "Really, Cora, you should get out more. Eve's Advocate is quite respected in both literary and charitable circles."

Strother looked utterly befuddled and a bit downcast.

"You went to Town to meet with your publishers," MacNamara said, stroking Hannah's knuckles. "You used the proceeds of your writing to fund the libraries and to keep Pleasant View in good trim."

"Also to assist Strother," Hannah said, "but only enough to keep him from going under. Papa and I agree that Strother is in need of management, and a healthy fear of the sponging houses is a useful tool in that regard."

A few years of having to make his own way in the world might have had an even more salutary effect. "I have another suggestion regarding the care and management of your brother."

Lady Standish merely regarded me. The instinct to protect and defend had apparently been silenced, particularly in light of Strother's willingness to sully the family name for new boots and a spanking high-perch phaeton.

"He ought to accompany your mother on an extended visit to her girlhood home. He should see where his maternal antecedents hail from, and he should ensure your mother's travels are all that is commodious."

"Scotland?" Strother expostulated. "You want me to escort Mama to Scotland?"

"I like the idea," MacNamara said. "Hannah?"

A look passed between Hannah and her mother. "You could meet James's family. He tells me they are quite nice. The earl is in failing health and might appreciate a chance to meet his prospective in-laws."

"Those in-laws weighed on my mind," I said. "The viscountess knows Debrett's, probably down to the last footnote and appendix.

She would not have overlooked James MacNamara's prospects, and yet, she disapproved of him as a suitor. Her first real conversation with me was to dissuade me from suitorly tendencies, when I would have been an excellent match." Though a cousin, and that had at first hidden the viscountess's true concern.

Cousins married legally all the time, to wit, the Royal Family had done in the present and immediate past generation. The more pressing issue for the viscountess was to either keep Hannah and her coin pinned down at Pleasant View, or to see her consigned by marriage to as distant a province as possible. The captain showed no longing to return to Scotland, and I was both local and socially prominent, at least in terms of standing.

"I would have sent Captain MacNamara to the Antipodes if I'd had the authority," the viscountess said. "He *encourages* Hannah's scribblings."

"The captain is truly a terrible man," Lady Ophelia replied. "He's a much-respected veteran of the Peninsular campaign, he looks after his fellow soldiers, and he's done everything in his power to ensure your brilliant daughter has a safe, inviting, private place to create her essays and do her thinking. What mother could possibly look upon such a scoundrel with affection or respect?"

Thank you, Godmama, for putting those sentiments so civilly.

"Scotland is beautiful this time of year," Carstairs wistfully observed.

"Scotland," said the viscountess, "is always beautiful. Perhaps a journey might be in order. I must discuss this with Lord Standish. Strother, you will see me back to Pleasant View."

"My lady is forgetting something." Hyperia spoke up evenly, and she was, as usual, entirely correct. "Something important."

"Mama, you needn't..." Hannah began, only to find herself pulled to her feet by the captain.

"She needs to," he countered. "She needs to if she wants to be welcome in our home. Otherwise, her grandchildren will never even see her portrait."

A dig perhaps, because Hannah's portrait had not hung on the walls of her own home, so obsessed was the viscountess at keeping her daughter from polite society's view.

As forward-thinking as the captain might be, he yet believed in holding wrongdoers accountable, and Hannah apparently agreed with him.

"Very well," the viscountess said. "Hannah, I apologize for any harm to you that might have resulted from my attempts to..."

Lady Ophelia cleared her throat.

"To stifle your creativity. You have a gift. You have been a loyal daughter and sister, and I owed you a different sort of support than I showed you."

Hannah looked to the captain, who smiled thinly. "Your apologies need work, my lady, but that suffices for the nonce. If our paths should fail to cross before your departure, enjoy Scotland."

~

"I'm still unclear on one point," Carstairs said when the door had been firmly closed on the viscountess and her son. "Our plan did not include Miss Stadler leaping out of a window and fleeing her captors, but you somehow put the notion in her head."

Miss Stadler, who might have spared my sensibilities by arguing to the contrary, merely grinned. The captain, leaning on her perhaps a bit more than necessary, also disdained to intervene.

"How would I have suggested anything to anybody when my every word was plain to Miss Stadler's captors?"

Hyperia cocked her head. "Jules, have you been devious?"

"Please say yes." Lady Ophelia paused in the pouring out of six servings of brandy at the sideboard. "I have long known you harbor the potential. Vindicate my hopes on this challenging day, dear boy."

Oh bother. The plan had worked. Why not own it? "I hate sieges," I said. "Cannot abide the loss of life, the sheer tedium, the cruelty to those besieged... I tried resorting to Marcus Aurelius first."

"That business about..." Carstairs furrowed his handsome brow. "The sun will soon set and you with it?"

Hannah nodded, smiling hugely. "Tell them the rest of it, my lord."

Lady Ophelia handed around servings of spirits. "For our nerves."

I accepted mine with good grace. "I left out the crucial portion on purpose. The whole quote runs something like this, loosely translated: 'Your days are numbered. Use them to throw open the windows of your soul to the sun. If you do not, the sun will soon set, and you with it.'"

"I love that part," Hyperia said. "'Throw open the windows of your soul to the sun.' A beautiful sentiment."

Hannah lifted her glass a few inches. "The most important part, and his lordship purposely left it out because he knew I'd notice the omissions. Windows... windows that had been thrown open by Mr. Carstairs's marksmanship."

Carstairs nosed his drink. "But you kept maundering on... Something about..."

The captain took up the narrative. "His lordship resorted to John Donne, quoting from 'The Sun Rising.' 'Busy old fool, unruly sun. Why dost thou thus, Through windows, and through curtains call on us?' Hannah, of course, knows the whole verse by heart, and there was another mention of windows. Clever, clever woman."

"James, you flatter me," Hannah said, looking more pleased than coy. "The Downings were plastered to the wall across the room from me, awaiting the next volley, so out I went, exactly as his lordship intended, safe in the knowledge that I would be running away from the line of fire."

Bullets could bounce and ricochet. They could hit a glass target that sent lethal shards spraying in all directions. I took a risk, suggesting Hannah Stadler avail herself of the open windows. I had also gained insight into the range and depth of her acuity before I took that risk.

"Miss Hannah assessed a suggestion," I said, "and used her great good judgment to act in her own best interests. Shall we offer a toast to Miss Hannah and to all who are safely returned to their loved ones?"

Carstairs sent me a sidewise glance but drank dutifully. He offered to see to having Lady Ophelia's coach brought around, and Lady Ophelia made her exit with him. If she did not know of the Hampshire Carstairs yet, she would soon have their entire lineage back to the Domesday Book.

"I have just this moment," MacNamara said, "decided upon a gift for my bride. Hannah, what do you think about refurbishing your granny's cottage as a sort of dower property?"

"The place needs a serious airing," she said. "The poor books... Half of them are mildewed. Gran would hate to see the state of the place now. From the outside, it looks cozy enough, but the inside is in a sad way."

"We will rectify matters, then, and consult Lady Dewar as to the particulars. Caldicott, the rumors about you were not exaggerated in the least. My thanks, and if you can think of a way to put Carstairs's situation to rights, you will have my eternal gratitude and probably his too."

I was not about to meddle in Bryson Carstairs's *situation*.

Hyperia took my hand. "Julian, what is the captain alluding to?"

"We'll leave you to discuss the specifics." Miss Hannah parted from her swain long enough to kiss my cheek, pat my chest, and sigh. "I have had an adventure. I ought to be swooning or taking to my bed, oughtn't I? Instead, I am considering penning a novel about desperate, pigheaded young men and plucky women, and oh, James... Might we have a meal sent to the fishing cottage?"

"Oh, of course, my dear. I don't know as you've met Coombs. Prepare to be smitten. The man can whip up a feast from bread, apples, and a splash of cognac. I kid you not..."

They wandered from the room, arm in arm.

"This fishing cottage will soon acquire a comfortable bed," Hyperia said.

"Already installed. Perhaps writers are inclined to frequent naps."

Post-battle nerves were setting in. Relief, also a somewhat shaky acknowledgment of all that could have gone wrong and profound gratitude that it hadn't.

Not for Miss Hannah, and not—at least not yet—for Hyperia and me.

"Is Mr. Carstairs in need of an investigator?" Hyperia asked.

"Perry, might we sit?"

"The morning has been long," she said, leading me to the sofa. "I worried for you. Carstairs warned us that he'd be practicing his marksmanship. He has promised himself that on the anniversary of Waterloo, he would always practice his marksmanship, though the actual date is still a fortnight in the offing. To hear the blast of a gun, then another and another... How did you not go mad in the first five minutes of every battle?"

"Some of us did, and the gun smoke made it all nightmarishly worse." I slipped an arm around her shoulders. She rested against my side. "Have you considered our earlier discussion, Perry?"

"About your restored animal spirits?"

No beating about the bush with my darling intended. "Yes."

"I'm sure you'd rather have all your faculties in working order, and the possibility of a recovery was always there. You are an exceedingly resilient creature, Julian Caldicott."

I needed a moment to follow the logic: The possibility of my recovery had existed when she'd agreed to marry me.

"The possibility is now a reality. If you cried off—"

She jabbed me with her elbow. "Do not use that phrase ever again within my hearing, please. What couple expects their entire situation to remain unchanged for years? Do you suppose your father would have abandoned your mother if she'd become incapable of bearing children?"

"Of course not." He'd not exactly honored his vows as a young husband, and Mama had offered him some turnabout, but he and Mama had sorted themselves out, eventually.

"Julian, for today, can we not simply be grateful for another investigation happily concluded and for a couple who face a brighter future because of it? Can that not be enough for the present? Think of where you were two years ago, and be grateful you survived the battle. I certainly am."

Which? Ah, she referred again to Waterloo, and like one far gone with fatigue, I only in that moment realized the import of what she'd said about Carstairs and his vow to practice his marksmanship annually.

"Waterloo." June eighteenth. Napoleon's final defeat. Wellington's great victory.

"Yes, Waterloo. The horrible climax of the horrible Hundred Days after we thought the Corsican monster had finally been vanquished once and for all. June eighteenth should be a national day of bewilderment, if you ask me. For every family rejoicing in Wellington's victory, other families must mourn the cost of his triumph. I don't know how our former soldiers stand it, now that so many of them are left to beg in the streets. They were heroes, if you believe the press. What sort of nation leaves her heroes starving under Parliament's nose?"

A national day of bewilderment was an excellent idea. "Perhaps you should write a pamphlet."

My darling gave me a stern perusal. "You had better not be jesting, Jules. I know what your years in uniform cost you. I am a good writer. All of Healy's tutors liked my essays very much, though I wrote them under Healy's name, of course."

Hyperia was asking my permission to publish her sentiments. She did not need my permission, except that she was that considerate, that much my ally, and her topic of choice was that personal to me.

"Write so passionately that Eve's Advocate will be inspired to even greater literary feats."

"Perhaps I shall." Hyperia subsided against me, her weight a comfort and a pleasure.

A sense of dread eased. Not a specific dread, but the sort of dread that knew the enemy was on the march and well provisioned. My creeping dismals, my restlessness and ill humor... They were part bewilderment, part preparation for a battle I still fought in my nightmares.

In future, I would not let the eighteenth of June ambush me. I would arm myself with good company, with gratitude for the blessings of victory, and—Carstairs was no fool—a bit of marksmanship for old times' sake. A battle plan to keep bewilderment from any more victories.

"For today, I am not merely content," I said. "I am very pleased with how events have progressed, and I love you, Hyperia West, very much."

We indulged in some sweet kisses and some of the spicier variety. We both had much to think about, and awkward discussions were likely to ensue from time to time, but our regard for each other remained fixed, and Hyperia was right: For today, that was blessing enough.

The captain did take my suggestion to consult Dr. Hugh St. Sevier and with good results, though the healing took time. Fortunately, the captain's lovely wife, ably assisted by a quantity of books, rendered the convalescence something of a prelude to a delayed wedding journey.

And as for Bryson Carstairs, he was, indeed, in a bit of a situation in want of investigation. That, of course, is a tale for another time!

Made in the USA
Las Vegas, NV
07 August 2025